W9-AVL-208

kisses
AND LIES

ALSO BY LAUREN HENDERSON

Kiss Me Kill Me

Adult Fiction

Tart Noir (anthology, edited with Stella Duffy)

Exes Anonymous

My Lurid Past

Don't Even Think About It

Pretty Boy

Chained

The Strawberry Tattoo

Freeze My Margarita

Black Rubber Dress

Too Many Blondes

Dead White Female

Adult Nonfiction

Jane Austen's Guide to Dating

kisses
AND LIES

LAUREN HENDERSON

DELACORTE PRESS

Published by Delacorte Press
an imprint of Random House Children's Books
a division of Random House, Inc.
New York

This is a work of fiction. Names, characters, places, and incidents
either are the product of the author's imagination or are used
fictitiously. Any resemblance to actual persons, living or dead, events,
or locales is entirely coincidental.

Copyright © 2009 by Lauren Henderson
All rights reserved.

Delacorte Press and colophon are registered
trademarks of Random House, Inc.

Visit us on the Web! www.randomhouse.com/teens

Educators and librarians, for a variety of teaching tools,
visit us at www.randomhouse.com/teachers

Library of Congress Cataloging-in-Publication Data
Henderson, Lauren.
Kisses and lies / Lauren Henderson. — 1st ed.
p. cm.
Sequel to: Kiss me kill me.
Summary: Orphaned British teenager Scarlett Wakefield postpones her
romance with the handsome son of the school groundskeeper in order
to travel to Scotland with her American sidekick, Taylor, in search of
clues to the murder of a boy who dropped dead after kissing Scarlett.
ISBN 978-0-385-73489-9 (trade)—ISBN 978-0-385-90486-5 (lib.
bdg.)—ISBN 978-0-375-89185-4 (e-book)
[1. Mystery and detective stories. 2. Murder—Fiction. 3. Friendship—
Fiction. 4. Wealth—Fiction. 5. Orphans—Fiction. 6. England—Fiction.
7. Scotland—Fiction.] I. Title.
PZ7.H3807Kk 2009
[Fic]—dc22
2008034711

The text of this book is set in 12-point Goudy.
Book design by Kenny Holcomb
Printed in the United States of America
10 9 8 7 6 5 4 3 2 1
First Edition

Random House Children's Books supports the
First Amendment and celebrates the right to read.

TO EVERY TEENAGE GIRL OUT
THERE WHOSE FIRST KISS
DIDN'T QUITE GO AS
SHE'D HOPED IT WOULD . . .

Acknowledgments

Many thanks again to my fantastic editor, Claudia Gabel, who has worked so hard at getting this book as good as it can possibly be, and who deserves a great deal of the credit for it. To my wonderful agent, Deborah Schneider, who is quite literally always there for me. I am so lucky to have you two fabulous chicks in New York City looking out for me.

Big thanks also to Sonia Slater, great lawyer and testamentary expert, who tracked down the help I needed to write the complicated entail around which a crucial part of the plot revolves.

PART ONE: ENGLAND

one

SETTING UP AN AMBUSH

"Show me something!" Dan says. He's laughing; his eyes are bright with excitement. I've never seen anything as handsome as him before. I could stare at him all day.

But instead, I kiss him. For a few seconds, it's perfect. His lips are so soft, I could melt into them, and his arms, briefly, briefly, are heavy around my shoulders. My first kiss. I've never been this close to a boy in my life. My head is swimming with all the different sensations, the taste of champagne on his mouth, the lemony smell of his soap, the musk of his skin. . . . I'm shivering from head to toe.

I feel like I'm about to faint, and as my legs begin to wobble, suddenly he's gone.

I stumble.

I fall and I keep falling. I know how to fall, from gymnastics, but this is different, because I'm completely out of control, my limbs flailing. I fall for miles, down a deep, deep well, like Alice in Wonderland. Cold stone around me, cold breeze blowing, an utter sense of loss that a moment ago I was pressed against Dan's warm body, and now I'm all alone. I land with a thud that knocks the breath out of me, on a soft squish of body, and it's such a shock that I scream.

And then I realize what I've landed on, and I scream even louder.

It's Dan. He's lying under me, and he's colder than the stone. He's dead.

My kiss killed him.

And the police are banging down the door to arrest me.

. . .

"Scarlett! Scarlett!"

I wake up screaming, but I don't know what words I'm yelling.

"Scarlett!"

My aunt Gwen's pounding on the door.

"You're screaming again! Wake up!"

Aunt Gwen tries the door. It isn't locked, which is a mistake on my part. She storms into my room. I hear her before I see her, because I'm still really disoriented and my eyes are crusty with sleep. I rub them to clear them out. Even that's hard, as I'm still trippy from my dream.

When I manage to open my eyes, I keep blinking. Aunt Gwen's a scary sight by day. By night, she's like a monster from a children's book. The hair sticking up like a deranged puffball, the warty forehead, the watery eyes . . . Ugh, I just emerged from a nightmare and dropped bang-slap into another one.

"Scarlett!" she yells, though there's no need because

she's standing right over the bed. "You were screaming in your sleep!"

"I was having a nightmare, Aunt Gwen," I say, flinching. "I'm sorry I woke you."

"I have a very busy day tomorrow! I have geography tests to invigilate for the lower fourth!"

Only Aunt Gwen would use a word like *invigilate* at—I squint at the clock—4:30 in the morning.

"I said I was sorry," I repeat. "I can't help having a nightmare."

She huffs loudly in disbelief. It's a famous Aunt Gwen noise; I've heard students imitating it in the corridors.

I can't help getting cross now.

"I can't help it," I protest. "I really can't."

Aunt Gwen knows what happened to me this summer: she knows a boy I was kissing dropped dead at my feet. How can she expect me just to push that aside as if it never happened?

Aunt Gwen huffs again, even louder. She doesn't care about what happened to me. She just wants to get her sleep. And she hates me.

But that's okay, because I hate her, too.

"This has *got* to stop," Aunt Gwen grumbles loudly. "I've had enough, d'you hear?"

She turns and stomps out of the room. I hear her slippers slapping back along the corridor, and the sound of her bedroom door slamming shut.

This does have to stop. That's the single thing Aunt Gwen and I agree on. I just don't know how.

. . .

"It's so weird that you started having these dreams *now*," Taylor says, pushing open the heavy glass door of the coffee shop with the effortless ease of a girl who does fifty push-ups before breakfast. I walk in and she follows me, holding the door till the person behind her, a man in a suit, can catch up to take it from her. He doesn't say thank you. Taylor promptly lets the door go, and he staggers back under its weight.

"You're welcome," she says to him.

He goes bright red, still off-balance and struggling with the door, and to complete his humiliation, we both snicker as we walk toward the counter.

"I think I'm dreaming about Dan now because I *can*," I say. "Does that make sense?"

"Uh-uh." She shakes her head.

"What I mean is, before, I thought I killed him, right? But now I know it wasn't my fault he died, maybe I feel free-er to dream about him," I try to explain.

Taylor, who usually doesn't go for any kind of deep psychological exploration—she's an action girl through and through—actually looks as if she's thinking this theory over. Her heavy dark brows draw together over her green eyes in a frown of concentration, and she shakes her head, making her short dark hair look even shaggier, a gesture she does unconsciously when she's thinking hard.

"It was a huge deal," she concedes. "I mean, a guy dropping dead at your feet. I guess the weird thing is that you never dreamed about it before."

4

"Exactly! But now I can."

In the mirrored glass behind the counter of the coffee shop I see the man in the suit, standing behind us in the queue. He looks appalled, and he's actually backing away from us a bit.

I can't blame him. It's not exactly the kind of conversation you expect to hear in Latte-Licious from two sixteen-year-olds, is it? Death and nightmares and blame and guilt? Especially when one of those sixteen-year-olds has just shown how much stronger she is than you. Taylor's got a swimmer's build, with naturally wide shoulders, but all the upper-body work she does means that she looks pretty intimidating, and her fleece emphasizes that, making her look even fitter and sportier. Me, I did gymnastics for years, so I'm pretty fit too, but unfortunately, for purposes of intimidating people, I'm naturally curvy, with a layer of fat that Taylor doesn't seem to have. You'd expect Taylor to be able to chin her own weight; you'd be amazed to see me do it, though I can, easily. So we make a pretty good team, I suppose. Taylor's the obvious muscle, while I can look all girly and fool people into thinking I'd cry if I chipped a nail.

I look briefly at myself in the mirror. I've made an effort today, because of who we're meeting. I've got mascara on, which emphasizes my blue eyes, and lip gloss, and I've put on big twisty silver hoop earrings and clipped my dark hair up in a twist that makes me, I think, look a bit older than I am. I'm wearing a V-neck dark pink cashmere hoodie that's slim-cut and shows off my boobs, and tight jeans tucked into leather boots, to show off my legs. I feel a bit self-conscious, because people are looking at me, but that's what happens when you show yourself off.

I haven't dressed up in ages, not even this much. Because the last time I dressed up, very bad things happened indeed. I fall silent as we wait for our turn to order, thinking about how my life has changed in the last six months.

Six months ago, I was at a different school: St. Tabby's, the trendiest, smartest all-girls' school in London—though I, and my two best friends, were probably the most boring, untrendy girls in the whole sixth form. Until Plum Saybourne, the reigning princess of St. Tabby's, invited me to a party.

I thought I was finally being picked out, seen as being special. I thought Plum had looked me over and decided that I was pretty enough to join her carefully selected court of glossy rich Plum-wannabes. I abandoned my two best friends on the spot to join Plum's court of admirers. What a fool I was—it turned out that I'd only been invited because some boy in their group fancied me. I was a party favor for him.

But at the party, Dan McAndrew, the most handsome boy in West London, captain of his school cricket team, striker on his school soccer team, dazzling as the lead singer in the band that all the girls had mad crushes on, poured me a glass of champagne and asked me to go out onto the terrace with him.

I had had a mad crush on Dan McAndrew ever since the first time I saw him. Of course I went.

We sat down on a bench and talked and drank champagne.

He asked me to do some gymnastics for him, and I walked up and down the terrace on my hands, totally and completely showing off to get him to like me.

And it worked. Because he kissed me.

It was the most beautiful thing that had ever happened to me. And then it was the most terrible, because suddenly he started gasping for breath and then he collapsed in my arms and then he died. Of an allergic reaction. He usually carried an EpiPen, a sort of injection for emergencies, and if he'd had it on him he would have been saved.

But he didn't.

I was blamed for his death, though no one could work out what had killed him. I was expelled from St. Tabby's, because Dan's death was all over the newspapers, and the headmistress hated all the journalists crowding round the building, taking photographs of the pupils. I was sent back to the school my grandmother runs, at our stately home in the countryside outside London. Wakefield Hall. It's a minimum-security prison for swotty girls. I have to live with my aunt Gwen, who, as we've seen, loathes my guts.

It was the worst time of my life. Even worse than when my parents died, because I don't remember much about that—while I remember every single thing about Dan's death and the aftermath, much as I try to forget.

And then I met Taylor, and we started investigating how Dan really died, and I sneaked into the apartment of the girl who'd thrown that party—Nadia Farouk—and I worked out that someone had put peanut oil in the crisps I had eaten that night, which meant when I kissed Dan I had peanut oil on my mouth, which he was violently allergic to. Someone tried to poison him, and I ended up being their weapon.

That didn't go down well with me at all.

In Nadia's apartment, I read her diary—I know, not exactly a brilliant thing to do, but there was a murder to solve, which I think does justify reading people's diaries—and in it she'd written that she saw Dan's EpiPen in Plum's handbag the night of the party. And that meant that Plum must be involved somehow in the plot to kill Dan.

Taylor and I talked it over and we decided that we needed help from Nadia. So here we are, setting up an ambush for her.

When you set up an ambush, you need bait. I look at my watch to make sure the bait's not late in arriving.

"It's early yet," Taylor says, seeing my gesture. "She'll be here."

"You're sure?"

"Oh yeah. She's more scared of us than she is of them."

"Sometimes you sound like—I dunno—like you're in the CIA or something," I comment.

Taylor smirks.

"Thanks," she says. And to the girl behind the counter: "Two lattes, skim milk, easy on the froth."

"I'm sorry?" the poor Latte-Licious employee says, baffled. She's a redhead, with lots of freckles, and a nice smile that vanished as soon as Taylor started giving her order, because when Taylor orders coffee, she always forgets that she lives in England now.

"We'd like two lattes, please," I cut in. "Made with skim milk, if you've got it, and not too much froth, if that's okay."

"Oh right, no problem," the girl says, smiling with relief at someone talking English to her, rather than New York American.

"I keep telling you," I say to Taylor, "the more you try to speed things up by ordering superfast and all New York-y, the more you actually slow things down. No one understands a word you say. And you have to put in a lot of 'pleases' and 'if you don't minds' and stuff like that, to be polite."

Taylor sniffs. "British people are just really *slow*," she says crossly.

We take our lattes and find a table, the most tucked-away, discreet table, half hidden behind the sweep of the counter, where no one could possibly see us unless they were walking through the whole shop looking for someone. Ten minutes later, the bait comes in. We can see her, because we're positioned so that we can watch the entrance in the mirrors that run in a strip all round the walls of the coffee shop—one of the reasons we chose this place for what Taylor calls, in CIA-like terminology, the rendezvous.

The bait goes up to the counter, orders a coffee, and when she gets it, stands there looking hopeless, as if she's waiting for someone else to tell her what to do. Which pretty much sums Lizzie up. She's in our class at school, but you don't need to spend more than ten minutes with her to see that she's the kind of girl who stands around waiting for other people to tell her what to do. If you told her to jump, she wouldn't even ask how high. She'd just do it. And then probably complain that it was hard to do in heels, and it had messed up her hairstyle, and could she put down her Pucci handbag before she did it again.

Taylor starts to get up, but I motion for her to stay seated. The mood she's in, she'll scare Lizzie so much that the poor girl will dissolve into a puddle of tears on the coffee shop floor. Instead, I push back my chair and go over to where Lizzie's hovering.

"Hi," I say.

She jumps without even being asked.

"I'm here!" she says nervously.

"Fantastic," I say encouragingly.

"Where did you come from? I was looking for you, but I couldn't see you."

"We're tucked away over there," I say, leading her over to the section Taylor and I have picked out for her to sit—in the middle of the coffee shop, behind a pillar, so that once Nadia has sat down, it will be hard for her to make her escape. We did a preliminary reconnaissance on this place last week, scouting it out to make sure it was a good location for this crucial meeting. It's a big and busy coffee shop in Victoria, near the big train and bus stations, with enough people coming in and out on a Saturday afternoon so that there are always plenty of free tables. Sure enough, I find a nicely positioned four-seat table for Lizzie with no difficulty at all.

She sits down and fixes nervous eyes on me. As usual, Lizzie's very made up, her eyes carefully lined and her blond highlights freshly done, smelling of lovely perfume. At first glance you would think she was in her mid-twenties. And then you look more closely, and you see that she's my and Taylor's age, just with more makeup on her face right now than I've owned in my entire life. (I'm not even counting Taylor in this—she'd break your arm before she let you come near her with a mascara wand.) It's very much the style of Plum's coterie—they're all beautifully groomed. Though she goes to Wakefield Hall, Lizzie hangs out with the smart set of St. Tabby's, due to the fact that her father has bags of money and Lizzie has bags of social ambition. But Lizzie, as with everything, tries so hard that she over-does it. And as a result, they look down on her. Who can re-spect someone who tries too hard?

Lizzie spots something over my shoulder and gasps.

"It's her!" she exclaims. "It's Nadia!"

I duck down immediately and scamper across the room, hoping that turning my back to the door will mean Nadia doesn't spot me. I slide into my seat opposite Taylor, who nods, confirming that Nadia's arrived. Despite her cool, Taylor is goggling a bit. She's seen Nadia only once, on a stakeout across Knightsbridge, never this close up.

"Wow, she looks like a *model* . . . ," she sighs almost wistfully.

I sneak a glance in the mirror along the wall. Wow in-deed. It's been awhile since I've seen a girl our age looking like that—Wakefield Hall girls favor clothes that don't get in the way of knees under desks and elbows on piles of books. In other words, scruffy jeans and sweaters. A world away from Nadia's slim cropped trousers, suede ankle boots, and artful layers of semitransparent black sweaters hanging elegantly off her thin, pale brown limbs. Her hair is glossy and dark and swishes subtly as she walks. Nadia is as polished and shiny as a Ferrari, and keeping her that buffed and sleek probably costs almost as much. She looks around, sees Lizzie, and crosses the room toward her, pulling out a chair and sitting down at the table.

I look at Taylor. She holds up her hand, telling me not to be impatient. We watch as Nadia puts her bag on the table, as she settles into her seat, crossing her legs, one arm over the back of her chair, looking haughtily round the room like she owns this entire chain of coffee shops and isn't that impressed with how they're being run. Lizzie's demeanor is visibly awkward: she's ducking her head and fiddling madly with her coffee spoon. If Nadia bothered to read the signals Lizzie's all-too-clearly sending out, she'd see immediately that something was up.

But Nadia tends to be oblivious to anything that she doesn't think directly affects her. Which means that it's probably unnecessary for Taylor and me to take all the precautions we do. We slide out our chairs, leaving our half-drunk coffees behind, and split up to cross the room toward our target, each taking different trajectories, aiming to approach Nadia completely unobserved. Taylor reaches the table first, taking the chair next to Nadia, boxing her in. Nadia turns to look at her, clearly astounded that someone should take the liberty of sitting down next to her without being invited.

Her beautifully glossed lips part, obviously about to give Taylor a severe reprimand. Then she sees me sitting down across from her, and they sag open in a gawp of surprise.

"*Scarlett?* What are *you* doing here?" she says, completely shocked to see me.

And I think I see something else in her dark eyes too. I think I see guilt.

"We need to talk about your not-so-anonymous note," I say, watching her closely. Her eyes waver and I know I'm right. It *is* guilt. Because she knows I didn't have anything to do with Dan's death, and she never told anyone what she saw that night—the EpiPen in Plum's handbag.

Nadia starts to stand up, reaching for her bag. Taylor puts a hand on her shoulder and pushes her down. Nadia turns to her in outrage.

"Who are you? How *dare* you touch me?" she hisses in fury. But between clenched teeth: she doesn't want to make a scene.

"You need to sit here and listen to what Scarlett's got to say," Taylor says, her voice flat and uninflected and all the scarier for that.

Nadia narrows her eyes. "*You!*" she hisses, glaring at Lizzie. "You told me you had a secret about Plum you wanted to tell me. You set me up!"

Lizzie's face crumples.

"They *made* me, Nadia," she wails. "They *made* me! I didn't want to!"

I glance at Lizzie to check how she's doing. Lizzie's eyes, squinched up in their frames of eyeliner and mascara, are darting from me to Nadia. I can tell she doesn't know whose side to take, and it's confusing her so much that

13

she has all the telltale signs of someone who's about to cry: her mouth is puckering up, her cheeks are flushing, her eyes are beginning to water. Bad, bad, bad. The last thing we need is Lizzie throwing a scene and distracting us, possibly fatally, from getting the information we need from Nadia.

Coming to a quick decision, I say sympathetically, "Lizzie, why don't you go? You look really upset."

"I just feel so caught in the middle—" Lizzie sobs, grabbing her bag. She looks at Nadia, checking that she's okay with Lizzie leaving. But Nadia just shrugs one slender shoulder at her, clearly not feeling the need for her support. Gratefully, Lizzie jumps up and runs off, looking overwhelmed. Wow, she really doesn't like conflict.

Lizzie has no idea that I have any connection to Dan's death. I certainly haven't told her, but I wonder if Plum and Nadia might have. But, talking to her at school, I can tell she's entirely innocent of any knowledge that I am the Kiss of Death Girl. I don't think Plum and Nadia really talk to her at all: they just use her for her platinum credit cards and the fact that her father owns a ton of restaurants and trendy clubs. And in the whole time I've seen Lizzie, she's never had anything but a tabloid or fashion magazine in her hands. From her babble, it's obvious she uses the TV and Internet purely to watch her favorite American shows, all gossip and glitz. I don't think she even knows what the news is. No wonder she's never realized that my leaving St. Tabby's and coming to Wakefield Hall, and Dan's mysterious death, are intertwined in any way.

As Lizzie makes her escape, Nadia pushes back her chair and stands up again.

"I'm leaving, too, and you'd better not stop me," she snaps. "I've got no interest in anything you have to say. Especially since you got me here under false pretenses."

But this time Taylor doesn't touch her. Instead, she says, "Oh yeah? Try to walk out of here and we'll call the police and tell them you know Dan was murdered."

I put my phone on the table. "I've got the number of the inspector who questioned me right here," I lie.

Nadia would go white if her olive skin would allow her to. Failing that, the blood bleaches out of her cheeks, and under her carefully applied blusher I see her turn pale. She sits down very slowly, like my grandmother when she's feeling her age.

"I don't know what you're talking about," she says, but it's clearly an automatic denial—there's no conviction in her voice.

"Oh yes, you do." I lean across the table and fix her with a hard stare. I can't believe I'm doing this: I'm intimidating Nadia Farouk, who, in the whole time I was at St. Tabby's, could intimidate *me* simply by casting a dismissive glance in my general direction.

But I am. It's working.

"I . . . ," Nadia starts, and then her voice trails off and she looks down at her hands, which she's twisting together on the table. She fiddles with her bracelets—they're gold, like all the Middle Eastern girls wear, the yellow metal gorgeous against their cappuccino skin.

15

Taylor starts to say something, but I hold up a hand and, miraculously, she hushes. This is my battle. I have to fight it myself, not always rely on Taylor to be my muscle. No matter how well she plays the part.

"You've got fifteen seconds to start talking," I say, reaching for my phone. "Then I'm ringing the inspector." I fix her with my stare again. "And don't try to lie," I add. "We know all about you seeing Dan's EpiPen in Plum's handbag the night of the party."

Silence falls. Nadia seems utterly shocked for a moment, but then she sighs, a long, deep sigh as though she wants to get something heavy off her chest.

"Okay," she says. "I'll tell you everything I know."

The way she says it, I believe her. Taylor and I lean forward expectantly.

"But in return," she continues, with a slightly sarcastic edge, "since you're such *super–spy girl detectives*, I want you to do something for me. . . ."

"YOU'VE CHANGED, SCARLETT"

Six months ago I was getting dressed for a party. And now here I am, doing exactly the same thing, but with all the difference in the world. Six months ago, I was desperate to look as pretty as possible, to fit in with Plum and Nadia's group, and to attract the boy I'd had a crush on since the dawn of time—Dan McAndrew.

Well, we all know how that one turned out.

Six months ago, it was all about pleasure. Now, it's business. I look at myself in the mirror, and I see that my jaw is set with determination. Though it takes a second to recognize myself. The last time I wore this much makeup was—you guessed it—six months ago. And it was in this same hip Notting Hill boutique that I was taught how to dress and how to paint myself prettier without looking like a clown.

I was a more-than-willing student. Unlike Taylor, who, unsurprisingly, is absolutely refusing to wear any makeup whatsoever.

"Just a little bit of mascara?" the salesgirl is coaxing. "It'll really make those green eyes pop!"

Taylor's look is the visual equivalent of a snarl. I have to give the girl major points for persisting.

"And maybe just a tiny bit of blusher?" she continues. "I've got these great gel sticks. You'll hardly notice it."

"Then what's the point?" Taylor snaps.

"Taylor," I say soothingly, "you've got to blend in a bit. You can't turn up at a trendy party in a club looking like—um—looking like . . ."

I'm not as brave as the salesgirl, clearly, because Taylor turns her stare onto me, daring me to finish my sentence, and I feel her eyes are popping quite satisfactorily without the aid of any mascara.

"It's all about individuality nowadays," the girl says cheerfully. "No one's trying to make you look like anything but yourself, okay? But just see what this does. . . ."

And she actually dares to reach out with a stubby pink stick and draw a line on each of Taylor's cheekbones. I'm amazed when she pulls her hand back with the wrist still intact. But, miracle of miracles, she does, because Taylor is, despite herself, looking at her image in the mirror, and both she and I can see that the blusher has made a small but significant improvement. It's given just a touch of color to her Irish-white skin. Taylor has such strong features she'll never be pretty, but, with her well-refined brows and cheekbones, plus those long green eyes, she could be really striking if she'd let herself make the best of her looks.

And push her hair back off her face a bit.

"That isn't bad," Taylor admits grudgingly, and to my amusement, she actually does push her hair back off her face, as if she heard my voice in her head. Or realized that she's actually got a face worth looking at.

"Want to try a tiny bit of mascara?" the girl suggests.

"Well . . . maybe . . . ," Taylor mumbles, blushing under the blusher.

I walk away, feeling that Taylor would rather not have me witness her this vulnerable. I honestly think she'd rather have me watch her being tortured than learning how to apply mascara.

In the full-length mirror set into the pale blue walls, I survey myself. I'm wearing a layered top, not unlike the one Nadia had on yesterday in the coffee shop. (I didn't set out to copy her—the salesgirl picked it out for me, which goes to show how on-trend Nadia is.) It's a sort of off-white, with silver threads running through it, and it's so delicate that I'm nervous I might shred it with any sudden movements, but it's fantastically pretty and it makes me feel glamorous and sexy but not like I'm showing too much skin, or cleavage, or anything that might make me feel embarrassed. It comes to my hips, and underneath it I'm wearing a gray suede miniskirt, silvery crocheted tights, and ankle boots with lots of straps and buckles that jingle when I walk and honestly make me feel a bit silly but that, I have been assured, are What Everyone Is Wearing at This Precise Fashion Moment in Time. My hair is pulled to one side in a ponytail, and the salesgirl told me to buy curling irons so I could twist it into one big loose ringlet falling over my right shoulder.

I haven't even got any makeup on yet, and I think I look

really nice already. I haven't seen myself dressed up like this since the night of Nadia's party. And while there's a part of me that is a little ashamed to admit this, I like it.

All of a sudden, I find myself wishing Jase could see me now. Jase Barnes is the grandson of Ted Barnes, the head gardener at Wakefield Hall, where I live now. More importantly, Jase Barnes is the incredibly gorgeous boy who I can't stop myself from thinking about when I'm not thinking about Dan. I don't have tons of experience when it comes to this romantic stuff, but I think that Jase might have a bit of a thing for me. This is based solely on the fact that he didn't exactly push me away when I kissed him recently.

I shake my head frantically, hoping that it'll block all images of that kiss with Jase from my mind. Taylor and I have an important mission tonight, and I need to get ready for it. As soon as I focus only on that, I see a difference in myself from six months before. Then, I was wide-eyed, unable to believe that I actually looked pretty enough, trendy enough, capable enough of fitting into Plum and Nadia's social circle enough that people wouldn't laugh and point the moment I walked in the door. Now, I've kissed a boy, and held him as he died in my arms. I've been blamed for it, and I'm in the middle of a battle to prove his death was at the hands of someone else.

No wonder there's a tougher look in my eyes.

"Hey," Taylor says gruffly, appearing behind me in the mirror.

She isn't half as dressed up as I am—she absolutely refused to try on a skirt. In fact, I don't think Taylor even owns one. I only know she has legs rather than prosthetics because I've seen her work out in gym shorts. But she's wearing low-cut jeans that show off her stomach, flat from thousands of sit-ups, and a bright red T-shirt with dull gold embroidery over one shoulder. The salesgirl was able to get Taylor to push her hair back behind her ears, and somehow Taylor looks a few years older and a lot more sophisticated. By the embarrassed tone in her voice, I can tell that Taylor sees it, too.

I know better than to shower her with compliments.

"You look cool," I say.

"So do you," Taylor responds.

We stare at each other in the mirror for a moment.

"Is this going to cost a ton of money?" Taylor asks eventually.

"Two tons," I say.

She cracks a grin. "Gotta love that trust fund, right?"

*   *   *

Nadia's deal with us was simple. Well, the deal was simple. The story behind it wasn't.

"I throw up sometimes, okay?" she said, lowering her voice, so we had to strain to hear her over the clatter of cups and chatter in the crowded coffee shop. For someone who was glaring at us so boldly before, she was refusing to meet our eyes now: she was fidgeting with her gold bangles, her slick of shiny hair falling over her face. "I'm not bulimic or anything," she went on, "because I don't do it every day. Or anything like every day."

She paused here, as if she was daring us to challenge

this, but neither Taylor nor I did. Without wanting to sound too cold, we weren't there to save one pampered rich girl from her own low self-image problem: we were there to solve a murder. Which sort of took priority.

"Sometimes I eat that bit too much and it just helps," Nadia continued, still sounding defensive. "Everyone complimented me when I lost weight when I got the flu, but I started putting it on again, and then I realized if I just—you know—every so often—"

"What do you want us to *do?*" Taylor broke in impatiently. "Flush the john after you've finished barfing?"

Nadia's head jerked up, and her big dark-penciled Persian eyes flashed jet-black daggers at Taylor.

"Well, thanks for the *sympathy,*" she hissed, turning her shoulder on Taylor. "*You* know what it's like at St. Tabby's, Scarlett. Everyone's so horribly competitive." She grimaced. "You wouldn't believe the kind of stuff that goes on."

She seemed to be waiting for something, so I prompted, in as sympathetic a voice as I could manage:

"Oh? Like what?"

"Like *filming me doing it,*" Nadia hissed again. "Can you *imagine?*"

"Someone *filmed* you throwing up?" I asked incredulously.

She nodded. Even under the bright coffee shop lights, which washed me and Taylor out and gave us dark shadows under our eyes, Nadia's skin was golden and glowing. I couldn't help admiring it, even as I wondered whether I could detect a hint of something sour and acid on her breath.

"Plum did," she said quietly. "On her phone. We were feeling like we'd overdone it at brunch, and we thought we'd, you know, *puke*." She whispered the last word. "We went into her bathroom to do it together and I went first. I had no idea what she was doing—I mean, why would you think anyone would *film* you? And then, the next day, she showed it to me. She said it was just a joke, but I *begged* her to delete it, and she wouldn't, and ever since, when I don't go along with her, she makes this gesture, like she's sticking one finger down her throat, and I know she's saying if I don't do what she wants, she'll show everyone."

"So what do you want us to do about it?" Taylor asked, frowning in confusion.

"Get it back!" Nadia's voice rose hysterically. "I want you to get it back!"

I could see that something about Taylor was making Nadia freak out, so I asked Taylor to go fetch us some more lattes.

"Fine," Taylor said gruffly, obviously annoyed that I'd sent her on an errand in the middle of our power play.

Once Taylor was out of earshot, my suspicions were confirmed.

"Your friend's really, *really* butch," she said disapprovingly. "And completely classless."

I narrowed my eyes at her. "That's pretty funny coming from a girl who pukes in the loo on a regular basis."

Nadia seemed almost impressed by my comeback. She looked at me properly for the first time, one of the up-and-down, thorough surveys that St. Tabby's girls only bestow on girls they think are their rivals in some way.

"You've changed, Scarlett. You've grown a backbone."

"I had to," I said simply.

Nadia nodded. "It must have been really hard," she said. "Dan, I mean."

For the first time, Nadia revealed a sympathetic expression. Even so, there was no way I was letting down my guard in front of her.

"It wasn't a barrel of laughs," I said brusquely.

Nadia raised her eyebrows. "Well, when I remember you at St. Tabby's—"

"What exactly do you want us to do about Plum?" I cut in.

Nadia looked a bit taken aback that I'd dared to interrupt what was doubtless going to be a humiliating account of what a wimp I used to be at school. The only time I stood up to Plum was when I was clearing my stuff out of my locker, and that wasn't exactly typical of my behavior there. Besides, she bullied me with a big group of girls around her, which really drove me to it.

"I want you to steal her phone," she blurted out. "So I can delete that video."

I stared at her, bewildered.

"Plum's bound to have uploaded it to her computer," I pointed out.

But Nadia was shaking her head so vigorously that her earrings were trembling glints of gold through her blue-black hair.

"Plum's had her computer hacked into before," she explained. "So now she doesn't keep anything really private on it. She wants total control of that video, so she won't

24

send it anywhere someone else might get hold of it. Then she wouldn't be able to, you know, sort of hold it over my head."

"Some friend," I said dryly.

Nadia's eyes narrowed, and she started to say something, but she bit it back.

"How are we supposed to steal her phone?" I asked. "Plum knows me, and after the last time I saw her, I'm pretty sure she won't let me anywhere near her."

I had shoved Plum into a locker. I didn't hurt her or anything, and she had her entire gang grouped round me, bullying me, but Plum wouldn't exactly see that as justifying my actions.

Nadia was looking blank.

"And besides, the phone must be really precious to her, if she keeps incriminating stuff on it," I added, thinking out loud. "Hmm, how can we make this work?"

I drummed my fingers on the table, which always helped me to think, though I knew it was annoying for everyone else. Nadia, however, had the good sense not to complain: after all, my brain was spinning fast in an attempt to help her out.

"I know!" I exclaimed eventually. "I'll distract her, and Taylor can take the phone. Seeing me will be a great distraction—especially after last time. She'll be spitting blood at the sight of me. We'll just have to work out someplace we can do it so Taylor can get close to her bag without her noticing. And without getting caught," I added. "Obviously—the last thing we want is Taylor getting arrested for stealing."

"Well, we're going clubbing tonight . . . ," Nadia suggested, a bit dubiously.

"Perfect," I said firmly.

My brain told me that this would be a great opportunity—dark, crowded, Plum probably tipsy and thus less likely to notice her phone disappearing. And besides, it was striking while the iron was hot. I was on fire to push ahead with solving Dan's murder.

My nerves, however, were screaming in protest. The idea of going clubbing—me! clubbing!—in any kind of venue that was a regular hangout for girls like Plum and Nadia filled me with complete and utter dread and fear. This was miles out of my league. I swallowed hard, telling my nerves to shut up.

"Will Taylor be okay with that?" Nadia said doubtfully, turning to look over at Taylor, who was eyeing us carefully from the coffee pickup line.

"Taylor," I said to Nadia, turning back to look her directly in the face, "wants to be a PI."

"A what?"

"A private investigator. She takes it really seriously. She'll do anything she needs to do to get the job done."

"If you get that video back, so I can delete it," Nadia said, clasping her hands together in a kind of prayer, "I'll do anything I can to help you, Scarlett. *Anything.*" Her big dark eyes were wide and imploring. "I helped you already, didn't I?" she reminded me. "I got Lizzie to leave you that note, because I felt guilty everyone was still blaming you. Please, Scarlett. Get that video for me. And I'll tell you everything I know about that evening. I promise."

I believed her. Because I was sure that video existed—Nadia wouldn't make up something that embarrassing. So I was sure she'd do whatever she could to help us out. And even after we'd helped her, I was equally sure we'd get the truth from her about the night Dan died, because if she broke her promise, we'd go to Plum and tell her it was Nadia who arranged for us to steal her phone and delete that video. And I wouldn't want to be Nadia if Plum knew that. Her wrath would be terrifying.

Of course, Nadia could try to lie to us. But I trusted myself and Taylor to sense if she was lying, and pressure her for the truth. Taylor, as she herself says, has a built-in bullshit detector. While I was drumming my fingers, I was thinking this all through. I tested it now, in my mind, and it hung together. I nodded to myself, satisfied with my calculations.

After all, it wasn't as if Nadia had asked us to do anything bad. We'd take the phone, and if Nadia was telling the truth, we'd find that video, delete it for her, and make sure Plum got her phone back ASAP. That was it.

How could that possibly go wrong?

Three

"WHO WANTS TO SEE MY KNICKERS?"

It's just as dark in Coco Rouge as I imagined it would be. And even louder. For the first time in my life, I fully understand the expression "I can't hear myself think." If this place were drawn in a cartoon, it would have "Boom! Boom! Boom!" written above it, and wiggly lines around to show the whole building shaking with the force of the music they're playing.

The bass line is throbbing all around us, as if we just stepped into a gigantic heart. And the decor's like being inside a heart too—the walls are red and shiny, the upholstery crimson and plush, the carpet dark purple. Inasmuch as I can see the decor, that is, because the club's already heaving with rich young people a bit older than us, dressed to kill and gripping fancy glasses filled with expensive cocktails.

Taylor and I snatch a glance at each other, and I don't know which one of us looks more intimidated. Tell us to climb a rope or jump out of a window or smuggle ourselves into a penthouse, and we'll grab at the chance. But dress up and act like a cool clubber . . . that's a real challenge. I feel like everyone we pass is staring at me and laughing, because I look all wrong. And, from the way Taylor is setting her jaw and slouching awkwardly, she feels exactly the same.

I look around, though, and with the sensible, reasoning part of my brain, the part that isn't panicking, I can see that what we're wearing does fit in here quite well. Taylor, in her embroidered T-shirt and low-cut jeans and DIY shaggy haircut, looks a bit too indie for this crowd, like she should be carrying a guitar. But she's slouching in such a cool way that she makes everyone else look overdressed.

And my miniskirt and long layered top are exactly right—I can see a girl across the room wearing a dress that's very like my top, falling off one of her shoulders just the way mine does. I always feel self-conscious going out with what seems to me like a lot of makeup on—mascara, lipstick, blusher—but you get into a place like this and you realize how under-made-up you are by comparison. I like my red lipstick, but I wish I'd put on more eyeliner now. There are a lot of girls here wearing more makeup than clothes.

The guys are in jeans and shirts, looking a bit boring by comparison. I don't think this is my kind of place—I'm not that keen on the music, which is loud and thumping and all sounds exactly the same, and the boys are too posh to be sexy. They're all really pink-faced and chinless.

It was ridiculously easy to get in here. Lizzie led us up to the velvet rope, bypassing the line, and a man dressed in black from head to toe lifted the rope and beckoned us forward. It was that simple. Lizzie walked through as if she'd been doing this all her life—which she probably has, considering her dad co-owns this place—and we followed, trying to pretend that we had, too, and probably failing dismally.

But I'd spent so much time at St. Tabby's watching the nasty games that Plum's coterie played that part of me still believed that this was a setup, in revenge for us luring Nadia to the coffee shop this morning, and that Plum and Nadia would be waiting when we showed up, having schemed with Lizzie to humiliate us, laughing at us for even thinking that we might get in somewhere as cool as Coco Rouge.

Well, it wasn't a setup. Operation Video-Puke Deletion is well and truly on.

Grimly, we follow Lizzie through the packed club, a series of rooms that open onto each other, full of playful screams and loud, pounding, drivingly sexy lyrics. Girls are backing up and shoving their bottoms into boys' crotches in imitation of the dancers in hip-hop videos, the boys roaring with laughter.

"If they could *see* themselves," Taylor yells in my ear.

I pull a face in response. No one's getting me to dance, I swear to myself. I'll die before I become one of those white girls trying to pretend they're black. It's completely and utterly embarrassing. Oh yeah—did I mention that everyone in here is white? Literally everyone. The only black people here are the bouncers. But the music's all sexy black R&B. Very odd.

We're held up by a particularly raucous group of girls with long shiny hair, sloshing colored martinis and dangling earrings around with equal abandon. As we maneuver past them, doing our best not to get drenched in flying orange liquid, I can't help staring at them in envy. They do look fake: they've got tons of makeup on, and they're dressed very tartily—though expensively, Versace rather than the knockoff high street version—but they're all undeniably, fantastically beautiful, tipsy and staggering as they are. I remember something I read once which said that if you call someone plastic, what you really mean is that they're prettier than you are. This is the moment when I realize how true that statement is.

Distracted, I lose sight of Lizzie, and I'm struck with panic. Suddenly this dark red club feels like hell on earth. Without Lizzie, without our mission, we don't fit in here at all. Taylor and I are just a pair of average girls, not half as pretty—or plastic—as the ones here. I spin around, desperately trying to spot Lizzie, and then someone grabs me by the shoulder and pushes me. It's Taylor.

"Round the corner!" she shouts.

Sure enough, Lizzie's in the next room, standing in front of another velvet rope as another bouncer checks another list. Honestly, there's more security here than there is at some airports. She turns round and beckons to me and Taylor as the bouncer reaches over to unclip the rope. A girl to my right, one who's not getting in, eyes me up and down; I see her doing that glance where she checks out my entire outfit. Thank God I'm comfortable wearing short skirts—short anything, really. You can't do gymnastics for years without being totally comfortable hanging out for large amounts of time in a leotard.

The girl's looking at me really enviously now as we walk through, and the awful thing is, it feels really, really good. Not only are we in a club that people are still queuing to enter, but now we're in the inner sanctum, the VIP area. Nadia and Plum are hot, young, and in Plum's case, titled (she's an Honorable, because her dad's a peer). They get photographed at parties for *W* and *Tatler* and tons of other glossy gossip mags. They're It-girls about town. So they get in free, and they bring their crowd, and the club is even more cool because they're here. The VIP section isn't hidden away—it's on a raised platform, up a couple of shallow stairs, so everyone can see that Plum and her set are here, and feel cool to be in their company.

Even though they're not allowed into where they are.

It's a very weird system.

But I understand it. Sort of. Because although I know I shouldn't, I can't help feeling cool that I'm in the VIP area. And if it has that effect on me—someone who doesn't study those magazines as if they were a bible of information on how to dress and where to go and who to be seen with—it must be even more powerful on someone who does.

Like Lizzie, who's positively radiating pride and excitement as she runs up the steps to the booth where Plum is holding court. Taylor and I immediately duck down at a side table, much less conspicuous than Plum's, which of course is the most central on the entire dais area.

"That's her," I say, nodding over at Plum. My back's mostly turned to her, and I doubt she'll spot me—the place is rammed, and by the brief glance I had of her, she's very merry already.

Ugh, how I hate that girl. When I was at St. Tabby's, Plum either ignored me or laughed at me and my lack of fashion sense. She mocked my boobs when they suddenly sprouted, and she only took any notice of me when Simon fancied me and she wanted to do him a favor by telling Nadia to invite me to her party. I was just so much girl-meat to Plum, to be thrown at a boy she wanted to keep happy, because apparently Simon has more money than God. And after Dan died, Plum screamed that I was a killer, claimed to have been his girlfriend, and led her entire court at St. Tabby's in a systematic campaign to send me hate e-mails and texts and generally try to drive me into hating myself even more than I already did.

I'm really glad that Nadia's given me the opportunity to thwart Plum in some way. Even if it's a minor revenge for all the pain she's caused me.

"The one in the middle with the sequins?" Taylor confirms.

I nod.

"Wow," Taylor says. "They always say that English girls are scruffy, but these ones all look totally Upper East Side."

"What's that?"

"Princesses," Taylor says concisely.

"There's a countess up there, actually," I tell her. "The blond one. Sophia Von und Zu Unpronounceable."

Taylor raises her eyebrows. "I never saw a countess before," she says. "I must tell my folks, they'll get a kick out of that."

"Ross! Simon!" Plum screeches, loud enough for me to hear her even over the roar of chatter and the boom of the music. I am horribly familiar with Plum's voice, though. In

33

my nightmares, I sometimes hear her screaming "You killed him!" at me.

I twist around further, so the two boys coming up the stairs don't see my face.

"That's Simon, the blond one," I hiss at Taylor, leaning far over the table.

She's quick to rememeber. "The one who liked you— you were invited to the party so he could try to get off with you?"

I nod.

"And the other one, Ross, thinks the world revolves around him," I add. "Is he still spotty?"

"Like he's got measles."

Her head swivels as she watches their progress.

"Okay, they're at Plum's table now," she says. "No one's looking over here."

"Cool so far," I hiss back. "Now we have to work out a way to get Plum's phone—"

But just then, a crash of breaking glass behind me makes us both jump. I chance a look round and see Plum climbing up onto the table. The sequins turn out to be a minidress which I have to admit, due to her extreme thinness and her elegant face, she actually manages to make look elegant. On me, with my figure that goes in and out a lot more, I'd look as tarty as if I was trying to snag a footballer for a night and then sell my story to the tabloids. Her chestnut hair is styled in a fringe cut, her greenish eyes are darkly rimmed with eyeliner, and her lips are glossy and pale. She looks sort of sixties: it really suits her. But then, everything seems to suit Plum. I can't help being envious.

Everyone around her is yelping with excitement and cheering her on.

"Go, Plum! Go, Plum!" Ross is shouting, in a beery voice that suggests he's already trashed.

"Who wants to see my knickers?" Plum screams, fiddling provocatively with the hem of her minidress.

"No *way*," Taylor says, looking at me incredulously.

"I bloody do!" Ross yells, his face now completely red, which means that his skin has flushed the same color as his spots.

Everyone's looking over at Plum now. She's dancing, which is no mean feat considering her heels must be four inches high, and there are still quite a few glasses left on the table. Shimmying back and forth, she does a couple of squats, sticking out her bottom, which would work better if she had one worthy of the name, and pops her hips back and forth. Taylor totally cracks up.

"Ohmigod," she says between sobs of laughter, "that's the worst booty dancing I have *ever* seen in my life—"

But I interrupt her, because I have suddenly had a brilliant idea.

"Taylor!" I say urgently. "Get under the table!"

"Why?" She stops laughing, baffled. "Nobody knows my face but Lizzie and Nadia, and they're not going to say anything! It's *you* that—"

"No, not to hide! Not this table!" I correct her impatiently. "To get Plum's phone! Grab it out of her bag!"

Most girls would freak out on the spot at that proposition. Not Taylor. She sizes up the situation and sees instantly what I mean:

1) Plum is on the table.
2) Everyone else has jumped up to stand around it, clapping and cheering her on.
3) They're all drunk and collapsing with laughter.
4) Their entire attention is focused on Plum.

Therefore, no one should notice Taylor sneaking through their midst—or hopefully, if they do, they'll be too hammered to realize what they're seeing.

"Marc Jacobs bag, chestnut, big limited-edition buckle with MJ on it, barrel-shaped, two big side straps," she recites with utter seriousness.

I bite my lip so I don't crack up and offend her. Taylor is so fashion-illiterate she might as well be running over the combination of the safe she's about to open surreptitiously. We had to look up a picture of the bag online today, to make sure she recognized it. She pored over that photo like she was committing a secret formula to memory—and in a way, she has.

"That's it," I assure her. "Nadia says Plum takes it with her everywhere, because it's a limited edition."

Taylor briefly rolls her eyes: she has no time for people who care whether a bag is a limited edition. But then, she doesn't own a single handbag.

"Okay, here I go," she says, standing up. "Watch my back."

"If it looks dodgy, I'll create a diversion," I promise, and I mean it, though all I can think of is waving to catch Plum's attention and yelling that her dancing is worse than a four-year-old's. That should do it.

But it's very much a worst-case scenario, because if Plum sees me here, and then her phone goes missing, she's bound to connect the two incidents, and then she'll come after me. Which is the last thing we want to have to deal with. So we're both hoping a diversion won't be necessary. My fingers are crossed so tightly I'm almost cutting off my circulation.

I turn to watch Taylor slipping through the crowd. She bends down, as if she's dropped something, and then she's simply gone, disappeared. Though she's big-shouldered and packed with muscle, Taylor moves surprisingly smoothly, and there doesn't seem to be a ripple in the crowd around where she ducked down.

Meanwhile, Plum is still giving the table-dancing everything she has, wiggling and shaking, her long hair flying from side to side as she tosses her head around in a way that I'm sure would make me want to puke my guts out if I had a few colored martinis inside me. Her skinny legs flash up and down, and when she does that squatting move again, which makes all the boys whoop, I'm pretty sure that everyone in front of her is definitely, as promised, seeing her knickers. I don't get why it's sexy to look like you're about to go to the loo—even her face is all twisted up like she's constipated—but clearly there's a lot about being sexy I'm just not aware of, because it's going down fantastically with the crowd.

Plum's halfway through popping out her bum again when it happens. Up till now, the situation's been fairly contained: Plum's lot are crowding round the table to watch her, people are looking up from the pleb section to see what's going on, but no one else seems that bothered—though I do notice the bouncers guarding the VIP area are looking over at the booth and talking into their headsets.

Then it all goes to hell in a handbasket.

It looks like the table's tipping under Plum's feet. She falters. The expression on her face changes from constipated to alarmed. She wobbles, and then she sits down heavily on the table, her legs shooting up in the air. The table tilts drastically. The drinks on it go flying, and everyone screams and jumps back.

Oh my God, what if Taylor's underneath it? Forget getting caught, she could be badly hurt! I'm on my feet, running toward the table, all concerns about getting spotted by Plum forgotten in my concern for Taylor. As I push into the crowd I see Nadia right by the table, her hands outstretched. It looks like she's trying to steady it. Ross is reaching out to help Plum, who's trying to stand up, but just then the table does a huge heave, and her heels slip on the surface, probably from all the spilled sticky alcohol. She does a spectacular half spin, her arms flailing, looking like nothing so much as a figure skater on drugs. Despite the gravity of Taylor's situation, I start giggling—I can't help it—and someone next to me starts giggling too, and swiftly the entire group is howling with laughter.

Ross has grabbed Plum by one arm and is hauling her off the table. She slips and spins around as he grabs her, and her feet kick the air. People start screaming and ducking as her long pointy heels whip scarily close to them. I duck down too, partly not to get a heel in my face (I notice that Plum is wearing ankle boots like mine, which goes to show how spot-on the salesgirl at the boutique was in advising me to buy them), and partly to see if I can spot Taylor. It's such a free-for-all by now, though, that there are so many bodies down here with me I can't see anything at all. I try to crawl, but someone bumps into me from behind and I get stuck.

A deep voice is booming above the table and suddenly there's a wave of shoving and pushing. Panicky, I manage to get my feet under me and stand up, scared I'm going to get trampled, and as I come up level with the table again I see several bouncers, head and shoulders taller than everyone else, their big black-clad arms reaching out to clear the area. One of them is yelling:

"Everyone *back up!* Back up *right now!*"

I still haven't seen Taylor, which is making me frantic for her safety. I try to slip under the arm of the bouncer in front of me, but he catches me and pushes me back roughly. And just then, on the other side of the area they're trying to clear, half hidden behind the burly shoulder of another bouncer, I see a shock of blond hair, ruffled up messily. Below it is a pink and white face, its eyes round with shock, its mouth open ditto, and as its eyes meet mine, its lips move and it mouths *"Scarlett?"*

Oh God. It's Simon. Simon, who had a crush on me and got me invited to that fateful party where my life went completely off the safe and sensible rails on which it had been running up till that point. Simon, who tried to chat me up at the party, but was sent packing by Dan. Simon, who's still calling *"Scarlett!"* at me and struggling to get past the

39

bouncer who's holding him back, which would be funny if the situation weren't so dire, because it's like watching a Chihuahua trying to fight a rottweiler.

My only hope is to get out of here right now and pray that Simon thinks he made a mistake in recognizing me. At least I've had the presence of mind not to acknowledge him in any way. I slip back till I'm completely concealed behind the huge bulk of the bouncer beside me, and then I just keep going, retracing my steps, down the stairs and out of the VIP area. At the back of the room, I turn to get a last look at the chaos still raging up on the dais. One of the bouncers has grabbed Plum and is frog-marching her down the steps.

I know I should get the hell out of here, but I can't resist waiting for a moment to see what happens next.

"No dancing on tables!" the bouncer's yelling at Plum. "House rules! No dancing on tables!"

"Don't you know who I am?" Plum screams in fury.

"You could be Princess Beatrice and you still couldn't dance on the table!" the bouncer booms back at her. "Now settle down, or you'll be barred for life!"

Ross runs down the steps and starts saying something to the bouncer. I see him reach into his jacket pocket and I assume he's going for his wallet, trying to bribe him so he won't bar Plum. Reluctantly, I turn away. I still can't see Taylor up in the VIP area, so I duck into a side room and pull out my phone, thumbing out a frantic text:

U OK?!

No immediate answer. I wait for what seems like ages. By now, everyone's heard that there's been a riot in the VIP area, and people flood toward the archway that leads into it till a couple of bouncers appear and block the way. A few people emerge, but not Taylor. I'm on tenterhooks by now, all kinds of scenarios frantically running through my head: she's been injured, she's trapped under the table, she's been caught going through Plum's bag and hauled off by the bouncers, who are calling the police. My heart is pounding madly, my phone sweaty in my hand. It feels like hours before my phone finally buzzes with a message, and I stab so urgently at the button to see it that I miss, hit the wrong one, and it takes me ages to get back to the text menu and finally see:

MEET ME OUT BACK

Oh, thank God. I tear through the crowd, which is hard because everyone's pouring the other way, but I make it through by dint of much shoving and pushing and I run up the stairs and out and duck under the velvet rope and stand there for a minute, not knowing which way to go, till I have a brainwave and pant to the doorman:

"Where's the back exit?"

He jerks his head to the right. I take off, running as well as I can in these heels, and just as I turn the corner of the building someone grabs me and I yelp, spinning round, and Taylor's voice says:

"*Run!*" We both shoot back the way we came, to the

front of the club, where Taylor—who's faster than me, because she's not wearing heels—makes for a taxi that's just dropped off a group of partygoers. She grabs the door they've just slammed and hauls it open again even before the driver's had time to switch on the orange For Hire light.

We slump on the seat, gasping for breath.

"The bouncers started putting everyone out the back," Taylor pants. "I suddenly realized Plum might see you—"

"Where to, ladies?" the taxi driver interrupts, turning round to look at us through the opening in the glass. He's quite old, with silver hair and a jolly face. "On to your next party?"

"No, we're done for the evening," Taylor says.

"Oh, what a shame," he says, making a tut-tutting sound. "Two pretty ladies like you should be dancing till dawn."

I giggle, mostly at Taylor's appalled expression at being called a pretty lady. Fishing in my bag, I pull out the slip of paper on which I've written Lizzie's address, and read it out to him.

"All righty," he says, setting the cab in motion. "Home, James, and don't spare the horses!"

I look at Taylor.

"Did it go okay?"

"Yes and no," Taylor says, still keeping her voice low. "I got the phone, I deleted the video, that's all done—*but*, there's a situation with the handbags."

"*What?*"

Taylor sighs.

"Limited edition, my ass. There were two bags *exactly*

the same under that table," she says. "When Nadia saw Dan's EpiPen in Plum's bag, she could've made a mistake. It might not have been Plum's bag after all."

"*Two?*" I'm so incredulous I can barely get the word out.

Taylor nods grimly.

"Oh my God!" I exclaim. "That means—"

"Yeah." Taylor's had more time to think this through than I have. "It might have been someone else besides Plum who took Dan's EpiPen."

I stare at her, my heart sinking.

"This is awful," I say.

Taylor nods glumly. I slump back into the corner of the taxi. This is so miserable. Twenty seconds ago, I was flying. Operation VPD had gone fantastically: we were well on course to find out everything that Nadia had to tell us, getting closer to solving the mystery of Dan's murder. And now, it feels like we're back to square one.

Plus, it might not even be Plum who killed Dan. I realize I was really hoping to find out that Plum was guilty. Plum's such a bitch; it would make complete sense for her to be a killer. She even had a motive—she was so keen on Dan she told people she was his girlfriend, which totally wasn't true. If she was jealous of his flirting, that could have made her want to kill him . . . couldn't it?

But now that I think it over, I have to admit, reluctantly, that maybe it isn't *that* strong a motive. And the way Dan was killed was so sneaky. Poisoning the crisps with peanut oil, positioning them in front of him . . . I don't see Plum carrying out a plan that cunning. She'd be much more likely to stab someone in a fit of temper, or push them off a cliff, and then claim it was their fault for provoking her.

Everything I thought I knew for sure has just dissolved. I slump further into the corner of the taxi seat, curling up in a ball. We're no closer to solving Dan's murder than we were at the start of the evening. All this for nothing. I'm so disappointed I could burst into tears.

four

"ARE YOU IN THE POOL?"

"Cannonball!" Taylor yells, and hurls herself into the air, arms wrapped around her knees. The next second there's a gigantic splash that temporarily blinds me. Crossly wiping my eyes and blinking, I see water pouring over the edge of the pool and running into the channel cut into the marble drainage surround. Shock waves from the impact lap around me; it feels as if Taylor's displaced half the water in the swimming pool.

I'm not in the mood for cannonballs. To be honest, Taylor's obsession with them is annoying me. I'm still pretty depressed about the fact that I thought I was getting close to solving Dan's murder, and now I'm back to square one again. It's okay for Taylor, because it isn't personal to her. But this means everything in the world to me, and I've just been dealt a crushing blow. I really think Taylor could be a bit more sympathetic. Instead, she isn't even noticing that I'm paddling around in the shallow end, dispirited and list-less. She's hauling herself out of the water again for another cannonball instead. I turn away so I don't get a faceful of water this time.

"*Cannonball!*" she yells again, just before another half-ton of water shoots out of the pool in her wake.

I suppose it's not her fault that investigating Dan's death just isn't as important to her as it is to me. For Taylor it's something to do to relieve the crushing boredom of life at Wakefield Hall Maximum Security Prison, and, of course, a great opportunity to train up in those PI skills she wants to improve. And sometimes she forgets that to me, this is much more than just a way to kill time. I mop the spray from her impact out of my hair and reflect that, in the end, I'm the only person I can truly rely on a hundred percent. That's only normal, I suppose. We're all alone in the end.

But I hate acknowledging it.

Suddenly, watching Taylor cavort around in the deep end, a deep rush of loneliness washes over me. Am I over-relying on her? Maybe I am, if the fact that she's not focusing on this disappointment as much as I am is upsetting me this much. Perhaps I need to lean less on Taylor and stand more on my own two feet. I was so happy to make friends with her because when I met her my old friends had dumped me (my own fault, so I shouldn't really complain). Taylor doesn't have anyone else either: she's as much an outsider at Wakefield Hall as I am. After some initial mistrust and hostility, it's amazing how quickly we've bonded. But have I rushed things too much? Do I need to get more balance in my life and not assume that Taylor will always be there for me?

Ugh, too many questions, and all of them miserable. I

dive underwater to shake them off, swimming slowly along the bottom of the shallow end, wishing I could stay down here forever and never have to come up to face the problems on the surface.

Believe it or not, we're in the basement of Lizzie's house. Which, besides the heated swimming pool, has a private cinema, game room, and, for all I know, a bowling alley and tennis court as well. When we realized we would have to stay in London tonight—because we couldn't go out late to a club Saturday night and get back to school at two in the morning—Lizzie offered to put us up. It took us both by surprise, as, to be honest, we haven't really been that nice to her. But she was quite excited by the idea.

"Lizzie doesn't really have any friends, does she?" Taylor said earlier. "When I asked Mademoiselle Fournier if I could stay over at Lizzie's tonight, she sounded happier that Lizzie had someone to stay with than that I had someone to visit."

"Honestly, I could have told my aunt Gwen I was staying with a pedophile I met when he picked me up in the knickers section of Marks and Spencer's, and she wouldn't have batted an eyelid," I said sourly.

"Yeah, but your aunt Gwen hates you," Taylor pointed out with brutal frankness.

"She doesn't think much of Lizzie, either. She sniffed when I said who I was staying with. And when I said she was a friend of ours, I know she didn't believe me."

Taylor shrugged. "Well, maybe we're the closest she's got."

"That's pretty sad. We should be nicer to her."

Taylor pretended to gag, but beneath that tough exterior

is a slightly—*slightly*—softer heart, and she was actually quite polite to Lizzie this afternoon as Lizzie proudly showed us to our rooms. (Yup, we have one each, and they're huge, and they're both en suite. All this in Chelsea, the most expensive area in the whole of London. Lizzie's dad clearly has more money than God.)

We didn't realize there was a swimming pool, though. Lizzie was too absorbed in showing us her built-in handbag and shoe cupboards, plus her wet room and Jacuzzi. We found that out from Lucia, the Romanian live-in housekeeper, who let us in when we got back from the club.

"You want something to eat?" she asked, stone-faced, when we'd finished apologizing for making her get up to let us in. ("Is okay. Is my job. Miss Lizzie say perhaps you not come back with her.")

"No, that's fine," I said wistfully, kicking Taylor, who always wants something to eat. But I knew if we said yes, Lucia would have to get it for us, and she had clearly got out of bed to let us in—she was in her dressing gown and slippers, and her eyes were all blurry with sleep.

"You have drink?" Lucia asked. "Watch film in cinema? Swim?"

"I'm sorry," I said blankly, "I must have misheard you, but I thought you said . . ."

Five minutes later the lift doors pinged open, and Lucia led us out and down a beautifully tiled corridor. She pushed open a door. We gasped.

"Hot towels there. Swimming clothes there. Sauna there," she pointed, though we were too mesmerized by the

48

delicate cloud of steam rising off the bright blue water of the swimming pool to really focus on her directions. "Toilet also." She indicated the far side of the pool, which is set in pale pink–tinged marble. "Behind the pillars." Those were marble too, of course.

"Thank you so much," Taylor said fervently.

"No problem." Lucia actually cracked a tiny smile. "You good girls. Not drunk. I not smell drink when you talk."

"Um, thank you," I said, profoundly grateful we hadn't had a cocktail in Coco Rouge.

Lucia turned to leave.

"You drink water now," she said over her shoulder. "For the sauna."

"Yes, Lucia," we chorused.

I surface from my underwater swim, wishing my aunt Gwen were more like Lucia. I don't mind a bit of tough love. And Lucia was nicer to me than Aunt Gwen's been my whole life.

"Show me how you spin round so fast in that somersault you do on the trampoline," Taylor calls, pulling herself out of the pool with one smooth flex of her powerful upper body.

"I'm not really feeling like it," I mumble, treading water.

"Oh, come on, Scarlett!" Taylor puts her hands on her hips. "I know tonight was disappointing, but we're in a *private swimming pool*—that's got to cheer you up a bit!"

Now I feel like I'm being a misery guts, and dragging Taylor down with me. Guiltily, I instruct her:

"You need to get into the tuck as fast as you can. Snap

your arms down like you're throwing a ball, and by the time they come down, your knees should be tucked tight into your chest."

"Throwing a ball," Taylor says, raising her arms above her head and trying it out. "Okay, here I go!"

She runs toward the edge of the pool, jumps up, tucks up, and in that precise moment a voice booms out from nowhere, bouncing round the tiles and marble so loudly that Taylor's tuck somersault goes completely haywire.

"Are you in the pool?" the voice says.

Taylor throws out her arms wide, I don't know why, but it completely stops her spin, and she lands facedown in the pool, her arms splayed wide and her knees still tucked up to her chest. I laugh so hard I double up. The expression of total shock when she comes up again makes me laugh even harder. And I don't even feel bad about laughing at her. After all, not a minute ago she was lecturing me about needing to cheer up.

"Are you in the pool?"

"Aaaah!" Taylor gasps for breath, coughing out water. To my shame, this is somehow even more funny than the belly flop. Maybe it's because I've never seen Taylor be anything but in complete physical control of herself.

"Are you in the pool?" the voice asks again.

"Who the hell are you?!" Taylor shouts back. Her face is bright red: she's literally livid.

"It's Lizzie!"

"Stop screaming at us!" Taylor yells.

"Sorry, it's the intercom! It makes everything sound really loud! I'm coming down!"

50

Lizzie bursts through the door a few minutes later, all excited. I bet Lucia would have smelled drink on her breath.

"Hey!" she says, beaming. "Are you enjoying the pool? Isn't it great? And what about that scene in the club! Wasn't it crazy? Plum had a complete meltdown! I was scared, but it was really exciting, too! And how did your top-secret mission go? Did you find everything out?"

"Not really," I say, sighing. "It turned out to be much more complicated than we realized."

"Oh, that's a shame!" Lizzie actually looks disappointed on our behalf. "I know, why don't I make some popcorn? And we can have cocoa with mint Baileys and marshmallows in it? That's my favorite!" She claps her hands in glee, like a little girl. "I'll go and start the popcorn machine. Meet you in my living room. Take the lift to the third floor and turn left, all the way down the corridor. Ooh, this is going to be so much fun!"

"I never thought these words would come out of my mouth," Taylor says as the door bangs shut behind Lizzie, "but I gotta say, sometimes being Lizzie's friend seems like a really good deal."

. . .

Naturally, the pool changing room is well stocked with fluffy toweling robes and assorted spa-type slippers, so ten minutes later we're curled up in front of a roaring fire in Lizzie's sitting room, mugs of hot, minty, and slightly alcoholic cocoa in our hands, a bowl of popcorn between us, and the very comforting popping sound of another batch cooking up in the machine. This is the life.

Or it would be, if I weren't feeling, very strongly, that tight little knot inside my stomach, which is the perpetual reminder I have of Dan's death. That knot's always with me, but sometimes I don't feel it as much as others. Right now, it's like a stone in my stomach, hard and cold, because I'm so disappointed about tonight.

But also, I'm really enjoying this coziness, and my cocoa is so delicious it's competing with the tight knot for attention. It's weird feeling torn like this.

That's another reason I'm so keen to solve Dan's murder. I want to be able to feel just one feeling at a time. I want to get rid of the stone in my stomach.

"I feel like we're in a ski resort in Colorado," Taylor comments, blowing on her drink.

"It's cozy, isn't it?" Lizzie beams. "Sometimes I make my cocoa and take it into the Jacuzzi to watch TV. That's lovely too, though you can't see the fire. So what was the problem tonight?" she continues, so happy to feel she's at the center of something that her eyes are shining like headlights.

Here's the thing: we can't tell Lizzie anything important, as she'll just babble it to everyone she knows in an effort to show off how she's in our confidence. She knows, of course, that something's going on between us and Nadia, something secret and complicated and important. Still, everyone involved has kept her completely in the dark. But Taylor and I had a quick brainstorm downstairs, and we decided that there was one issue on which Lizzie might actually be helpful. It's her special subject, after all.

I sigh. "It sounds silly," I say, "but Nadia wanted our help. You see, there's a boy she likes, and she thinks he likes her. Only she's not sure. And a few nights ago, they were out at a club, and she was sitting with Plum's handbag next to her—"

"The Marc Jacobs limited edition!" Lizzie interrupts excitedly, eager to show off that she knows Plum's wardrobe.

"Exactly. And she thinks this boy thought it was *her* bag—Nadia's, that is—and put in a note for her."

This part of the story is very weak indeed. I mean, who leaves notes nowadays? I keep talking quickly before Lizzie starts to realize it doesn't quite make sense.

"Only the thing is, it wasn't Plum's bag after all—she got confused, 'cause quite a few girls have the same bag, apparently, but she didn't realize. So she really wants to find out who's got the same bag and see if any of them got a note in it that wasn't meant for them."

I look dubiously at Lizzie: is she actually falling for this? I didn't have time to come up with a better story. Luckily, the cocktails at Coco Rouge and the Baileys have dissolved any shred of common sense she might have possessed.

"That's so *romantic*!" she breathes. "And now he doesn't know that she didn't get the note, so he might think *she* doesn't like *him*. . . . It's sort of like Romeo and Juliet, isn't it?"

"Um, yeah," I say, tilting my head to one side and trying to make my eyes go misty. This also means I avoid catching

Taylor's eye, which I don't think will be a good idea if I want to keep being convincing. I leave it a moment, then say thoughtfully:

"I don't suppose *you* have any idea who else has that bag, do you?"

Lizzie almost jumps up and down in glee, her Baileys cocoa slopping dangerously near the edge of her mug.

"Of *course* I do!" she says excitedly. "Sophia has one! She only got it last month, her sister gave it to her because she was bored with it, but Sophia really likes it, she takes it *everywhere*, even if it doesn't really go with what she's wearing. . . ."

"Sophia Von und Zu Whatsit?"

"Yes, it's funny, because you know how Plum *hates* it when people have the same thing as her, it's sort of a rule that you don't have anything the same, right? But Sophia really, really wanted to keep the bag, and *apparently*, when she came into school with it"—Lizzie puts down her mug and leans forward in her velvet armchair, all excited to be telling us what she considers a prime piece of gossip—"she put it under her chair so Plum didn't see it straightaway. And then Sophia invited Plum that morning to come to their schloss with them for half-term. Which is amazing, apparently, it's like an entire castle in Austria and it looks like something out of a fairy tale, and Sophia's family are really, really posh and fantastically well-connected, so Plum's been dying to get an invitation there for ages. So of course she said yes. And then Sophia reached down to get her bag and everyone saw it for the first time. And *apparently*, everyone went absolutely dead silent, but Sophia had just invited Plum to stay, so Plum didn't, you know, do anything about it. It was sort of like a bargain, know what I mean?"

"Yeah, I do. Okay, so Sophia has one," I prompt. "Does anyone else have the same bag?"

Lizzie's nodding vigorously. "Lucy has one. Lucy Raleigh." Lizzie's eyes go moony and puppylike, the way they do when she mentions Plum's name. Which is interesting, because I've never seen Lizzie look like this about anyone but Plum.

"Who's Lucy Raleigh?" Taylor asks.

"You don't *know?*" Lizzie is incredulous. "She's, like, *incredibly pretty and cool*. She's at St. Paul's Girls'. She was at the club tonight, did you see her? She was wearing a D&G top and Made by Lou jeans"—she stops for a moment, narrowing her eyes—"and," she finishes triumphantly, "a Guess jacket. I *think* it was Guess," she adds conscientiously. "I think she was the first person to have one of those bags. I haven't seen her with it for ages, though."

Sophia was at the party when Dan died, but that was six months ago, and according to Lizzie's story, her sister only recently gave her the bag. So she's in the clear. I must say, I'd have found it very hard to believe that Sophia had anything to do with killing Dan. I used to be in the same history class as her at St. Tabby's, and as a result, I know that Sophia has about as many brain cells as a newt. Organizing anything that complicated would be out of the question for her—the mental strain would put her in a coma for weeks.

"And no one else has one of those bags?" Taylor asks.

Lizzie shakes her head. "No one we know. They didn't make that many."

Well, that's definite. If there's one subject Lizzie's an expert on, it's handbags.

Suddenly, the coziness of Lizzie's sitting room turns suffocating. I've got a clue.

Taylor's eyes are gleaming: I can see she feels exactly the same. Lucy Raleigh. Who goes to St. Paul's Girls'. And is incredibly pretty and cool. Could she have anything to do with Dan's murder?

Oh, there's one more thing to clear up.

"Does Sophia's sister hang out with Plum's lot at all?" I ask, just to make sure there's no chance that the sister was at Nadia's party.

Lizzie looks amazed. "God, no! She's much older. She's, like, *married*!"

Well, that rules the sister out, which means we can completely concentrate on this Lucy Raleigh. My mood is improving by the moment: we have a real clue here to focus on. And in the taxi, I talked myself out of real suspicions of Plum. Maybe I'm wrong, but thinking it over, I do have my doubts that it's in Plum's character to carry out such a complicated and sneaky plot. Plum's all about direct confrontation. Maybe, if I find out more about Lucy Raleigh, it'll turn out that she's much more the type to kill someone in the kind of way Dan was murdered. . . .

"So you think that maybe Lucy got the note that was meant for Nadia?" Lizzie's asking.

Our blank expressions would completely expose us for

total liars, if it weren't Lizzie we were dealing with. We really have to work on our reflexes if we want to be super–spy girl detectives.

"Yeah!" I say, several beats too late, as Taylor chimes in with an overenthusiastic series of nods.

"Oh, I hope she gets together with him," Lizzie sighs wistfully. "It sounds *incredibly* romantic!"

five

I BLUSH ALL OVER REMEMBERING IT

"Elbows off the table, Scarlett. And sit up straighter."

I jerk myself up, horrified to realize I've committed an error as basic as propping my elbows on the table while at lunch with my grandmother. I must have been miles away.

"Sorry, Lady Wakefield," I mutter.

My grandmother has decreed that while I'm a pupil at Wakefield Hall, I have to call her Lady Wakefield at all times, so that nobody thinks I'm getting any special treatment from her. I sort of understand that if it were just in public, as she is, after all, the headmistress—but having to call her Lady Wakefield in private too is really odd.

"So, tell me about the friends you're making here," my grandmother instructs.

I've just forked up some peas and am chewing ten times before swallowing, a rule my grandmother insists on for good digestion. So it's a few seconds before I answer her.

"Um, I'm mainly friends with Taylor McGovern," I say eventually.

"The American girl with the archaeologist parents?" my

grandmother says, but it isn't really a question. She knows every single girl in the school from the moment they first step through the doors of Wakefield Hall. It's rumored that she has dossiers on everyone, and I wouldn't be at all surprised to find out that was true.

I nod, then remember this isn't considered a sufficient answer.

"Yes, that's her. She's quite sporty. We work out together a bit."

My grandmother nods, and cuts another bite of chicken. It's all bland food, again because of her digestion. Poached chicken, boiled carrots and peas and potatoes. Oh well, at least it's better than school food, which is the one consolation for having to spend every Sunday lunchtime with my grandmother in her private dining room, sitting up straight with my elbows off the table, practicing the arts of polite conversation and good table manners.

It's very hard to do both simultaneously, I find.

I look around me as my grandmother chews her chicken. She has a whole private suite of rooms which she chose when she was converting Wakefield Hall into a school, and naturally, she picked the nicest ones. The dining room is in the old conservatory, so it has a glass ceiling and partly glass walls. When it's raining it's really dramatic to sit in here and watch the water pour down over the roof, feeling safe and warm inside. The woodwork is painted pale green, and there are big plants in china pots arranged in niches around the room: like everything my grandmother does, it's simple and elegant. She uses it for big dinners for school governors and particularly favored parents (rich/titled/influential ones, that means) and so the table is huge enough to accommodate twenty people. It's always strange to be sitting at one end of it, our two places neatly set with the family Minton china and monogrammed silverware and crystal water glasses, with a whole expanse of polished wood stretching away from us, occupied only by branches of silver candelabra set at regular intervals.

It makes me feel incredibly self-conscious.

So does my grandmother, because she's so perfectly in control of herself. Her white hair, trimmed into a neat bob, is always smooth and elegant, much smarter than an old-lady bun at the back of her head. Her eyes are bright and blue and see everything, especially the things you don't want her to see. She wears pastel twin sets and tweed skirts and I've never seen her without her pearl necklace and earrings. They're family heirlooms, which is one of the reasons she always wears them; the other is that pearls should be worn as often as possible, because they get their luster from the oils in your skin. That's what my grandmother says, so it must be true because she's always right. Every movement my grandmother makes is precise, and she never says a word she doesn't mean.

You can see why it would be intimidating to have to spend every Sunday lunchtime with her, can't you?

"And how are your studies progressing?" she asks.

I writhe. This is so awkward—when your grandmother's your headmistress, too, how can I possibly answer that?

Then I have a stroke of inspiration.

"I'm really behind in Latin," I say. "I didn't realize it's taught much better here than at St. Tabby's."

My grandmother's ears prick up with interest.

"Really?" she says with a casualness that's about as believable as a cat telling you he's just sleeping outside a mousehole by coincidence. "Tell me more."

"Oh"—I spear, chew, and swallow a piece of carrot—"nothing, really. It's just that all the girls here are so far ahead of me. They've all been writing Latin for years. At St. Tabby's, we mostly translated it, we didn't do that much writing."

My grandmother lays down her fork and wipes her lips with her monogrammed linen napkin.

"I had no idea standards were so shoddy there," she says happily.

I nod, wide-eyed.

"I didn't realize that till I came here," I say, which may be overdoing it a bit, but it doesn't matter. Grandmother launches into an exquisite denunciation of lazy exam boards, modern curricula in general, and St. Tabby's in particular, which carries us all the way through the removal of our main-course plates, our gooseberry fool for dessert, and coffee (served in china cups so fine you can almost see the coffee through them—I'm always terrified of breaking them). St. Tabby's is one of the best girls' schools in the country, and for Grandmother to have found a chink in its armor has absolutely made her day. We're a competitive family, the Wakefields.

I congratulate myself on having found a subject for lunchtime conversation on which my grandmother can happily hold forth for hours. I'll find something else to criticize about St. Tabby's next week. And then I can just sit there and nod and avoid as much as possible having to practice the art of making polite conversation.

This pleasant mood lasts all the way out of my grandmother's private apartments, down the elaborate central staircase, and through the big main door of Wakefield Hall. Once in the fresh air, though, my mood shifts, no matter how hard I try to keep that feeling of elation. It's always hard for me when I have to go back to Aunt Gwen's.

I struggle with feelings of jealousy toward Taylor all the time. Because Taylor doesn't live at Wakefield Hall. Like the rest of the girls, she just boards here. She has a proper home to go back to, a cozy one where people are happy to see her, and probably make her breakfast. Even Lizzie, whose dad is never around, has that palace to live in and Lucia alternately coddling and tough-loving her. Whereas for me, this is it. A room grudgingly provided for me by Aunt Gwen, who copes by pretending I don't exist. And I can't say any of this to Taylor. It would be much too much poor-little-orphan-me.

I don't often think about my parents, because there isn't any point, and besides, I was too young when they died to remember them well. I just have snatches of memory, like those old-fashioned slide shows you see sometimes in films, where they project a bright image at you for a few seconds before someone clicks something and it snaps away to another slide.

I'm almost down the drive now, almost at Aunt Gwen's house, which is actually the old gatehouse, tucked away in a nest of trees beside the main gates. I wonder if I'm feeling strong enough to go through my special box, where I keep things that remind me of my parents. Photos of us, when I was little. My baby book. A scarf my mum knitted for me. It's not very good—it has a lot of dropped stitches—but I find that really endearing, because she was obviously rubbish at knitting but persisted anyway, because it was for me.

I pass the stand of cypresses that conceals the gatehouse from the drive, and as I round them and the house comes into view, I jump and nearly drop my bag, and all thoughts of anything but what's immediately in front of me are wiped from my mind.

Jase Barnes is sitting on the garden wall. Looking pretty hot in a bright orange shirt and black jeans.

He must be waiting for me.

Oh my God. What have I got myself into?

• • •

Last week, I sneaked into Nadia's flat. Which is when I found out that Nadia saw Dan's EpiPen in what she thought was Plum's handbag—and when I worked out that Dan was poisoned by peanut oil on the crisps. I ran all the way back from the Wakefield tube, so excited by my twin discoveries that I couldn't wait to tell Taylor everything I knew. Someone killed Dan. It really wasn't my fault that Dan died. And *that*, in turn, meant I could kiss a boy without being afraid that he might drop down dead at my feet, like Dan did.

So when I raced back to school that evening, and I saw Jase Barnes by the dining hall—gorgeous Jase Barnes, who every girl in the school must be in love with, but who seems surprisingly interested in me—I chased him down like a dog. I ran after him, and I made him stop, and I put my hands on his shoulders and reached up and kissed him . . . and then, thank God thank God, I ran away straight afterward without hanging round to embarrass myself even further.

Aaah. I blush all over remembering it.

But at least he didn't die.

Which is pretty obvious, as here he is, in the flesh, jumping down off the wall when he sees me with what I can't help hoping is enthusiasm. His bright golden eyes are gleaming. I hope he doesn't think I'm going to throw myself into his arms again. I don't think I have that quite in me right now.

"Um, hi," I say, walking toward him, because I have to, as he's standing between me and the gatehouse, and praying with every fiber of my body that I'm not so red right now that I resemble a tomato in clothes.

"Hey," he says, and I do think it's totally unfair that because he's the color of those soft caramel centers you get inside really nice chocolates, I can't tell whether he's blushing too. He does run his hand over his scalp, which is totally unnecessary, because his hair is tightly cropped in tiny dark curls, so maybe that's sort of the boy's equivalent of blushing.

We stand and look at each other for a long moment. I'm shifting from foot to foot, trying to find the words to say that I'm in a hurry and need to go inside Aunt Gwen's, because honestly, I'm wishing he hadn't come to find me. Of course,

I'm flattered, but this is just too confusing for me to deal with right now.

"I like your outfit," he eventually says, grinning.

Automatically I look down at myself, and am immediately struck with horror, because I completely forgot that I'm wearing clothes suitable for lunch with my grandmother, according to her very strict rules. Which are: a brown pleated skirt, a navy sweater, tights, and sensible shoes (*not* boots, which are *not* to be worn with skirts). No makeup—that goes without saying. I look like I just timetraveled in from the 1940s.

"I just had lunch with my grandmother," I manage to explain, sure I'm blushing even more. I'm cursing the fact that practically every time I see Jase, I'm either Sundaymorning scruffy or Sunday-lunch prim. Why couldn't I be all dressed up like I was last night when I bump into him, just once?

"It's very, um—" he starts.

"Ladylike?" I suggest.

"Well, that's one way of putting it," he says, grinning even more.

"I have to buy clothes just for seeing her," I find myself saying, so he won't think any of this stuff is actually something I might like. "I never wear anything like this the rest of the time."

"Not even the shoes?" he says, keeping a straight face, so I think for a moment he's serious, and look down at my shoes—brown leather, sort of loafers with a little stacked heel—before I realize that he's joking.

"Oh yeah," I agree. "I love these so much I cry when I have to take them off."

"I'd cry when I had to put them *on*," Jase says, and we both burst out laughing.

I meant to say hi, have a quick conversation, and then go inside as soon as I could. I don't want to be rude to Jase, of course I don't. He's utterly gorgeous, and though I don't know him that well, I've really liked what I've seen of him. I definitely want to hang out with him more, get to know him, kiss him again . . . but only when the dark cloud of Dan's death, still hanging over my head, has floated away for good. Awful and selfish as it sounds, I'd like to be able to hide Jase away in a cupboard so no other girl can get to him, and then take him out when I'm ready to play with him.

But Jase isn't a doll. A doll couldn't make me laugh despite myself, or lure me into the middle of a funny conversation when I intended to say a quick hello and goodbye. I'm more confused than ever.

"Um, I was wondering," Jase starts, and then grinds to a halt. He clears his throat. "Um . . . are you up to anything right now?" he asks.

"Well, I've got some homework to do . . . ," I say, and then I could bite my tongue off. How boring does that sound? And it wasn't what he was asking at all, I know that.

"Oh," he says, looking disappointed, and he shuffles his feet as if he's going to walk away.

"But that won't take all day . . . ," I hear myself adding quickly. "I've just got, um, a couple of hours' work to do."

Which is a total lie. I can't believe these words are

coming out of my mouth. Despite my best intentions, I just couldn't bear the sight of him walking away from me disappointed.

I must be the weakest-willed girl in the world.

"Oh, good," he says enthusiastically, a lovely smile lighting up his face. "Do you maybe want to go see a film or something later on, when you've got that done? There's the new James Bond in Princebury—it's on at four—"

"I've been wanting to see that," I say.

"Cool," he replies. "Meet you at three-thirty?"

I nod, still feeling that I should back out. I swore I wouldn't get involved with a boy in any way till I'd solved the mystery of Dan's death. *But now at least you know it wasn't your fault that Dan died,* says a wicked little voice inside me. *You didn't kill him, you're in the clear. Why shouldn't you go to see a film with Jase, just once?*

"Wear jeans and a warm jacket," he says, grinning at me. "It's a nice day, but it gets a bit cold on the bike. I'll be waiting for you down by the main gates."

I'm going on a motorbike to see a film with Jase Barnes. I can't believe this.

With trembling fingers, I search my rucksack for the door key. The idea of going on a motorbike with him is so dazzling it momentarily sweeps away any doubts I might have had. I let myself in and run upstairs to my room, throwing my rucksack on the bed and pulling open my dresser drawers, looking for an outfit to wear. That dark pink cashmere hoodie will be perfect—the style's casual enough to look like I haven't gone to too much trouble, but it fits really nicely. And the jeans I wore to ambush Nadia go with that really well. I can tuck them into boots again. Suddenly I realize I am planning exactly the same outfit to impress both Nadia and Jase. Is that weird, or ironic? Or does it just mean I haven't got that many cool-yet-sexy clothes?

I look at my watch: it's 1:30. I have two hours before meeting Jase. For a second, I wonder whether I should ask Aunt Gwen's permission to go out with him on the bike, and then I decide I'm being ridiculous: Aunt Gwen wouldn't care if I said I was going out with a whole pack of Hell's Angels to do some devil worshipping, as long as I was back for the dinner roll call.

But before I can get too excited at the thought of holding on to Jase as we zip through the streets, I feel a big lump form at the back of my throat. I remember how excited I was when Dan smiled at me from behind the bar in Nadia's flat.

So instead of picking out what earrings to wear, I'm sitting in front of my computer, searching for Lucy Raleigh.

That makes sense, doesn't it?

* * *

Beep! Beep!

I'm so deep into my online research that I completely forgot that I'd set my alarm so I could make sure I have time to get dressed and do my makeup before meeting Jase. I switch off the alarm without even taking my eyes off my computer screen. I've been scouring all the networking sites and I've got a ton of information here.

Crucial facts learned about Lucy Raleigh so far:

1) She really is very pretty: she has straight blond hair, round blue eyes, and porcelain skin. Her features make her look very innocent, but she's so trendily dressed and made up that she has just as sophisticated an aura as Plum. I think she's even more photogenic than Plum, too, which I bet Plum doesn't like very much.

2) All her friends are intimidatingly good-looking and grown-up-looking too.

3) Plum is a friend of hers online, as is Nadia, and all the girls from Plum's set at St. Tabby's. But reading between the lines of the messages left, it doesn't sound like they're close, more like they're sort of tactical allies in the battle to be more fashionable than anyone else. (Lucky for me, Lizzie isn't online friends with Nadia, Plum, or Lucy, so I'm safe on that front. Still, it's kind of chilling to know just how much these girls are using Lizzie, like Plum had used me, and it makes me feel kind of awful for using Lizzie too. However, I'm quick to remind myself that using Lizzie is a means to an end, and that once this is all over, I can try to redeem my character.)

4) Lucy has a boyfriend named Callum, but he doesn't seem to like being photographed. There are tons of pictures of Ross and Simon and those boys from the table-dancing night at Coco Rouge, arms wrapped round Lucy and Plum and Nadia, grinning madly at the camera, but I can't find any of Callum. His avatar is a cartoon

character I don't recognize, who looks a bit indie-punk, on a tartan background.

5) Callum has only one profile, and it doesn't help—he's never even filled most of it out. It just says his age—seventeen—where he lives—Ayrshire, in Scotland—and the music that he likes, mostly bands I've never heard of, with the same kind of indie-punk artwork as his avatar. His friends have barely posted any messages apart from a few initial hellos. Callum's obviously one of those people who create a page for themselves and quickly realize they're not that into it and they can't be bothered to keep it up.

6) But most importantly—there are a flood of messages the day after Nadia's party. Everyone is asking Lucy how she and Callum are doing, but Lucy hasn't responded to any of them. Callum wasn't at the party, I note. There are various comments straight afterward asking when he's coming down to London, and if Lucy's seen him yet, so clearly he was somewhere else—in Ayrshire, maybe, if that's where he lives. Still, it's strange how everyone seems extremely concerned about Lucy and her boyfriend, as though they had a very strong link to Dan.

I stare at the pictures of Lucy for a while, flicking through them till I come to one of her in a black backless dress—she's looking at the camera over one shoulder, posing sexily, to show off her bare back. There's just a tiny string holding the dress together at the back of her waist. Lucky her, not to have to wear a bra all the time.

And then I get a flash of memory, and I have the really strong feeling I've seen her somewhere before. I squeeze my eyes shut, trying to grasp at the flickering images that just shot across my subconscious. Girls in backless dresses, giggling, sitting somewhere—at a bar—was it at Coco Rouge? No, much longer ago than that. But I never go out to trendy bars, so it must have been—

At Nadia's party. That's where I saw Lucy. She was sitting with another girl further down the bar. She was giggling and flirting with Dan as he mixed drink after drink.

And when I ate those crisps, which had been laced with peanut oil, I was sitting at the bar, too. Lucy was right there, in perfect position to have slipped the bowl of crisps in front of Dan, hoping he'd eat some.

It doesn't prove anything. But it does make Lucy an even more likely suspect in Dan's death.

Still, what motive would she have for killing him?

I grab my mobile and ring Nadia, for the promised conversation in which she has to tell me everything she knows about the night Dan died at her penthouse. I have a *lot* of questions for her by now.

Ten minutes later, I put down my mobile and slump back in my chair, totally dispirited. Nadia turned out to be no help at all. The one thing I did establish is that she has absolutely no idea about the crisps. When I asked her if she'd noticed Plum going behind the bar during the party, Nadia was so taken aback that it was clear she had no notion of why I was asking the question.

Of course, I was asking because I wanted to see if Plum had had any chance to bring in the peanut oil and doctor the crisps with it. If it hadn't been so frustrating, I'd have laughed at Nadia's answer.

"Why would Plum be behind the *bar?*" she said, clearly amazed that I was asking. "Girls don't serve drinks at parties—boys do that!"

"Um, okay," I said cautiously, "but wouldn't there maybe be some reason—she might be going to get herself a glass or something—"

"God, no! She'd tell someone to get it for her. She might pour herself a drink, if there was an open bottle on the table, but that's about it. Most girls won't even open bottles, because it ruins their nails."

"*Right.*"

"I mean, honestly," Nadia said, quite getting into this explanation now, "of all the girls at the party, Plum would be the *least* likely to do *anything* like go behind the bar and get something. It would be *so unusual.* I tell you what—if she had, *everyone* would have noticed. I mean, Plum doesn't do stuff for herself, you know? She gets people to do it for her."

"Did she get there early?" I asked, grasping at straws. Maybe if she'd been hanging out with Nadia in the early stages of the evening, she could have nipped to the bar and doctored the crisps before anyone else arrived.

"Oh please!" Nadia said with a patronizing tone for my

stupidity. "Plum likes to make an *entrance*. She never gets anywhere early."

"Of course," I muttered, feeling like a complete idiot. "Um, what about Lucy Raleigh?"

"*You* know Lucy Raleigh?" Nadia sounded very skeptical, of course. How could a girl like me associate with a goddess like Lucy?

"Don't ask me any questions, Nadia," I snapped. "That wasn't part of the deal."

Nadia was quiet for a couple of seconds. "No," she answers eventually. "Lucy's like the Plum of St. Paul's. She doesn't lift a finger either."

"Did she have that Marc Jacobs bag with her?" I asked. "The one that Plum has?"

"Oh my God, you're *right*!" Nadia exclaimed, so loudly I had to hold the phone away from my ear. "I totally forgot Lucy had one too!" She paused. "You know, Scarlett, I thought I'd seen Dan's EpiPen in Plum's bag that night, but maybe I messed up. I mean, until you mentioned it now, I hadn't remembered Lucy. . . ."

Nadia's voice trailed off. She didn't know that I had read her diary, so she probably felt like she'd just made an unnecessary confession that cast suspicion on someone more powerful than her. Nadia recovered quickly and skillfully, though. No doubt something she learned from being friends with Plum.

"Forget what I said. Lucy didn't have a grudge against Dan, if that's what you're getting at. She'd never hurt him, because of Callum."

Interesting. My skeptical mind leapfrogs over Lucy and lands on her boyfriend.

"What do you mean by that? Were Callum and Dan close?" I asked, covering all the bases I could think of.

Nadia laughed. "Um, *yeah*! Everyone knows how tight they were. God, Scarlett. How *clueless* can you be?"

I flinch. The backbone that Nadia had said I'd grown has been sawed in half by that catty remark. I pause for a second to gain my composure but Nadia cuts in again.

"Is that everything you wanted to ask?" she said, a tone of haughtiness in her voice. "I'm late for an appointment with my masseuse."

Whatever shred of guilt Nadia may have felt at the coffee shop didn't seem to exist anymore.

"Wait, I'm not finished."

"*Yes*, you are," Nadia said, sounding annoyed. "I have to go."

"Don't forget, Nadia. Taylor and I did you a huge favor!" It was my turn to sound annoyed. "I don't think one flimsy phone conversation is enough to pay that off, do you?"

For some reason, this made Nadia giggle. It wasn't a very pleasant giggle, though. It sounded as if, somehow, she thought she'd scored one over me.

"That's true, Scarlett. I probably *do* still owe you. You and your friend were *amazingly* helpful," she said before hanging up.

A shiver of worry travels up my arms as I hear the sound of her giggle echoing in my ears.

Beep! Beep!

My alarm goes off again—I must have hit the Snooze

button. And I'm lucky that I did, because when I look at the time I realize I have a bare half hour till I'm supposed to meet Jase.

I sit there, staring at the computer screen with its images of Lucy out with her friends, and wonder if I'm doing the right thing, getting myself involved with Jase when I'm still so embroiled in Dan's murder and all its messy and possibly dangerous consequences. I contemplate meeting Jase and telling him I've just got too much homework this afternoon.

Then I remember that I'm sixteen. And I need to build *something* for myself that isn't connected to Dan in any way . . . or else I'll lose myself completely.

I slowly push back my chair from the desk, deciding that even teenage girls on vengeance missions should get out once in a while.

six

THE ONLY GIRL IN THIS WHOLE SCHOOL

I'm clinging on to Jase's waist as we weave effortlessly through the slow-moving cars. One thing about having done gymnastics for all those years: it means I'm not a screamy girly-girl on a speeding bike, not when I can see that Jase knows exactly what he's doing. I'm sure he's going extrafast to impress me, because that's what boys do, but he never takes a turn so quick that it freaks me out, or cuts in dangerously close to a car.

This is even more fun than the James Bond film—because in the film, exciting though it was, I didn't get to lock my hands around Jase's waist. I hoped he would hold my hand, or put his arm around my shoulders, but he didn't, which was a bit disappointing. Still, I knew that we'd get back on the bike again at the end of it and he'd glance back at me as I perched myself on the seat and reached my arms around him.

I can't believe I'm doing this, but I'm pretending that Jase and I have just met. Some baddies have started shooting at us so we've got to jump on his bike and flee the scene. They chase us, but we're too swift and smart for them. The country lanes whiz by in a blur of streetlights zipping past, one flash of sour yellowish light after another, cars that we buzz by, and I never want this to end. I close my eyes and lean right into Jase, his leather jacket crinkling against my face, his aftershave crisp and smelling of apples, sweet and delicious, and under the aftershave his own scent, which is even more delicious, darker, not like apples at all.

We're slowing down.

We've stopped.

I look around me, dazed. It takes me a little while to realize where we are, because, despite this being my family home, I've never used this road in my life.

Jase puts a gloved hand up to his helmet and slides the panel up. It's dark outside, but I can see he's laughing.

"You don't want to get off, do you?" he's saying. "You really like the bike."

I realize that he can't get off till I do. What an idiot I am! I scramble off more awkwardly than I meant to, and Jase kicks the stand out on the bike, swinging one long leg over and off. He removes his helmet, and I do the same with mine, hoping to God that my hair hasn't got too squished down.

"You're a speed freak, aren't you?" He puts his helmet down on the bike seat, and reaches out for mine.

"I love going fast," I confess, handing him the helmet.

He takes it, puts it down next to his, and somehow he does it so quickly that my hand is still out and he's holding it—oh, I see what he did, he took the helmet with his right hand and simultaneously came in with his left hand to hold mine, that's really smooth. Jase Barnes is holding my hand, and he's pulling it, very, very gently, but enough so that I find myself taking a little step toward him.

I have to say something. I don't know why, but I do. Because if I don't say something, he won't either, and what might happen then, in the silence, is too much for me right now. I'm scared he'll kiss me, and I'm not ready. Not yet.

"The film was great," I say brightly, as if we haven't said already how much we liked it.

"Which was better, the film or the bike ride?" he asks.

I don't even need to think about that one.

"Oh, definitely the bike ride. *Definitely.*"

Jase's face softens into the most beautiful smile.

"Really?"

"Yeah, I loved it," I confess. "It was so cool. I've always wanted to go on a motorbike."

"It's a great way to get around if you're in the country-side. But my family wouldn't let me have one, not for ages. My gran got completely wound up whenever I mentioned it. I saved and saved and finally I got one when I was eighteen. But she's still not happy about it."

"Was it worth the wait?" I say, almost at random.

"Of course!" He grins. "First time I went out for a spin I couldn't stop smiling all day. Literally. I looked like a clown. My gran kept telling me I'd catch flies in my mouth if I wasn't careful."

I giggle at the image.

"You were pretty good, considering it was your first time," he adds.

"Really?" God, I have to stop saying that. I sound like a moron. But I'm so overwhelmed by being so close to him that it's hard for me to get any words out at all, let alone a whole sentence. And I'm still struggling with the thought that maybe I should say goodbye now, and go, before things get more intense than this.

"Yeah," Jase confirms. "You didn't scream or tell me to go slower. And you leaned out really well."

His hand gently squeezes mine, and I melt a little.

We've come onto the grounds of Wakefield Hall through the back gate, up the service road. Jase has parked behind his family's cottage, where the Barnes family have lived for generations. Lights gleam through a few chinks in the curtains, allowing streaks of golden light through the windows. Beyond the cottage looms the big bulk of Wakefield Hall, the main building obscured from this angle by the modern block, and even the strip lighting in the corridors is far enough away, and gently blurred by the settling night mist, to seem cozy and inviting—light in the darkness, warmth in the cold.

It's completely silent, apart from our breathing and the creak of Jase's leather jacket. It's cold out here, but I warm up when I think about how everyone else is inside, either studying or waiting for dinner.

I'm the only girl in this whole school standing outside in the dark with a boy whose gloved hand is clasped around mine.

I shiver for so many reasons I couldn't list them all, not if you sat me down with a paper and pen right now and made me.

Jase and I are even closer now, because he's taken a step toward me, and I can feel his breath on my forehead, the leather of his jacket brushing against the front of my body.

And then I do it. I look up. Knowing what will happen if I do.

His breath is on my face now. There's a soft waft of menthol, and I think, *Not fair! When did he have a mint?* but I'd look a bit silly complaining about it. The next thing I know is that his lips are on mine, and I can't think any more.

I'm so glad I wore my boots with the three-inch heels, even though I thought they might make it hard getting on and off the bike. But I must have been secretly hoping for this, I must have thought that if Jase did kiss me, and I was in trainers, I would be so much shorter than him, and it would be awkward . . . whereas now, though my neck is craning up a bit, I can reach up and put my arms round his neck, pulling him even closer, feeling his body down the whole length of mine. He catches his breath and bites down on my lip and really pushes himself against me now so I almost stumble, and I find myself catching at him, hooking my foot against his leg so I don't fall, and somehow he's holding me even tighter, I can hardly breathe, but I don't care, it's like I'm breathing his breath instead of my own. . . .

Jase loosens one hand from the small of my back and pushes my hair back from my face. The leather of his glove against my skin is really sexy for some reason, I don't know why, and I catch my breath and notice that I'm tilting my head, pushing it into his hand like a cat does when you stroke it. He pulls his hand away, and I freeze, thinking I've done something wrong.

I'm still so new at this, so inexperienced, and I'm scared it just showed. Was that too much?

Jase is stripping off his glove with his teeth, not wanting to take his other hand from its firm hold on my back. I flush with pleasure as his hand, bare now, reaches back to my head, pushing back my hair, tangling in it, stroking it down, playing with it as he bends to kiss me again. I find myself going up on tiptoes to meet his mouth faster, not wanting to wait even that split second before his lips meet mine. I loved the feel of the leather glove, but his bare hand is so warm as it wraps around my head. It's so wonderful to feel the contact of skin on skin that I realize I want more of it. I pull my gloves off behind his head, one by one, and drop them to the ground, not even caring where they land. Now I can run my palms over his head, the warm soft skin of his neck, sliding my fingers down as best I can to feel the edge of his sweater, sliding them underneath.

His hands drop to my waist, feeling under my jacket, pulling up my sweater, my T-shirt, touching my bare back, and I gasp and jump because of the simultaneous shock of the cold air on my skin and the heat of his hands.

He misunderstands, and pulls back a bit so he can look down at me.

"Sorry," he mumbles. "Too much?"

"No . . . yes . . ."

I don't know what to say. My head's spinning. I can't get any words out at all. I want to pull him close and kiss him again, feel his hands on the small of my back, twine myself around him. But at the same time . . . I want to run away. I'm really confused by my own feelings.

To my horror, I suddenly find myself remembering my kiss with Dan. It's the last thing I wanted to pop into my mind right now, yet I can't help it. I know it was six months ago, but I don't remember Dan being this smooth, this good at kissing. Jase is making everything seem so easy. I want him to touch my bare skin, it seems so natural and right. And I don't remember having that feeling with Dan—but then, Dan and I were only kissing for such a short time, we hardly knew each other at all. Whereas Jase and I have been talking on and off for a while, making each other laugh, building a sort of connection, sitting pressed against each other on his motorbike. . . .

I've tensed up because my brain is insisting on making a series of awful comparisons between Dan and Jase, like a computer running a program that overrides everything else and won't stop, no matter how many buttons you press. Jase misunderstands my sudden tension. He tugs at the hems of my T-shirt and sweater so they fall back down, covering my back again. He rubs my back through the fabric, brisk strokes, not sexy now, and, despite the fact that I know he thinks I've stiffened up from the cold, not a past memory of a dead boy, I'm so grateful for his consideration that I could burst into tears. He's not being pushy; he's respecting my feelings, even though he's read them wrong.

The memories of Dan mercifully start to fade. My body relaxes in Jase's arms as my brain comes back to the present.

He's looking down at me, concern in his eyes.

"Warmer?" he says. "Sorry, it's really chilly out here for October."

"Yeah," I manage.

I look up, meeting his eyes, and at the sight of him a smile breaks across my face. No, not a smile. An idiotic smirk. I know if I saw myself in a mirror right now I would die of embarrassment. I duck my head so he can't see how stupid I look.

"It's okay," Jase says, leaning down. He whispers in my ear: "Scarlett? I'm happy too."

My arms tighten around his neck, and my head tucks into his shoulder as we hug. For a moment I feel really safe, enfolded in his arms. Ick, that sounds like something out of a romance novel.

A bell rings in the distance.

"Is that for you?" Jase asks into my hair.

I giggle.

"Yes, it's the special ring my grandmother does for me. She goes up to the bell tower and rings it herself."

"Cheeky!" He tickles my ribs. "You know what I mean."

I sigh. "Yes," I say, reluctantly pulling away from his warmth. I look up at him. "It's the dinner bell, I have to go."

"That bloody bell," Jase says, though with amusement rather than anger.

"I suppose you've got school all week?"

I nod. "But half-term starts on Friday," I inform him. "I won't be so busy then."

"Cool. D'you have a mobile?"

"Of course I have one," I say, a bit insulted. How sheltered does he think I am?

He pulls out his phone and I give him my number.

"I'll text you," he says, "and then you'll have mine." He clears his throat. "You could even send me a text back to say you got it."

"I think I could manage that," I say flirtily.

Wow. That came out just right. I know it did, because he gives me a sexy grin and says:

"Don't strain yourself, will you?" in a really nice, jokey way, and I come back with:

"I'll be careful. You know how delicate I am."

That makes Jase burst out laughing—he's seen me doing gymnastics on the Great Lawn and knows that if there's one thing I'm not, it's delicate.

And then we both jump, because the door of the Barnes house swings open so fast that it slams against the wall outside, and a man's voice yells:

"Jason! That you?"

The laughter drains from Jase's face so fast I don't even see it go.

"Yeah, Dad," he calls back, in a flat voice. "Just coming in."

Jase's father appears at the front door. With the light behind him, it's hard to see him clearly, but he's a stocky shape, with big burly shoulders, and I'd never have guessed he was Jase's dad from seeing his silhouette—though Jase has nice muscly shoulders, he's much longer and leaner.

"Well, don't lurk round outside, will you?" his dad yells, and I'm very taken aback to notice that his fists are clenched at his sides. His whole stance is menacing, and I just don't understand why. What are Jase and I doing that's so wrong? Why would it make him this angry?

Because he really *is* angry. He ducks his head forward, as if he's glaring at us, and involuntarily, I find myself flinching back.

"We weren't *lurking*, Dad," Jase protests.

"Oh yes, you were. You want to watch that! I'm likely to think you're a pikey and fire off a couple of shots at you and whatever little tart you've got out there with you."

"Dad!"

"You heard me!"

Mr. Barnes reaches out to grab the door handle, and as he does I can see him momentarily in the light from inside the room. He's red-faced, with short gray curly hair, and a nose that looks stubby and swollen. His eyes are small and sunk in pouches of flesh: he's not really fat, but he looks unhealthy, and a bit like a pig. An angry pig. I can't see any resemblance to Jase at all. Grunting with the effort, he stamps back inside, pulling the door shut behind him with a slam that makes its hinges squeak in protest.

I gape at Jase, shocked by what I've heard. He doesn't meet my eyes, though, and it's awkward. We stand in silence for a while. I'm expecting him to say something, explain away his dad's foul temper, but he doesn't.

At last, because I can't bear the silence any longer, I ask: "What's a pikey?"

"Like a gypsy," Jase mutters. "It's a word they use round here. We're not keen on them. Well, Dad isn't. He hates pikeys."

I clear my throat. "Does your dad have a gun?"

"A shotgun, yeah. For scaring crows. Dad's just joking about using it on people," he adds defensively.

But I don't think he was. And neither, I can tell, does Jase.

"I'm sorry about . . . ," he starts, but he trails off.

I know he's talking about his dad calling me a little tart.

"It's okay," I say quickly, ducking down to grab my gloves. "I should dash, I'm really late for dinner already."

He looks very grateful.

"I'll text you, yeah?" he says.

"Cool."

Thank God I have to run off for dinner roll call. I sense that Jase wants me gone as soon as possible, and I understand why. I run off down the path that leads to the dining hall, still shocked by what just happened. Jase's dad is horrible. It must be so nasty for Jase. I think of him having to go into that house now for his own dinner, and the picture that calls up is awful. I hope at least his mum is nice, but it must be awful for her too, married to a man who's such a bully, who'd shout incredibly rude things at people he doesn't even know who haven't done anything bad to him. And talking to Jase like that in front of me! That was horrible of him.

There's nothing good about being an orphan. Nothing. But sometimes, you meet a parent who's so unpleasant that for just a little while, you can't help thinking that being an orphan might not be the worst fate in the world after all.

seven

"DIETING IS FOR POOR PEOPLE"

"Ugh, cauliflower cheese for dinner *again*," Taylor complains. "I'm going to be farting all night."

"You and everyone else," I say glumly. "The dining hall was already getting a bit smelly."

"Sunday nights are just the *worst* for dinner here," Taylor says. "I can't believe we have to eat something called *spotted dick!*"

"It's called spotted because of the raisins in it," I explain, following her up the staircase.

"Yeah, but why is it dick?" Taylor's nipping up the stairs faster than me. I don't know how she can move that fast with a bellyful of cauliflower cheese and steamed pudding.

"No idea. But *dick* isn't a rude word in England."

We turn into the corridor and enter Taylor's room. She flops onto the floor; I collapse on the bed.

"I'm so full," she says, holding her stomach. "I feel sick."

"Me too." I pause. "Um. Sorry about that."

"Sorry about wha— Oh, *Scarlett!*"

Taylor jumps up and starts fanning the air furiously.

"I'm really sorry," I mumble. "This always happens to me with cauliflower. And brussels sprouts. Sorry. I'll open a window."

"*Jesus. Ewwwww.*"

"Sorry. Really sorry. I'll go out in the corridor next time."

"You better." She giggles. "Wow, you are so lucky you didn't have cauliflower cheese before you went on your date with Jase. Can you imagine sitting in the movie theater and farting up a storm?"

I can feel the blood draining from my face at this appalling scenario.

"Oh my *God*," I say. "I couldn't have gone."

"No, you couldn't!" Taylor is rolling on the floor, she's laughing so hard. "Can you imagine?" She puts on a fake English accent. " 'Oh, my darling Jase, how exciting to finally be alone with you'—*squit*—'Yes, Scarlett, I too have dreamed of this moment, my love'—*squit*—'Kiss me, Jase! Hold me tight in your strong manly arms'—*squit!*"

I'm actually pretty impressed with Taylor's ability to parody romance novels, but I can't show it, because I'm too busy grabbing a pillow and attacking her. Amazingly, she barely defends herself, because she's laughing so hard. I'm laughing too, of course, but Taylor's in absolute hysterics. So I have the advantage—which normally I never do, because she's as strong as an ox. I batter her with the pillow as she howls:

" 'My darling, what is that terrible smell? It's like a sewer exploded in the cinema'—*squit!*"

"Taylor! Scarlett!" someone yells behind us.

I turn to look over my shoulder. It's Lizzie. She looks frantic. Before I can ask her what the emergency is, however, she wrinkles up her nose.

"Ew, what is that *stink?*" she asks. "It smells like *drains*. Do you have a blocked-up loo or something?"

"*Squit! Squit!*" Taylor sobs with laughter. "*Squit!*"

I put the pillow over her face and sit on it.

"No!" Taylor yells from beneath the pillow. "Not your butt! Get that thing off me, it's a deadly weapon!"

She shoves me off with one powerful shift of her shoulders.

"Oh dear," I say feebly, my giggles fading as I tip off her, feeling a familiar sensation in my lower body. "Um . . ."

"Oh *no*. Scarlett!" Taylor wails. "Not again! Lizzie, do you have air freshener or anything like that?"

"I've got some scented candles."

"Get them," Taylor says. "Get them *now!*" And when Lizzie hasn't moved, Taylor bellows like a sergeant major: "*Go! Go!*"

Lizzie dashes out the door like a terrified dog.

"I'm really sor—" I start again.

"Save it, Fart Girl," Taylor snaps. "You better hope those candles are strong enough. Or you're sitting in the corridor for the rest of the evening."

* * *

"You have to see this!" Lizzie nearly cries in excitement, beckoning us to cluster round her laptop. She's been dying to show us what's on the screen, but Taylor wouldn't let her

89

until she'd lit the candles and put them on the windowsill. They're burning nicely, and I must admit, they do seem to be doing a good job of covering my toxic emissions. Ugh.

We're watching YouTube. Above the black screen are the words *Dieting's for Poor People*. Lizzie clicks on the Play button and the clip starts.

It's Plum.

My heart sinks. I was so enjoying this evening, horsing around being stupid with Taylor, memories of my lovely afternoon with Jase filling my mind. For a few hours, I've been like a normal girl: laughing with my best friend, being teased about a guy I might be starting to date. Since I snapped my laptop shut, it's been the nicest time I can remember for ages.

And now, I'm watching Plum, and it's plunged me straight back into the world of St. Tabby's, Dan McAndrew's death, and everything I managed to avoid thinking about this afternoon.

I let out my breath in a long sigh of regret.

Plum's sprawled on a big sofa, a smug smile on her face. The quality of the film is really bad (I assume it was taken on a mobile phone) and the sound isn't great either, but I can clearly see Plum's face as she sits up straight, flicks back her long mane of chestnut hair, and holds it behind her head with one hand at the nape of her neck. With the other, she reaches out for something on the glass table in front of her, and the camera tilts to capture it. She's holding what looks like a pencil—no, it's a straw, a short straw. She puts it to her nose. She leans over the table till she's hanging over it. And then there's a sniffing sound and she's sort of scraping the straw against the glass surface of the table.

"Can you *believe* it?" Lizzie breathes.

Plum puts the straw down, sits back up, and tilts her head back, wiping under her nose and sniffing again. Then she reaches for a pack of cigarettes, taps one out, and lights it.

"*God,* that's good," she drawls. "Coke and ciggies. Best diet in the world."

Someone off-camera makes a comment, and Plum laughs.

"God, no. Dieting's for poor people!" she says.

And, because that's the perfect end line, the screen goes black.

We gawp at each other in shock. I lean forward to check the name of the YouTube user who put up the clip, but it's just a jumble of letters and numbers, designed to make it impossible to guess the poster's identity.

"Three different girls sent me the link in the last five minutes," Lizzie says, her voice much higher than normal.

Evidently Lizzie's connection with Plum's circle is getting stronger, which is definitely worrisome. She's kind of like a ticking time bomb that way.

"Who put it up?" I ask her.

She shakes her head, her face blank. I believe her. She'd be blurting it out if she knew.

"Never a dull moment with this Plum, right?" Taylor says.

My phone buzzes, and I jump. A text just came in for

me. I'm so focused on what we just saw on Lizzie's laptop that I immediately think it's from someone at St. Tabby's, telling me about the clip of Plum. My heart leaps, hoping that it's Luce or Alison, my two best friends from St. Tabby's, who are still, as far as I know, furious with me because I dumped them to go to that fateful party of Nadia's, where I kissed Dan and he died. If Luce or Alison have decided to get in touch, that would be amazing. I grab for the phone.

But it's a number I don't recognize. I click on it.

HEY UVE GOT MY NO NOW. SO USE IT! C U @ THE WEEKEND. —JB

Wow. How could I possibly have forgotten that Jase was going to text me? I was sitting all through dinner on tenterhooks, waiting for my phone to buzz.

My face must be glowing with happiness. Taylor looks at me and guesses immediately who the text is from. She raises her eyes to the ceiling soulfully and puts both hands over her heart, miming it beating fast.

Lizzie doesn't notice anything: she's too involved in the drama of Plum being seen online doing drugs and laughing about it.

"She's in *such trouble!*" Lizzie says, breathing heavily in excitement. "Ooh!"

She grabs for her phone, which is loudly tinkling out a pop tune.

"I *know!*" she cries. "Yes, I *know! Unbelievable!* She's in *such trouble!* . . . Yes, I *know!*"

Taylor and I roll our eyes at each other. This will go on all night.

"Ooh, I've got another call coming in . . . hang on . . . ," Lizzie babbles. "Yes, I *know* . . . *Unbelievable!* . . . Yes, *everyone* must have seen it by now. . . ."

"I'm going back to Aunt Gwen's," I say, standing up.

"You want to read his text three hundred million times and then spend hours deciding what to write back," Taylor says with killer accuracy.

"No, I don't," I say unconvincingly.

"Liar," Taylor says amiably. She jerks her head at Lizzie. "You can't leave her here. I'm not having her sitting in my room all night going 'Yes, I *know!*' and '*Unbelievable!*' "

"Your English accent is getting really good," I say grudgingly. "Lizzie . . ." She's so absorbed in her conversation that she doesn't hear me. I pick up her laptop, close it, and give it to her, jerking my head at the door. She takes it and follows me out, still gabbling away enthusiastically. I can hear her all down the corridor, even though I'm heading in the opposite direction.

I scurry down the stairs, in a hurry to get back to Aunt Gwen's (I never call it home, because it isn't). Taylor wasn't completely right. I do want to read Jase's text over and over again—though maybe not three hundred million times— and then agonize about what to text him back.

But as I walk back, I realize just how much that video of Plum has really screwed me up. I can't stop thinking about Dan now, in that obsessive way that I used to do when I collected all the articles on his death and stashed them someplace safe where no one else could touch them (except for bloody Taylor, that is). I'm having this uncontrollable urge to rifle through the stack of newspapers and magazines again, although I haven't done that in a while. My gut is telling me that I'll find something there, but I don't know why. I must be going crazy.

I unlock the front door and creep in. There's a light on in the living room: Aunt Gwen must be watching the telly. But even if she were out, I wouldn't go in and curl up on the sofa. It's so much Aunt Gwen's place that I don't feel at home anywhere but in my room.

I go upstairs, my emotions such a mix at this point after the day I've had. I keep hearing Nadia's ridiculing voice, calling me clueless, mocking me because I didn't know Callum and Dan were close. Which makes me think all the more that I'll discover a link between them somewhere in my twisted assortment of articles. I rummage through my desk, remove a panel in the back of one of the drawers (my new hiding place, thanks to Taylor), grab my folder, and rifle through the articles one by one. I'm grinding my teeth so that I can stop my heart from pounding. Every time I see the bits about me ("16-year-old minor who cannot be identified for legal reasons") my pulse races. In the middle of the stack, I come to Dan's obituary. It's a bit wrinkled so I flatten it out with my hand. I read each word carefully. It's as though I'm looking at this with new eyes and no memories.

When I get to the last sentence, I stare at it, my limbs totally numb. My clenched jaw falls open and my heart pounds ferociously. Because my miraculous hunch has really paid off.

"Daniel McAndrew is survived by his parents, of Castle Airlie, Ayrshire; a sister, Catriona, 21; and a brother, Callum, 17."

Callum and Dan were *brothers*.

I drop the folder onto my desk, my head spinning like the wheels on Jase's motorbike. I have no idea what to do. For a second, I think about trying to meet up with Lucy Raleigh, but dismiss the idea almost immediately. How far would that get me? Even if I used Lizzie or Nadia to get to her, Lucy probably isn't stupid enough to reveal any motive she or, God forbid, Callum, might have for killing Dan.

I'm having trouble breathing, so I go into the bathroom and splash cold water on my face. I've never actually done this before, but people do it on TV all the time. It's even more of a shock than I was expecting. The sudden chill of the water calms me down and brings me a moment of clarity. And, staring at myself as the water drips down my face, an idea begins to form in my mind of what my next step could be.

I reach for a towel and dry my face, the idea getting clearer and clearer, like adjusting a camera lens to bring an object into focus. But the better I see it, the more frighteningly extreme it is. What if it works, and I have to deal with the consequences?

I'll just try the first step, I think. Just the first step. Then I'll decide later, once I'm through, if I feel brave enough to go ahead and finish what I've started.

I walk back into my bedroom, sit down at my desk, and take a few sheets of the former stationery that my grand—I

mean, Lady Wakefield—had printed for me when I turned
sixteen.

Dear Mrs. McAndrew, I write, my fingers quivering as I
scribble in my best cursive.

> I hope you don't think it's too ~~weird~~ strange
> that I'm writing to you, but I thought it was best
> to let some time pass before I got in touch. I really
> wanted to talk to you at the inquest, but you were
> so upset, I thought it might upset you even more.
> I really hope this letter doesn't upset you too
> much, either. But I felt that I ought to be writing
> it because Dan said something to me before he died
> and it was about you and your family. I would like
> to tell you all what he said. Also, I have some-
> thing that belonged to him that I would like to give
> back to you. If I could meet you and your family
> and do that, it would be ~~great~~ ~~amazing~~ ~~really nice~~

I sit for ages, staring at the heavy vellum paper. This is
proving really hard to write. All these lies. And even
though I tell myself that, by finding out how Dan died, I'm
doing what his parents would surely want, what happens if
it turns out that the truth of his death is something they
would much rather never have known?

I shiver.

> really kind of you to let me. I am having a very
> hard time with what happened, as you must be too.

96

I do feel that maybe by meeting up with you and ~~your family~~ Dan's brother and sister, and talking about it, we would all feel better afterward, even if it's ~~weird~~ difficult.

My phone number, address, and e-mail are below. Please get in touch with me when you can. I could come up to where you live if that's easiest. I hope you will say yes.

~~Best wishes~~ Very sincerely,

Scarlett Wakefield

I stare at the black ink for a while, thinking about what this means. I'm angling for an invitation to meet the McAndrews—the family of the boy who died in my arms. I remember Mr. and Mrs. McAndrew at the inquest, though I could hardly look at them, it was so upsetting. Mrs. McAndrew cried all the time, and Mr. McAndrew might have been carved from a single piece of granite. Am I really considering sitting down with them face to face and talking with them? Even if it's the one chance I have of getting close to Callum and Lucy?

I read the letter over. I don't think it expresses everything as well as I would want to, but it'll have to do. God, I think that was the hardest thing I ever had to write, harder even than the Tacitus essay last week, which strained my brain so much I thought blood was going to spurt from both my ears.

I'm trying very hard not to think about the fact that, if

this comes off and I find out that Callum is in any way in-volved, through his girlfriend Lucy even, that would be hor-rendous news for the McAndrews. I know that might be a possibility, awful though it would be. But not for a moment does it make me think I should stop here, while I still can, with the knowledge that I have no responsibility for Dan's death apart from having accidentally eaten the wrong thing and kissing him afterward.

I can't stop, though. I have to keep going. I have to find out the truth even if it burns me and everyone else involved with it.

Dan died in my arms. I'll do whatever I can to find out how that happened. I owe that to him.

And maybe when I find out the truth, I'll stop having nightmares.

eight

ROUGH JUSTICE

"Taylor! No *bouncing*! How many times do I have to tell you?" shouts Miss Carter. The last bit is clearly not a question, as she doesn't wait for a response, but continues: "This is *netball*. We do not bounce in netball!"

"Sorry, Miss Carter!" Taylor yells, shoving her hair back. Her face is corrugated into one enormous frown, her dark brows pulled down so far that I can barely see her eyes.

"You're in England now," Miss Carter says, rather unnecessarily, as I feel Taylor is all too aware of which country she's in.

"Sharon Persaud bounces in netball," I mutter to Taylor in an attempt to cheer her up. Like me, Sharon Persaud has a well-developed chestal area, but unlike me, Sharon has clearly not bothered to work out that she needs to wear a minimizer and a sports bra to stop her boobs swinging around like a pair of oranges being juggled by a blind person. The effect actually adds to Sharon's general scariness on the sports pitch—not only has she apparently taken out at least one girl's front teeth with her terrifying lavender hockey stick, but as she plows toward you, her boobs look like extra weapons, bouncing violently in all directions.

Taylor doesn't even snigger at my joke. She takes team sports incredibly seriously. Which I don't, not in the same way. I spent years and years doing gymnastics, which is really competitive, of course, but although technically you're on a team, when it counts it's just you and you alone out there on the bars or on the mat. I preferred it like that: being dependent on no one but myself, and trying to better my own best performance. It's funny, because Taylor is actually more of a loner than I am. But she loves team sports, which is why she's trying so hard to excel at netball. Even though, because she's used to basketball, she keeps trying to bounce the ball. . . .

"Right, net practice!" Miss Carter blows her whistle. "Blue team, stretches; red team, practice shots! Five minutes each team and then change over. Off you go, girls!"

Taylor and I, wearing blue tabards over our T-shirts and gym skirts, run over to the side of the netball court where the rest of the blue team is heading for stretches.

"Front splits?" Taylor suggests. We sit down facing each other on the cold tarmac, our legs wide. I put my feet against the inside of her thighs and we clasp each other's forearms. I lean back, pulling her toward me.

"Nose to the ground," I chant, "nose to the ground . . ."

"Ow!" Taylor says as I pull her forward, straighter and straighter.

"You're lucky I'm not sitting on your back," I say. "Ricky, my gym coach, used to come around and do that. Honestly, sometimes I thought something was going to *split*, he weighed so much."

"Scarlett! Taylor!" a familiar voice cries faintly.

Taylor pulls on my arms so I'm sitting upright again.

"Guess who?" she whispers. "It's the neediest girl in the world!"

"Be nice, okay?" I turn my head to watch through the net surrounding the court as Lizzie runs toward us across the grass of the hockey pitches. "All we do is bully her and make her do things she doesn't want to do."

"Yeah, well, she's like a Lab my aunt used to have. My cousins were really mean to that dog, they'd kick it and tease it and pull its ears, and it still ran after them, wagging its tail. 'Cause it would rather have negative attention than none at all," Taylor says cynically.

"Could you be any more depressing?"

"Plumgotexpelled!" Lizzie cries. "Plumgotexpelled!"

She crashes into the netting and hangs there, holding on to it with both hands, panting like—well, the Labrador Taylor was just talking about. To be honest, it'd be a fair comparison.

"Ijustheard! Venetiatextedme! Plumgotexpelled!" she gasps.

"Because of the YouTube clip?" Taylor asks.

Lizzie nods, winded. People in the smart set are finally letting her in enough and giving her real gossip, which she is obviously salivating over. This is not good. Still, I have to pretend I'm not bothered by this.

"Well, even St. Tabby's wouldn't exactly be keen on one of its pupils being filmed doing drugs," I say.

"That's not all!" Lizzie's recovered some breath, enough to allow her to space her words out a bit more. "It was *Nadia*! Nadia put that clip on YouTube!"

Taylor and I look at each other. I can see that she's processing this information as fast as I am, and coming to the same conclusion.

"It can't be a coincidence," Taylor says.

I shake my head.

"What can't?" Lizzie asks eagerly. But when we don't answer, she rushes on: "I can't believe Nadia did that to Plum! It's like they're at *war* now! I mean, they were best friends! But Nadia told Venetia it was her who did it! Isn't it *unbelievable?*"

A whistle blows practically in my ear.

"What's going on over here?" Miss Carter bellows—again, not really a question. "I said stretch, not gossip! Lizzie Livermore, stop distracting Taylor and Scarlett *right now* or I'll make you jog round the hockey pitches!"

Lizzie falls away from the netting immediately, eyes and mouth so wide with horror at the thought of jogging that everyone bursts out laughing. Miss Carter blows her whistle again.

"Switch over, girls! Blues shoot, reds stretch! And Taylor—"

"*No bouncing!*" the entire courtful of girls shouts back.

*   *   *

"You know what this means," Taylor says as we walk back to school after netball practice.

"Nadia used us," I say. "She got us to wipe that video from Plum's phone and then she put up the video she had of Plum."

"No question," Taylor says. "They must have been in this Mexican standoff."

"Mexican standoff?"

"It's like you're each holding a gun on each other, so neither of you wants to shoot 'cause then the other one would too."

"Why is that Mexican?" I'm as bemused by Taylor's American expressions as she is by our English ones.

"No idea. But anyway, that's probably what happened."

I nod. "That explains why Plum didn't show that video to anyone. I never quite believed that she wouldn't have sent it to a few people. So I guess Nadia couldn't show anyone the clip of Plum doing drugs—not until you deleted Plum's clip."

Taylor looks at me. "You pissed at Nadia?"

I think it over.

"Well, yeah, because it feels shitty to be used," I say. "And besides, if you'd been caught going through Plum's bag, you'd have been in real trouble."

"Ha! As if I would have gotten caught!" Taylor says cockily.

"But honestly," I admit, "Plum has always been an absolute cow to me. I can't be too upset that she's got her comeuppance."

Plum is an awful person. And she's only got what she deserved. I mean, there's no one in that clip *making* her do drugs, or say that diets are for poor people. . . .

"So, what? It's rough justice?" Taylor asks.

"I suppose so," I say doubtfully. "But it's still not right. No wonder Nadia laughed like a drain when she'd answered all my questions. She got what she wanted, and she didn't have anything that useful to tell us in return. *And* she sort of lied to us when she didn't tell us why she really wanted us to delete that clip of her throwing up."

Taylor cracks a grin.

"Don't worry," she says. "I wiped it off Plum's phone. But I sent it to mine. We've got the dirt on Nadia anytime we want."

I gawp at her.

"That's awful!" I say.

"But brilliant," Taylor says complacently. "I am an evil genius."

In her triumph, she automatically bounces the netball she's carrying, and immediately looks appalled.

"Some evil genius," I tease, "you can't even play netball properly!"

Then I duck as Taylor makes a grab for me, uttering dire threats about bouncing my head off the nearest wall. Out of the corner of my eye, I spot someone, and as Taylor makes another grab at me, I throw myself into a showy and completely unnecessary dive roll, lunging far enough away that I don't kick Taylor in the face as I fly into it. I land on the grassy verge and roll easily. I'm on my feet again in a couple of seconds, and as I come up Taylor's saying, sounding very indignant:

"Jeez, Scarlett! I was just messing. I wasn't going to hurt you or anything."

Then she sees Jase, and realizes why I was showing off. He's standing underneath a group of elm trees, a wheelbarrow and a broom propped a little way away, enough to suggest that he saw us approaching and walked out to meet us.

"Nice escape," he says to me, his eyes glimmering. "I was wondering if you needed any help."

I giggle. Ugh, it's the kind of giggle I only do with boys, and I hate it. I never sound this coy or pathetic with girls.

"No, she's not as scary as she looks," I reply.

"Yes, I am," Taylor says indignantly.

Jase laughs.

"I wouldn't like to get in a fight with you," he says to Taylor, which completely wins her over.

"Jase, this is Taylor," I say, and then wonder if I shouldn't have done that the other way around. Does it sound like Jase is more important to me than Taylor?

"Hey," she says, blushing only very slightly. "Um, we met before, in the maze."

I wish Taylor hadn't mentioned that, because when Jase found us in the maze, Lizzie was sobbing and we were standing over her, harshly interrogating her about the anonymous "It wasn't your fault" note, which turned out to be from conniving Nadia.

I try to nudge Taylor to get her to shut up about it, but the tips of her ears have gone pink, so it looks like she's realized it for herself.

"That was ages ago," I say brightly, trying to gloss over it.

Ugh. I start to fiddle with my hair, out of nerves, and realize to my horror that I put it in bunches today, which, as always, have gone curly from the damp weather. It's an old habit from gymnastics, because if you're doing forward or backward rolls, a ponytail on the middle of your head will bump on the ground and dig into you, whereas bunches never get in the way of anything. But bunches—particularly curly ones—make me look thirteen years old. Plus, I'm not wearing any makeup and I'm in a white T-shirt, brown gym skirt, and pale blue tabard over the top. It's the ugliest outfit you ever saw.

I hope Jase remembers how I looked on our date.

Behind us, I can hear the stream of netball players giggling and whispering as they trail past down the path that leads back to the changing rooms. I don't really blame them—I'd be doing the same thing. We barely see any men around here at all, apart from poor Mr. Theobald, the maths teacher, who for many and various reasons doesn't count as a man in any meaningful way. Jase Barnes is like catnip to a lot of very bored and frustrated cats.

And I'm the girl he stops when she's coming back from netball practice. I wish I felt more deserving, and less guilty. There's so much about me he doesn't know. If he found out everything, would he still look at me like he's about to push Taylor aside and kiss me?

"Your dad's the gardener here, right?" Taylor asks politely.

Jase grins, his white teeth flashing.

"Yeah—my dad and his dad before him. I'm following in their footsteps, you might say. Got my gap year now, so I'm sweeping leaves and saving up to travel. Then I start at agricultural college next year."

"Oh, cool," Taylor says enthusiastically.

While I really like it that Taylor seems to approve of Jase, I'm all too aware that Miss Carter won't—no way I'd be allowed to talk to a boy during school hours, even if he is working here. And Miss Carter can't be far behind us on the path. . . .

"We should get going," I say, pulling a face. "Our PE teacher's really strict."

Although this is nothing but the truth, saying that I have to go seems to prompt Jase into more than just making conversation.

"So, I was wondering . . . what are you doing later?" he asks, looking straight through me.

I've been doing so well being cool, and now I dig my nails into my palms to remind me not to gush with excitement. I didn't think I'd see Jase till Friday, half-term—we've texted a couple of times and sort of agreed to meet up then—and here he is asking to get together with me *today*. He must be really keen to see me. My whole body floods with warmth at the thought, even though it probably shouldn't.

"After school?"

"Yeah," Jase says, shifting on his feet and lowering his gaze, as if he doesn't care one way or the other what I say. But I know he does. "You free?"

I actually manage to be cool enough to turn to Taylor and look at her inquiringly, like I'm asking her if I'm free or not. She quickly grasps what I'm doing and says, "We haven't got anything planned."

I look back at Jase.

"Okay then, I'm free," I say casually, though my palms are slick with sweat.

"Great." His face lights up. "Want to go for a walk around the lake?"

"It's out of bounds," I say warily. "There's a gate, it's always kept locked—"

Jase grins and pats his pocket. "I've got the key," he says. "I thought we could have a bit of, you know, time on our own. . . ."

Oh my God, I can't believe he said that *at all*, let alone in front of Taylor. I guess it's clear that he and I aren't just going to have a talk about the weather. I must be blushing madly by now.

And I don't want to say no.

"I *would* like to see the lake," I manage, as if that's the only reason I'm accepting his invitation. "I haven't been there since I was little."

God, this is so embarrassing. It's like I'm admitting that I want to be alone with him so we can kiss again. Forget looking him in the eye—my head's ducked so far down now that I can barely see him at all. I know I said that I didn't think I should hang out with him too much until Dan's death is resolved, and I mean that one hundred percent. But the trouble is—that's when I'm not with him. When he's standing in front of me, asking me out, all my good resolutions melt like I did in his arms the other night.

"Meet me at four by the gate?" he suggests.

"Um, yeah." I'm torn between giving him a huge smile and dissolving into the ground with utter embarrassment.

I'm more than relieved when I feel Taylor grabbing the

back of my tabard and pulling me away—just in time, as Miss Carter's voice can be heard on the path behind us, telling the girls carrying the net of balls to hurry up and look lively.

"Ohmigod, you have a secret date with a superhot boy!" Taylor mutters.

"I *know*," I mutter back. I'm determined not to look over my shoulder to get a last glimpse of him, much as I'm dying to. "I can't believe he saw me in this stupid tabard."

Taylor grimaces.

"I know, gross. . . . But hey, he was probably looking at your legs anyway." She nudges me. "That forward roll you did, he probably saw your panties as well."

"Don't say panties! It's weird and creepy. Say knickers." I'm blushing all over. I hadn't thought of Jase seeing my big brown gym knickers (part of the very old-fashioned PE uniform) when I did the forward roll. I was just overcome with a mad desire to show off.

"Jase saw your knickers! Jase saw your knickers!" Taylor chants, till I can't bear it anymore and scream terrible curses at her, chasing her all the way back to the changing rooms, which at least lets off some of the head of steam that's building up inside me at the thought of seeing Jase this afternoon by the lake.

That's not the only head of steam that's been building up, though. Because I haven't told Taylor about the letter I sent to Mrs. McAndrew yesterday. I didn't know if she would think it was a good idea, but that's not why I didn't tell her.

It's more clear now than ever that I'm leaning on Taylor

way too much. She did all the hard work of getting Plum's phone and sorting out that video clip. She even thought of sending the incriminating evidence back to herself, which is probably why she makes a good partner. Taylor's always right there, more than eager to help, and maybe, lucky as I am to have a friend like her, I'm coming to rely on her so much that I can't do anything on my own.

I know Taylor's motives are only the best: she wants to be a PI, so this is great practice. She's bored to death here at Wakefield Hall, and helping me is a great adventure. And, now that we've become close, she wants me to solve the mystery of Dan's death for my own sake.

But I never *asked* Taylor to help me. She saw there was some secret I was trying to unravel, barged right in, and, I must admit, saved me from a fate worse than death—being busted by my terrifying form teacher when I was totally out of bounds. Still, I never chose to have her as a partner: she just started acting like one. And more and more, I'm worried that because she's so good at it, because she may well be better than me, I'm not proving to myself that, if Taylor wasn't around, I could handle this on my own.

Could I even have got this far without her? I don't know. And that's a very scary thought, because if I don't know, what does that say about me? Doesn't it mean that I'm not as clever and strong and brave as I think I am, or want to be? If we really are all on our own in the end, then I have to fight my own battles, don't I? The really important ones, at least.

Right now, I think that the more I, and only I, am responsible for finding out who killed Dan and why, the more I'll feel that I've earned the right to move on and put it all behind me. And moving on from Dan's death is the single most important thing in my life.

I can't consult with Taylor on every single thing. She's so strong and confident, she could take everything over without even meaning to. This is my investigation, my fight, and I need to take control.

But I know she won't see it that way.

nine

BALANCING ACT

"It's so beautiful," I say breathlessly. "I haven't been here for years and years."

I can't see Jase, who's closing the gate behind us, but I can hear a lilt in his voice as he says, "Yeah, it's lovely, in-nit? Seems a shame that nobody gets to use it. Your gran comes here sometimes. Oops, sorry"—he corrects himself as he comes up to stand next to me—"*Lady Wakefield*, I should say."

I giggle. "No, it's fine. She gets cross with me when I don't call her that too."

Jase stares at me incredulously. "Your gran makes you call her Lady Wakefield?"

I pull a face. "In term time, yeah. She says if I don't, dis-cipline will slip."

"*Right.* Your gran could be in a coma and she still wouldn't let discipline slip." Jase gives a belly laugh.

It's horribly true. But looking at Jase, standing on the lit-tle slope that leads down to the glittering surface of the lake, thoughts of my grandmother mercifully fade from my mind;

the excitement of the moment is too much for me to think about anything negative. It's a glorious autumn day, and the oak trees around the lake are deep shades of russet and gold, like quiet fires. The weeping willows dipping into the water are exactly as I remember them, their branches bending so elegantly they look like dancers leaning over the water. And the lake itself, with its central fountain of leaping dolphins, is one of the most calming sights I've ever seen in my life. There's something about still water shining in the sun that instantly makes you feel peaceful.

Or it would, if I didn't have Jase standing next to me, and every nerve ending in my body wasn't jumping, wondering when he's going to kiss me again. . . .

"We used to go out boating on the lake," I remember. "Me and my dad."

"The boathouse is over there," Jase says, pointing to a small building in the same gray stone as the balustrade that runs around the border of the lake.

"Oh yeah. Wow, everything looks so much smaller now."

"How old were you when you came here with your dad?"

"Only about four."

"No wonder it seems smaller now, eh?" he says. And, to my surprise, I feel him taking my hand. "You miss them a lot, do you? Your parents?"

I don't know how to answer this. No one's asked me that question that I can remember. I'm amazed that Jase is asking it, actually. And I'm really touched.

I clear my throat.

"I can't say I *miss* them, I suppose. They died when I was very little. I think I've sort of made up memories from looking at photos, if you know what I mean. But I miss having parents. My life would be so different if they were alive."

Jase squeezes my hand.

"And I can see from the photos that they loved me," I say, to my horror. Why am I telling him this? Tears are pricking at my eyes as I say the words. "So, um, that would be nice."

I mustn't cry. I mustn't cry. I'm sounding pathetic enough as it is. I stare ahead, blinking fast and breathing deeply, and manage, just about, to get my tears under control.

"I'm really sorry," Jase says after a few moments. "I shouldn't have asked you that."

"No, it's okay." I take another deep breath. "No one ever does ask about my parents, so I liked that you did."

"Can't be much fun for you, living with old Scratchface," Jase says.

I turn to look at him, feeling safe to do that now I've got my tears under control.

"*What* did you call her?"

He grins at me, unabashed. "Old Scratchface. Your aunt. That's what I used to call her when I was little. I was never allowed onto the Hall grounds proper—we had to keep to our garden. But I used to sneak in sometimes, to explore, and God, wouldn't she tear me off a strip if she caught me! I used to have nightmares about her, tell you the truth."

I giggle. "Scratchface," I say appreciatively. "That's perfect for Aunt Gwen." I realize something. "That's why we never met before, when we were little. Because you weren't allowed anywhere on the grounds. I never even knew there was another kid here."

"I knew about you," Jase says. "Saw you wandering all over the place, actually. But I never let you see me when I was exploring, because then I'd really get into trouble. With my dad too. No fraternizing with the Wakefields, they're too posh for the likes of us, that's what he always said."

Oh dear—Jase has mentioned his dad. I can tell he didn't mean to, not after the incident a couple of nights ago, but now he's all tensed. He must still be embarrassed about it, because his hand slips out of mine. It's my turn to feel sorry for him about his parents.

Sensing that we need to change the subject to something a lot lighter, I walk down the slope to the edge of the lake, and jump up onto the balustrade. It's only about a foot high, and wide enough to walk along easily.

"I wish we could come here more," I say wistfully. "We could buy some boats and row, or punt, or something."

Jase runs down the slope and jumps up next to me.

"It's all health and safety now, isn't it?" he says, reaching for my hand again, his momentary gloom forgotten. "You can't do anything, because if something went wrong somebody would sue you."

"That's really stupid," I say.

"Well, maybe you should change things. Talk to your gran." Jase looks at me. "This'll all be yours one day—you should have some say in what goes on."

I goggle at him.

"I can't even *think* about that right now." I stare over the lake. I suppose I *will* own all of this one day. But the responsibility feels completely overwhelming like a huge coat thrown over my shoulders, one that's much too heavy for me, and I can barely stand up in it, let alone walk.

"Sorry," Jase says, squeezing my hand. "I just completely freaked you out, didn't I?"

I nod.

"Scarlett—"

It's so nice hearing him say my name that I involuntarily turn to him and smile. The sun is behind me, and the sunlight melts in his eyes, turning their amber into liquid pools of gold. Just like the sunlight, I melt looking at him. His hand clasping mine is warm and strong, and on his palm I can feel the calluses from all the gardening he's been doing. He raises his other hand to shade his eyes from the sun, and I say, idiotically:

"It's very bright, isn't it?"

Jase just smiles. He takes a step toward me, and I find myself taking one toward him, till we're nearly touching. He lowers his head, and I tilt mine up. It's like a dance, we're so smoothly choreographed. His lips touch mine and we kiss, very gently. My heart bounces in my chest as if Taylor were playing basketball with it. We drop each other's hands— again, just as if we were choreographed. I reach my arms up to his neck and Jase's arms lock around my waist. We pull each other closer. Our feet shift, and Jase must have gone a little off the edge of the balustrade, because he wobbles, which makes me wobble. The next thing I know we've torn our arms away from each other, because we need them to balance with.

I'm okay—if there's anything I'm used to after years of gymnastics, it's balancing, and the balustrade is much, much wider than a balance beam. But Jase actually teeters for a couple of seconds, his arms flailing wildly in the air, and I can't help it—I start giggling. And this one isn't a girl-to-boy giggle, it's a full-on, you-look-silly giggle.

In an effort not to fall into the lake, Jase leans way over to the other side, so far he overbalances and has to jump back down onto the grass again. He stands there looking up at me, and I can see he's a bit cross. I try to stop laughing.

"Sorry," I say. "You just looked a bit funny."

"I'm a lot taller than you," he says grumpily. "It's harder to balance when you're taller."

I jump down too, not wanting him to stay grumpy.

"I did balance beam for a long time," I say, hoping this will salve his wounded pride. "I can balance on anything."

"Oh *really?*" His face creases into a huge smile. "Come on, then!"

He grabs my hand and pulls me into a run. We tear across the grass, around the wide curve of the lake, past a drooping cluster of weeping willows trailing their leaves in the water, all the way round to the far side, where a large and majestic oak is standing close to the water's edge.

Jase grabs a branch and swings himself up, finding knotholes in the trunk with his feet. I can tell he's climbed this tree many times before, because he knows the way up as easily as if he were climbing a ladder. I'm right behind him, careful to avoid his feet. Wow, men's feet are so enormous—Jase's, in his trainers, look like boats. He reaches a fork and straddles it, reaching down a hand to help me up. But I don't take it.

"I'm fine," I say, grasping a branch above me and letting it take all my weight as I walk up the trunk to a branch I can stand on.

"You don't need me, do you?" he says, and there's disappointment in his voice as well as grudging approval.

I'm supposed to need him, I realize. I'm not supposed to be strong enough to climb this big tree on my own. But I didn't want to take his hand, I wanted to do it all by myself. Ricky, our gymnastics coach, would only spot you if you really needed it; he'd watch you like a hawk to make sure you were okay, but he would never just help you for the sake of helping you. But then, Ricky was our coach. Whereas Jase might, maybe, one day, be my boyfriend. Big difference.

And maybe it's nice that someone who might one day be your boyfriend wants to help you?

But by now I'm standing on the branch, so it's too late. I smile at him, and thank goodness, he smiles back.

"That's the one," he says, grinning. "Want to try balancing properly? I used to walk along that when I was smaller."

I look down the branch where it grows away from the tree. Wide and sturdy-looking, it reaches out over the water. Wow. That would be exciting.

"Is this a challenge?" I ask.

"Yeah. I thought I heard you just say you could balance on anything," he says, his eyes glinting.

"Okay," I say, "what do I get if I do it?"

"Anything you want."

"And what do *you* get if I don't do it?" I ask, knowing the answer already.

"You have to kiss me."

"Ewww!" I say. "Yuck! I don't want to have to do *that*!"

For the first time, I'm allowing myself to really enjoy this. The teasing and the flirting. It's even more fun than it looks in films and on TV, because in real life, you have to come up with the dialogue yourself, and there's a whole adrenaline charge in trying to be funny and clever and sort of sexy, pushing someone away to bring them closer.

Which is what I'm doing now. I could tell that when I said, even teasingly, I didn't want to kiss Jase, that made him want to kiss me more. He's sitting in the fork of the tree, legs wide, leaves dangling past his face, one arm curled round a branch, grinning at me, and I put my chin in the air and stand up straight, take a deep breath and let it out—you should never hold your breath while balancing, it makes the body nervous—turn my back to him, and set out along the branch.

I wish I weren't wearing trainers. I'm used to balancing in bare feet, and the trainers don't let you feel the surface beneath you half as well.

An overhanging branch. I duck my head and move beneath it, slow steady steps, and as I emerge the full panorama of the lake is stretched out before me, silver water shining in the sun. I wish the marble fountain in the center were switched on. There's something so lovely about water playing in a fountain. But the sight is still beautiful enough to make me catch my breath. I stand there, soaking it in. And a warm rush of pride fills me. This is the

Wakefield Hall lake, on Wakefield Hall grounds, and one day, probably, it will be all mine. I can't imagine my grandmother leaving it to Aunt Gwen—she's so mean to Aunt Gwen, making her live in the tiny gatehouse, treating her like just another teacher.

I would feel sorrier for Aunt Gwen if she weren't so mean to me in her turn.

I'm a Wakefield, I think, and this is where I belong. My great-great-grandfather built this lake, and one day, maybe, I'll inherit it. And if I do, I'll turn the fountains on every day and watch water shoot out of the dolphins' mouths and up into the sky—

"What the hell is going on?"

Totally shocked, I jump and nearly topple into the water.

I look down. There's a man standing below me, hands on his hips. His face is bright red with rage: he's glaring up at me, his eyes squinched into puffy slits of fury. I know who he is by the sound of his angry voice and his stance, his hands in fists by his side. But I would never have guessed otherwise that he was Jase's dad. He doesn't look anything like him. Nothing at all.

"Dad!" Jase yells. "It's Scarlett! She's—"

But Mr. Barnes totally ignores him.

"You get down from there right away, you little tart!" he screams while reaching up and grabbing the lower leaves of the branch I'm standing on. Then he does his best to shake it.

Mr. Barnes must be mad, I think. Completely mad to do something this stupid. Because even someone as trained and as skilled as I am at the balance beam can't possibly stay upright while some maniac is shaking the branch I'm standing on. In a split second, I assess my options. I can't run back down the branch, not with him shaking it. If I fall backward, I could crack my head open, or land on the ground and really hurt myself. The only safe thing to do is . . .

The branch rocks dangerously beneath me. One foot slips out from under me.

"*Scarlett!*" Jase shouts desperately.

With the other foot, I push away from the branch, diving forward. As I fly through the air, I realize I have absolutely no idea how deep the lake is. I know you can row in it, which means it has to be a few feet deep—I hope—I *pray*—because by now I'm completely committed to my dive, aiming out into the middle of the lake, avoiding the fountain—

I hit the water. The cold shocks me like a slap. Immediately the water pulls down at my clothes, and the next second my hands bang into the bottom of the lake. Terrified that my head's going to be next, I manage to push away into a sort of somersault, rebounding off the bottom. My heavy, water-soaked limbs flip over my head, and I splash and land awkwardly, clumsily, but more or less safe.

I get my feet under me and stand up, gulping air. I reach up to push my hair out of my face, my arms weighted by the water in my clothes. My lovely cashmere sweater that my grandmother gave me, which I wore to look pretty for Jase! I hope it'll be okay. And then I think what an idiot I am for even remembering my sweater at a time like this. I look over to the edge of the lake. Jase has jumped down from the tree and is running toward me. His dad grabs him, and they grapple together.

Jase is yelling, "Dad! Let go! I have to see if she's hurt!"

"She'll be fine," Mr. Barnes shouts. "She was asking for it, silly little mare! Dancing around on that branch, showing off for you!"

"I *dared* her to—Jesus, why does it *matter* why she was doing it?" Jase struggles to get free from his father's grip. "You could have *killed* her, Dad, you stupid bloody—"

"Don't you talk to me like that!" his father bellows, raising one hand.

Jase grabs him by the wrist, stopping the blow. They stand there, strength against strength, locked in a weird kind of stasis. I don't move either. I stand there in the middle of the lake watching them, unable to believe my eyes. Unable to understand why Mr. Barnes is acting like this.

Jase suddenly lets go of his father's wrist and ducks. The pent-up force in his father's arm makes him fly forward, over Jase's bent back, and he hits the grass as Jase pushes him away and sprints toward me. I should move. I'm up to my chest in cold water, freezing, but I stand here and watch Jase as he takes a flying leap and lands in the lake.

"Gaah!" he yells, shaking his head, water droplets flying from his tight curls. "Cold!" He wades toward me, taking long strides which the water impedes, so it's like watching him walk in slow motion.

Behind him, his dad is getting to his feet.

"*Jase Barnes! Come back here right now!*"

"Are you okay?" Jase calls urgently to me. "Scarlett?"

I look down at my palms, which are grazed and just

starting to bleed a little from being scraped along the rough bottom of the lake. The water must be slowing the bleeding down a little, so maybe the damage won't be so bad. It doesn't look terrible. But then, I'm probably in shock.

"I think so," I reply.

"You *flipped!*" he says.

"I did that deliberately," I explain, "so I wouldn't hit my head—"

"God, I thought you hit something in the water. . . ."

His face is so anxious, so concerned, that despite the drama and craziness of the situation I can't help but feel happy he's so worried about me.

"*Jase!*" His father is still shouting from the edge of the lake. "Get away from her!"

"Dad, do you know who this is?" Jase says, slow-turning to look at him. "This is Scarlett Wakefield! Lady W's granddaughter! If anyone's got a right to be here, she does!"

For a moment, I think it's all going to be resolved. Mr. Barnes, standing so bullishly glaring down at us, his fists on his hips, his face red and swollen, is going to realize what an awful mistake he's made thinking that Jase had brought one of the Wakefield Hall girls to a place that's so strictly out of bounds. He's going to apologize and reach down a hand to help us out of the water. He's going to—

"I know exactly who she is!" he yells. "Scarlett Wakefield!" He points at me. "If I ever see you hanging round my son again, I won't answer for my actions. You stay away from him, or it'll be the worse for you!"

That's it. That really is it. I stride through the water, amazed at how fast I'm moving, anger giving extra power to my legs. I grab at the balustrade and haul myself out of the pond with a whoosh of water flooding off my clothes, the lake catching at my completely drenched trainers and refusing to let them go till I kick it away from me. I climb up and stand on the balustrade, where I'm taller than him: I'm not jumping down onto the grass, where he can tower over me.

"This is *my* land," I say. "Mine and my family's. I'm a *Wakefield*, and you're nothing but a bully. And when you tell me what to do on *my* land, you've gone too far." I raise one sodden arm and point at him. "If you ever threaten me again, if you ever come *near* me again, I'll tell my grandmother and you'll get sacked." I'm panting for breath after my near run through the lake, but I can hear how serious I sound nonetheless. "Don't think I won't do it, because I will. I swear to God I will."

Mr. Barnes is staring at me with his jaw dropped. I stare back, my eyes narrowed, refusing to let him intimidate me.

Finally he mutters something that I'm sure I don't want to hear, and turns away.

"Jase!" he screeches over his shoulder. "Lock up and get back to the cottage. I've still got words for you!"

He's walking away. I've done it. I've bested him.

But as I look at Jase wading across the lake, I know it's been at a heavy cost.

Because Jase won't meet my eyes. In order to stand up to his father, I had to remind both the Barneses that we're not equal here. I'm a Wakefield, and the Barneses are the gardeners who've worked for my family for generations. We're not equal at all.

I blame Plum for behaving like a spoiled princess, but isn't that what I just did? Okay, I may not exactly be spoiled, but didn't I just use my princess status? With my rank, I intimidated Mr. Barnes, and even though he definitely needed to be intimidated, it still feels like a hollow victory, because it may have ruined everything between me and Jase.

If there was anything left to ruin, of course. Because his psycho dad might have succeeded in doing it all on his own, even before I jumped up on my pedestal and started laying down the law.

. . .

Jase and I part ways after he locks the gate. I walk down the path that will take me round the tennis courts, behind some hedges. Hopefully, I'll be concealed all the way back to Aunt Gwen's house.

I don't turn back to look at Jase. What would be the point? He certainly won't be turning back to look at me.

I squelch home, my feet so wet that I eventually take off my socks and trainers and carry them. The tarmac path is rough underfoot, but I barely notice. I can't believe how bad this afternoon has turned out. How could this happen? How could something so nice go so badly wrong? Why does Jase's father mind so much that we're hanging out together? My head's spinning with questions and I have no way of answering any of them. I want to cry. I want to lie down on my bed and burst into tears and never stop crying.

I can't help wondering if Mr. Barnes knows anything about me and Dan's death. Could he have heard my grandmother and Aunt Gwen talking about it? Is that why he doesn't want me around Jase? I could understand that, I guess. But that wouldn't explain his incredible hostility, or the fact that he could have killed me when he shook the branch I was standing on. It wasn't as if he caught me kissing Jase and dragged me off him, after all. That would make sense. But putting me in that much danger—it's insane.

My phone rings as I let myself into the gatehouse, and I sprint upstairs faster than I've ever run, thinking it might be Jase. No one else will be ringing me: I don't have any friends but Taylor, and she wouldn't want to risk interrupting me in the middle of my date with Jase. I'm counting the rings desperately as I hurtle upstairs—there are five and a half before it goes to voice mail. I tumble into my room and snatch at the phone at four and a half rings. There isn't enough time to see who the caller is, just enough to thumb the Answer button and say, breathlessly, "Hi!"

"Is this . . . Scarlett Wakefield?"

It's a woman's voice. Not Jase. I bite back the tears and say, "Yes," wondering who it can be.

"Scarlett . . ." She takes a long, slow breath. "This is Flora McAndrew. Dan's mother. My husband and I got your letter by this morning's post, and we've been talking things over."

I want to sit down, but I can't, and not just because I'm soaking wet and dripping on the floor. I'm totally gobsmacked as I go through to the bathroom, the phone clamped to my ear, not wanting to miss a word Mrs. McAndrew's saying. I can't believe she's ringing me so soon:

126

I posted the letter only yesterday morning. I didn't expect to hear from her for at least a day or so—that's always assuming she decided to get back to me at all. The first-class post must be a lot better than I realized.

"It was . . . nice to hear from you." Her Scottish-accented voice is hesitant. "We were wondering—well, what you wrote about wanting to meet us, and talk about his last minutes, really struck a chord with me. I know we saw you at the inquest, but we were so overcome with grief that we barely took in anything you said. And if you have something of Dan's that you'd like to return to us . . ."

I sit down on the edge of the bath, clutching my mobile tightly, like I did with her son's limp body.

"So we were wondering," she goes on, "would you like to come up here for a few days? To the castle? Dan's brother and sister will be back for half-term, you could meet them and maybe answer any questions they might have about Dan's"—she gulps hard, but recovers herself—"about Dan's last moments?"

I can't say anything. My throat has temporarily closed up.

"Scarlett?" Mrs. McAndrew asks, sounding very nervous. "Would you like to come? I thought this Friday to next Monday, a long weekend. Or maybe you have plans for half-term already. . . ."

Through some act of God, I finally find my voice.

"No," I say, swallowing hard. "I don't have plans."

I also don't have any time to think about whether or not I can go through with this, which is what I told myself I'd do before sending the letter to the McAndrews. Honestly, I thought I'd be capable of taking this next step, but now I'm unsure and scared.

None of that matters, though, because Dan's mother is waiting patiently for an answer.

My teeth are chattering with bitter cold and anxiety, but hopefully she doesn't hear that when I say, "Thank you very much for asking me, Mrs. McAndrew. I'd really like to come."

Ten

"WE'RE SUPPOSED TO BE PARTNERS!"

"Lizzie Livermore?" My grandmother stares at me, her lips slightly pursed, one hand raised, turning the pearls in her necklace. "I'm not quite sure I approve of this new friendship, Scarlett. A perfectly pleasant girl, but a follower, not a leader. And she has neither brains nor breeding."

"It's not really a friendship, Grand—*Lady Wakefield*," I correct myself.

Mistake! *Beep beep!* Mistake! My grandmother jumps right on that one.

"Not really a *friendship*? Then why, after staying with her last Saturday night, are you proposing to spend part of your half-term break with her as well?" she inquires, her blue eyes narrowing.

I recoup quickly.

"She's very nice to me, and I miss London," I say convincingly. "But mainly"—I look away here, as if it's hard for me to say the next part—"mainly it's because I can tell Aunt Gwen doesn't want me around too much. I really don't think she'd like me kicking round the house for a whole week with no school to go to. She's used to having it to herself. I thought it would be easier on her if I went away for part of the time."

I've been saying this mostly to a portrait of a Wakefield ancestor in a crinoline, her hair in unflattering ringlets, holding a parasol and a small dog and looking rather uncomfortable, which hangs on the far wall of my grandmother's office. It's always weird looking at the family portraits, because they're either the spitting image of my grandmother or of me. Which I expect means I resemble her more than I realize.

Ooh, that's a scary thought. I glance back at my grandmother, picturing her at my age, with my dark curls. It's impossible, though. I can't imagine her a day younger than she is now. And are my eyes really that bright shade of turquoise? I don't think so. Mine are paler, more aquamarine. And my skin isn't as pale as hers—Grandma is as white as a piece of copy paper. She definitely has more striking coloring than I do.

To my surprise, I see that her expression has actually softened. She's stopped turning her pearls as well, which is always a good sign.

"I see," she says, slowly, as if she's saying it more to herself than to me.

"Taylor McGovern is staying here this half-term 'cause—*because*—her parents are still on their archaeological site and she can't go and visit them. So when Lizzie invited me, I thought—"

My grandmother holds up a pale, wrinkly hand.

"There's no need to explain further, Scarlett," she says. "You may go to stay with Lizzie."

"Thank you, Gr—*Lady Wakefield*!" I exclaim enthusiastically.

Then I wonder if I've sounded too keen at the prospect of spending my short holiday with Lizzie. But my grandmother isn't suspicious: she looks rather sad, actually.

"Scarlett?" she adds as I'm on my way out of her office.

Holding the door, I look back. Seated behind her huge mahogany desk, my grandmother should look tiny by comparison. It's the desk that used to belong to the Wakefield men, made in the Victorian era, with a green leather studded top, very faded now. Desks for ladies of that period are tiny little things, with fold-down tops and a series of pretty little pigeonholes for party invitations and dressmakers' bills. I know, because Grandmother has one of them, too.

But, sitting behind this monster of a desk, in a very modern swivel chair, Grandmother looks like the queen of all she surveys. Her white hair's shining, her pale blue cardigan with pearl buttons is neatly done up over a pristine white blouse. She's a modern version of all the Wakefields in the portraits. The office is paneled in mahogany and painted dark red where there isn't paneling: it's supposed to be imposing, so parents and badly behaved girls summoned before the headmistress are daunted as soon as they walk in. But that's just an extra. My grandmother doesn't need this setting to be imposing. She can manage that all on her own.

"Yes?" I say, almost expecting some words of consolation at my having to live with Aunt Gwen.

"Just make sure you don't become too influenced by Lizzie Livermore," she says firmly, adjusting some papers on the desk. "She's a very silly, flighty girl without a thought in her head, and she's much too concerned with fashion and frivolity. And her father's the height of nouveau riche. Not a connection I want for my only granddaughter."

"No, Lady Wakefield," I say dutifully, closing the door.

I can't help grinning to myself. My grandmother really is as tough as old boots. Trust her to get in a comment like that at the end, just when I thought she might be letting down her guard a bit.

I just hope I've inherited half her backbone.

* * *

Lucky it went so well with my grandmother. Because it went as badly as it could possibly have gone with Taylor. She's furious when I tell her about Mrs. McAndrew's invitation. I've seen Taylor angry before, but not like this. A few weeks ago, she didn't really know me, and it wasn't personal. Now, it is.

"How could you not tell me you were writing to her?!" she yelled at me. "We're supposed to be *partners*. We're in this together!"

"Try to understand, Taylor. I just need to do this on my own for a while," I explain.

Taylor's fists are resting on her hips, her legs planted just as firmly a couple of feet apart. All of her muscles seem to be bulging, and Taylor has a lot of muscles. She's frowning so much her thick dark eyebrows are almost joining up. Anger has made her look like a cartoon version of herself.

"I'm not saying you should have sat down with me to write the letter," she continues, "but you could at least have *told* me you were sending it! Or that you found out that Callum is Dan's *brother*. Jesus!"

"I'm sorry," I say. "Look, I wasn't deliberately cutting you out or anything like that. After I read the obituary, I just had an idea to write to her and I sat down and did it and posted it off straight away, that's all . . ."

"You still could have told me," she insists.

I feel really guilty. Taylor has helped me out so much in trying to find out who killed Dan and put herself on the line for me many times. She even took the risk of going through Plum's bag, when if anyone had caught her, she could have been arrested. For a moment, I wonder if shutting her out was absolutely necessary.

"I thought we were a *team*," she's saying furiously. "I thought you felt the same way."

I look at her helplessly.

"I don't know if I *can* always be a team on this," I blurt out. "You didn't even *know* Dan, Taylor. You weren't there when he died. But I was. I'm the one he was kissing—I'm the one everyone thought had something to do with killing him. This is really personal to me and I need some space to deal with it on my own." I pause for breath, shocked by what I'm saying. I've never realized this before, not so clearly, but now it's put into words I realize how true it is. I'm begging her to understand.

"You could at least have asked if I could come up to Scotland with you," Taylor complains.

"I couldn't do that!" I exclaim. "It's just going to be me and the family there—I'd have felt ridiculous asking if I could bring a friend."

"Whatever," she says coldly. "Have a great time in Scotland solving *your* mystery." She puts a nasty spin on the *your*, and I can't blame her. "Don't bother to send a post-card," she adds sarcastically.

Then Taylor McGovern, my only true friend, turns and stomps away.

eleven

DOUBLE TAKE

Whistles blow. People shout and slam doors. I almost expect to see puffs of steam rolling down the platform. There's something about a long train journey that makes me think of a scene from a film—the train pulling out of the station, a journey beginning that may change your life. I should be hanging out the window, waving goodbye to someone with a handkerchief in my hand. But there's no one on the platform to see me off, because I told Lizzie to go, after her fussing round my compartment nearly drove me mad.

She thinks I'm going to stay with friends from St. Tabby's that my grandmother doesn't approve of, which is why I had to use her as cover. I hinted that there was a boy involved, which of course got her sentimental heart beating extrafast, and naturally explained why I needed to organize a clandestine stay in Scotland behind my grandmother's back. I must say, I haven't found a lie yet that Lizzie won't swallow.

I wish Taylor were waving me goodbye. Or, even better, sitting in a bunk above mine. But I doubt Taylor will even hear my name mentioned at the moment without spitting.

I do seem to have a special gift for alienating my friends.

The train jerks into motion. I know it isn't pistons and steam engines and men shoveling coal into open fires anymore, but it feels like it for a moment, as the carriage rattles and creaks beneath my feet. I sit down on the berth and watch through the window as the Caledonian Lowland Express slowly pulls out of Euston, London's lights sparkling orange and white against the dark midnight sky.

"Tickets please!"

I get up and struggle momentarily with the catch of my compartment door, finally managing to open it. A conductor stands there, the strap of his ticket machine straining across his stomach. He looks at my ticket and says, "Traveling alone?"

I nod. He makes a harrumphing sound. I don't know what it means.

"Cooked breakfast from six for first-class passengers in the lounge car," he says. "If you want something to eat now, you'd better make tracks for the buffet in ten minutes or so. We're going to run out of sandwiches, I can tell you that for nothing."

"I had dinner already," I say.

He harrumphs again. "Sensible," he says. "Couple of stops before Glasgow, but nothing to worry about. I'll give you a knock at seven, before we get in. Make sure you're all right."

I manage a smile at him by way of thanks. He heaves up his ticket machine, which has slipped below his potbelly, and waddles on down the corridor. I close my door and go back inside the compartment. The bed is all made up; my suitcase is stowed away. I should put on my pajamas, brush my teeth in the basin, and go to sleep. But I'm not tired. I sit back down and stare out of the window again. We're heading north out of London, the concentration of central-city lights already fading. We've got all of England's back-bone, and some of Scotland's, to travel up till we get to Glasgow the next morning.

I'm mad to be doing this. I'm mad to be going at all, of course, but in the more narrow scale of things, I'm mad to be going up to Ayr on the night sleeper—which means two trains, because there's a change at Glasgow station at seven in the morning, when I'll be bleary-eyed with sleep. I could have flown to Prestwick airport and got a taxi from there to Castle Airlie: that's what Mrs. McAndrew suggested.

But I couldn't face that. It would be such a short flight—I'd be there in an hour. Somehow, I needed more time for the journey, more time to acclimate to the terrifying situation I'm getting myself into. When I found the overnight sleeper, it seemed perfect. Lizzie said it would be romantic. But then, Lizzie's an idiot. How can it be romantic, when I'm by myself in a single berth?

At least I can afford a first-class compartment, so I don't have to share. I barely use my trust fund, and anyway, my grandmother's secretary, who gets the bills for my emergency credit card, never raises a fuss about my spending. Sometimes I wonder how high I could go before she would.

I reach for my phone. But then I remember what the time is. I want to ring Taylor, but it's too late, and I don't know if she'd talk to me anyway.

I tried to talk to her after our row, but she didn't

acknowledge my existence. I rang her and e-mailed her in an effort to find another way through, but she blanked me out. And then, for the next couple of days, I was overwhelmed with organizing myself for the trip to Castle Airlie, working out the train up to Ayr, wondering what to bring. I thought I might ring Taylor once I was there, to tell her how it was going, ask her for advice. . . .

But I'd really like to ring her now. I feel very alone suddenly, rocking gently from side to side in this train compartment, traveling all the way up to Scotland by myself.

I pull off my jeans and slide under the covers, not bothering to put on my pajamas. I can't deal with being naked right now, not even for the brief time it would take me to strip off while I'm changing. I don't even brush my teeth. I turn off the light and lie there in the hard uncomfortable bunk, thinking about what I'm going to face tomorrow morning.

There is Callum McAndrew, Dan's brother, who just might be responsible for Dan's death. That's an awful thought, but someone did murder Dan, and the trail seems to lead back to his family. Lucy, Callum's girlfriend, was at the party—and Nadia saw Dan's EpiPen in what might well have been Lucy's handbag. It would have been pretty easy for Lucy to get Dan's EpiPen from him. All you'd have to do would just be to ask him if you could look at it for a minute, just out of curiosity, and then create a small diversion and "forget" to give it back. I checked out Lucy's online profile again, and discovered she lives in Ayrshire too, so I'm hoping she'll be around a bit hanging out with Callum while I'm there.

Even though I have a couple of new suspects, the motive is still unclear. Why would anyone have wanted to kill Dan? When I thought it was Plum who had killed him, her motive was incredibly weak, and to be honest, the more I think about it, the less I see Plum as a sneaky murderess. Plum never does anything without an audience. It would be completely out of character for her to secretly plot and execute such a clever plan to kill someone and then never breathe a word about it. Like I said before, if Plum was going to commit a murder, she'd stab someone or push them off a building in front of a crowd of people and then announce loudly that it was all their fault in the first place.

And Nadia's sure Plum never went behind the bar.

It's much too much of a coincidence to think that the person who had Dan's EpiPen in her handbag isn't the person who killed him. This was a well-orchestrated, carefully worked-out plan. So, with Plum looking increasingly unlikely as a suspect, Lucy Raleigh, with her connection to Callum, is the best possibility I have.

My brain is racing so much with all this speculation that I'm sure I won't be able to fall asleep. I close my eyes, and immediately the rocking motion of the train, plus the exhaustion and stress of the last few days, tip me over and I fall into sleep as easily as turning off the night-light.

• • •

I wake up in a panic a few hours later, because the train is grinding and shifting and the noises have given me an awful nightmare. Then I remember that we stop at a station called Carstairs, where the Lowland Express splits into two directions, one for Edinburgh, one for Glasgow. Once I remember, I'm reassured that I haven't overslept completely and ended up in some railway siding in the Highlands.

Although I had wanted it this way, it's no fun doing this on my own. I have to look after myself the whole time, instead of having someone else with me to help me and cheer me up. Since I fall asleep again on that self-pitying thought, I toss and turn restlessly. I'm more than ready to get up at six and stumble down the corridor to the dining car. It's actually quite nice and old-fashioned and I think the waiter feels a bit sorry for me, because he keeps asking me if I want anything else, topping up my coffee and juice, and giving me extra bacon rolls and croissants. Nerves and greed make me eat the lot. At the end he slips me three minipackets of shortbread, saying, "In case you get hungry later, then!" with a wink.

By then I'm so buzzed on a potent cocktail of coffee, fried pig meat, sugar, and complex carbohydrates that I cope with the arrival at Glasgow and the change to the train for Ayr without much panic. Especially as the ticket collector makes sure that I know which platform I'm going to. Everyone is sort of taking care of me now, which is nice, and it makes me feel a bit less lonely than I did at five o'clock this morning. But as the little local train chugs down toward Ayr, stopping every five minutes at another little local station, any thoughts of loneliness fade as a much more pressing emotion floods in.

Fear.

What on earth have I done? What have I let myself in

for? All the McAndrews are going to hate me, and I wouldn't blame them if they did. Besides, as an extra incentive to get the McAndrews to meet me, I've told Mrs. McAndrew that I have something of Dan's I wanted to give back, which was a total lie. I'm gambling that I can sneak into Dan's room and fish something out to give her, but what if that doesn't come off? What if Dan's room has been cleaned out, or what if someone catches me at it? Should I just pretend I left it at home? But then what should I say it was?

By nine o'clock I'm in such a state of nerves that I seriously consider not getting off the train at all, just sitting still till we get to wherever it terminates and working out how to get back to London from there as quickly as possible.

"The next stop is Ayr," the crackly loudspeaker says. "Next stop Ayr. Please take all your belongings with you when leaving the train."

In my heightened state of nerves, it sounds like it's saying "Abandon hope all you who are prepared to die," and my hands are actually shaking as I pull down my suitcase from the overhead rack.

The train chugs into Ayr station and pulls, groaning, to a halt. The doors take so long to open that I find myself hoping there's a malfunction, they won't open at all, and we'll just have to go on to the next stop.

But then, with a tired old whoosh, they finally slide open and I lug my suitcase out onto the platform, pull up the handle, and tug it in the direction everyone else is going, toward the exit, my heart beating so fast and heavy it's almost unbalancing me. Mrs. McAndrew said someone would come to meet me at the station, but she didn't say who. Maybe he or she will be holding a sign that has KISS OF DEATH GIRL written on it. Wouldn't that be priceless?

However, when I walk out through the gate, I see my escort straightaway, but I do a double take because I don't actually believe what I'm seeing. He's leaning against a car, hands in his jeans pockets. He's tall, with wide shoulders and long legs, wearing an old cable-knit sweater which was once probably a cream color and now is so faded it's almost colorless. His jeans are equally old and battered, and his work boots are mud-stained. His dark brown hair's close-cropped, and his eyes are gray, the color of lake water, fringed with dark lashes so thick that if he were a girl, you'd think he was wearing mascara. His dark brows are pulled down, and his jaw is set and sullen, his shoulders hunched.

He didn't want to come, I can tell that immediately.

That observation pops into my head a split second before I feel my legs begin to buckle under me. My head's spinning. I can't breathe. Someone behind me exclaims as I start collapsing, but I can't make out what they're saying.

All I can see is Dan. Dan McAndrew, the boy who died last summer after I kissed him.

Dan McAndrew's ghost is leaning against that car, looking as if he would rather be anywhere but here.

And then my legs give way completely, and everything goes black, and I can't see anything. Not even Dan's ghost.

PART TWO: SCOTLAND

Twelve

THE BEST THING THAT COULD HAVE HAPPENED

I'm lying in something so soft that this is how I imagine it would be to float on a cloud. Soft and yielding and very very deep. I feel miles down, coddled in layers and layers of fluffy cloud. My eyelids are so heavy it's as if they have weights on them.

I can't open my eyes, but I can hear voices. Loud voices, but not right next to me. Muffled somehow.

"I can't believe no one told her!"

"I thought she would know—"

"How would she know?"

"She might have known—"

"Someone should have told her *anyway*, just to make sure—"

A third voice cuts in, much lower, but it silences the other two.

"Will you two stop squabbling!" it hisses. *"You're right in front of the puir wee girl's room!"*

Something creaks. It's a door opening. I hear footsteps, and I force my eyelids open, blinking because it's bright. I see little flowers, lots and lots of little blurred blue flowers on a white background. The flowers come into focus, filling my vision. I try to turn my head and find that I can, and as I do the flowers slide sideways and I see a room. Big window with heavy blue curtains drawn back, wooden floors, a pale blue rug by the bed.

The footsteps reach me. It's a woman in a corduroy skirt and a green jumper. The bed must be very high, because I can see a lot of her body even though I can't tilt my head yet.

"Oh good," she says in a very comforting voice, "you're awake. The doctor said to come in and check on you. She would have been worried if you were passed out much longer. You hit your head a wee bit when you fell, apparently."

"Passed out?" I manage.

"Och yes, dear, you fainted. Right in the middle of Ayr station. Causing such a commotion, I can't tell you. You puir wee thing!"

She sets something on the table by the bed.

"Do you feel you could sit up, hen?" she asks.

I nod. She leans forward and helps me, putting pillows behind my back so I'm propped up.

"That's better, isn't it? I brought you a nice cup of tea, do you think you could take some?"

"Yes, please."

She reaches to the bedside table, picks up a little tray, and sets it on my lap. There's a milky cup of tea in a big cup and saucer, and a plate of what looks like chocolate slices. I pick up the tea and drink it down so fast I surprise myself.

"Thirsty, aren't you?" says the woman, smiling. "Eat

something too. It's millionaire's shortbread, I made it myself. The doctor says you need to get some sugar down you. For the shock."

Dutifully, I pick up a piece of chocolate slice and bite into it. There's caramel under the chocolate, and shortbread under that. It's delicious.

"Tasty, eh? Good girl. Tea and shortbread, there's nothing like that for setting you up again when you've had a shock."

Listening to her has been very calming, a soft gentle flow of words that I sense she doesn't need me to respond to. But everything's coming back to me now: the boy I saw just before I fainted. Dan, leaning on the car. I saw Dan's ghost. The teacup rattles on the saucer—it's a miracle I don't drop it. I look at her in panic.

"I saw . . . ," I babble. "I saw . . ."

"Och, hen, you saw puir Dan's twin brother, didn't you now? No one told you he had a twin, did they? That was Master Callum you saw at the station, not a ghost. That's what you were thinking when you fainted, wasn't it now?"

I put down the cup on the tray and burst into hysterical tears. The next thing I know, she's taken the tray from me and is sitting on the bed, hugging me. I sob into her woolly shoulder, a great flood of sobs that I'm completely unable to control.

"Moira, is she all right?" says another woman.

"She's just had the shock of her life, Mrs. McAndrew," answers the woman who's hugging me. Moira. "But now she knows it was Master Callum she saw, she'll be doing much better. Won't you, hen?"

I nod into her shoulder, which is completely damp by now.

"Scarlett?"

I raise my head and make an awkward drag across my eyes with the cuff of my own sweater. Mrs. McAndrew, Dan's mother, is standing by the bed.

I remember her from the inquest: It would be impossible to forget her because her coloring's so striking. She looks like she's out of a fairy tale, not a real, flesh-and-blood person. She's very thin, with white white skin and red red hair. Her eyes are slightly slanted and greenish. I remember Mr. McAndrew, too—he was big and dark, his features all dragged down and saggy from grief. I realize that Dan and Callum must take after him, at least physically, because he was tall with big shoulders, just like his sons.

Callum wasn't there at the inquest, of course. I could scarcely have failed to notice him, could I?

Though Mrs. McAndrew's face is drawn and weary, she's looking at me with concern, I can tell.

"Scarlett, I'm Flora McAndrew," she says, her Scottish accent much lighter than Moira's burr. "I'm so sorry no one told you about Callum. I think we all assumed you knew already that Dan had a twin. . . ."

I shake my head.

"What's done is done," says Moira, handing me a handkerchief. "Blow your nose, hen."

"Are you feeling better?" Mrs. McAndrew asks as I honk into the hankie. "It must have been an awful shock, seeing Callum like that."

"Yes, thank you," I say, lowering the hankie.

She manages a sort of smile at me. "You had a long journey up here, you must want to wash and change. Why don't we leave you alone for a little while? Moira's unpacked for you and put away all your clothes. There's a bathroom just next door, and you've got fresh towels on the dresser. Why don't you have a shower, or whatever you want, and come downstairs when you're ready?"

I realize that my scalp's itchy and I'm probably a bit smelly. She's absolutely right—I really need to wash.

"Thank you," I say again.

Moira stands up and smiles at me. She has bright red hair, so bright it must be dyed, cut in a raggedy bob a bit like a doll. But from the lines on her face, she must be at least fifty or sixty. Oddly, the hair color suits her. She has very bright blue eyes, and they're twinkling at me now. It's a real smile, unlike Mrs. McAndrew's, which is definitely forced.

I don't blame Mrs. McAndrew for not being able to smile at me properly, I reflect as the two women leave the room, closing the door tactfully behind them. I don't know if I'd be much good at smiling at the girl who might have killed my son, even if she didn't mean to. But one very positive thing has come out of my fainting fit on seeing Dan's twin brother. By complete chance, I've arrived at Castle Airlie as a victim, needing to be looked after. Someone who needs sympathy, rather than the mistrust I'd expect considering the circumstances.

I remember the voices I heard before Moira came in. Nobody realized I didn't know Dan had an identical twin, so nobody thought to tell me. It wasn't their fault, but it meant I got a terrible shock, and needed taking care of. So they're starting off on the wrong foot with me—and that gives me a lot of extra leeway. I'm in a much better position to ask questions than I would be otherwise. As I climb out of bed and start pulling off my creased and rumpled and, yup, slightly smelly clothes, I realize that, weirdly enough, seeing Dan's ghost is the best thing that could have happened to me.

*　*　*

I hope my clothes are okay. Both Moira and Mrs. McAndrew were wearing A-line skirts and sweaters, in an old-fashioned, we-live-in-the-country sort of style, and sensible chunky shoes. It's actually the kind of thing I wear to lunch with my grandmother, but I didn't bring any of those clothes here. I decided to put on a pair of jeans (dark blue, not black, because you're not supposed to wear black in the country), a dark gray sweater, and a bright blue T-shirt that's almost the same color as my eyes. And turquoise earrings, ditto. I think I look smart enough without being over-dressed, but for all I know, I've got it completely wrong. It's really hard to work out what to wear when you're staying with people you don't know that well. If you get it wrong, it's so obvious that you don't fit in, and then they're never really that friendly with you for the rest of the time you spend there.

I cross my fingers that I've got it right.

But it may never be an issue, as I may fail to find a way downstairs and be marooned up here in this corridor forever. "Come downstairs when you're ready." It sounds so easy, doesn't it? But I've been wandering along the corridor for ten minutes now, looking for a staircase, and I still haven't found one. This place goes on forever. I thought I was about to find a way down when the corridor took a sharp left and became, for several meters, a sort of gallery, with small windows looking out over a rich marsh-green landscape outside. But at the end of the gallery, there's nothing but another endless corridor hung with pictures, just like the one my room is on. There are doors on either side that I'm much too nervous to open.

I have to keep going, though. I shut my bedroom door behind me, and I'll never recognize which one it is. I can't go back even if I wanted to.

Downstairs, I can hear voices, but I can't work out where they're coming from. Still, I think I'm getting nearer. At the end of this corridor, it turns left again—that's weird. I feel like I'm going in a circle. And then the perspective opens up unexpectedly to a huge landing. I've found the staircase, and it's doubled. Two wide wings of stairs, carved from ancient oak, carpeted in a very faded pale blue and red pattern, swoop away from each other out over the great hall below, return to meet each other, and then join in one dramatic final descent to the hall.

This is a Scarlett O'Hara staircase. I'm not dressed for this. I should be wearing a huge crinoline skirt and carrying a fan. I pause at the top of the closer flight of stairs, getting up my nerve for the scary task of making this descent to meet the McAndrews, when a door below me slams and a boy's voice yells:

"This is *bullshit*! She shouldn't be here!"

I freeze.

"Callum, *please* . . ." I hear hurried footsteps, a woman's heels clicking on a wooden floor.

"I had to *pick her up and put her in the car!*" Callum McAndrew, Dan's twin brother, yells. "I didn't even want to *talk* to her. You shouldn't have made me go and collect her from the station."

"I thought it would be easier for you—you'd have a bit of time alone with her—"

"Well, you were wrong, Mum, weren't you?" he says bitterly.

"Oh dear," Mrs. McAndrew wails, "I hope I haven't made a dreadful mistake! I thought it would give everybody closure to meet her and talk about Dan . . . and she said she had something of his she wanted to give us back—"

"I don't give a damn what she's got of Dan's!" Callum yells. "What could she have? She hardly knew him. And this whole closure thing's ridiculous, Mum! You know we all think it's ridiculous. Nobody wanted her here but you!"

"Your father thought—" Mrs. McAndrew starts weakly.

"Dad will go along with anything you say, Mum. You know that. Catriona and I always thought it was bollocks to invite her."

I'm overwhelmed with the urge to run away and hide in my room for the next two days. The level of hostility Callum McAndrew has toward me is really intimidating. But then I think of my grandmother sitting behind that enormous desk, her spine as straight as if it were made from steel. My grandmother, who took over Wakefield Hall when my grandfather died, and single-handedly turned it into a school to stop it being sold out of the family. She's never run from a fight in her entire life.

If I've inherited anything from her besides my Wakefield looks, hopefully it's that courage. I have to start walking down the stairs; I might as well confront the worst as soon as possible. Slowly, reluctantly, I take one step down, and then another and another, my trainers making no sound on the carpet.

"Cal?"

Though this new voice is muffled, it's a girl, definitely younger than Mrs. McAndrew. It must be the sister, Catriona.

I hear a door swing, and another set of footsteps. Craning over the edge of the balustrade, I see her crossing the enormous hall below me. It's like a gigantic living room, with a fireplace at the far end that's big enough to roast a whole horse in. The stone floor is partly covered here and there with carpets which would fill a normal room, but in this huge space, they look like small bedside rugs. There are groups of sofas, upholstered in velvet and big floral patterns, and lots of occasional tables holding silver candelabra and flower vases. The girl weaves her way around a couple of ancient-looking high-backed armchairs and I see her clearly: pretty, blond, slim, wearing jeans and a white sweater, her hair pulled back in a smooth ponytail. Although it's standard country wear, her jeans are the latest cut and fit her perfectly, while her sweater, with its high ribbed waist and elegantly puffed shoulders, is obviously by some very expensive up-and-coming designer. She looks as if she'd smell of delicate, subtle perfume only available from a handful of sophisticated boutiques.

"He's very upset, Lucy," Mrs. McAndrew says rather unnecessarily.

My ears prick up. Lucy Raleigh, Callum's girlfriend! Wow, it was definitely worth coming to Castle Airlie. In my first few minutes here, I've already found her. Relief rushes through me: this visit's obviously going to be as painful as lying on a bed of nails, but it won't be for nothing.

Lucy says in a worried voice, "Cal, sweetie . . ."

She disappears from view underneath me. They must all be standing at the foot of the stairs.

"I wish she'd never come here," Callum says viciously. "I wish she'd hit her head when she fainted and—"

"*Callum!*" booms a man's voice, so deep it resounds even in this gigantic space, as does his heavy tread on the wooden floor. "That's enough!"

I turn on my heel. The last thing I want to do is walk into a fight between Callum and what I presume is his dad. A memory of Jase grappling with his father snaps into my mind, and though I can't imagine that Callum and his dad are going to come to blows, that memory is so awful that it makes me want to run away till any conflict is over. I see Jase, so clearly that it brings a lump to my throat. I remember him struggling with his father on the grassy verge of the lake. I remember him wading through the shallow water, his face set and angry, to check if I was all right. I remember his soft lips on mine.

And then I push those memories down, stamping them

away. I have to keep my focus on Dan right now. Thoughts of Jase will distract and weaken me—boys seem to have that effect, I've noticed before. One thing at a time. First I have to deal with the McAndrews and solve Dan's murder. *Then* I can set my attention to working out why Jase's dad is so hostile to me, and seeing if I can win Jase back.

Callum and his dad are shouting at each other, and, as the subject of their argument, I definitely don't want to go downstairs to face that. I decide to sneak upstairs again till it's over: I'm sure I can make it back up the carpeted stairs without anyone in the hall below noticing me. But, as I look up, I see movement in the gallery above me.

Someone's there. And they'll see if I run away.

I'm trapped.

So I take a deep breath and walk down the rest of the flight of steps, to the point where it takes a ninety-degree turn, merges with the other wing of the staircase, and becomes a double-wide, imposingly dramatic final descent into the hall.

There they all are, at the base of the staircase. Mrs. McAndrew, thin and pale, with that flaming head of red hair: her long white hands are twisted together as if she were wringing them. Mr. McAndrew—I know it's him, because I recognize him from the inquest. Older and graying at the temples though he is, now I see him again I realize how much he looks like Dan and Callum. And there's Lucy, reaching up to touch Callum on the arm, so pretty and innocent-looking, with her porcelain skin and wide-set blue eyes, that it's hard to believe Dan's EpiPen might have been in her handbag when he was killed.

Finally, I summon up my courage and look at Callum, Dan's twin. Glowering with anger, his strong dark brows pulled together, his green-gray eyes gleaming, his arms folded across his chest. Strangely, though his resemblance to Dan is uncanny, I can see the difference between them now. Dan was so happy-go-lucky, concerned to charm everyone, always cracking a smile. Callum looks like he's never cared in his whole life what anyone thought of him and isn't going to start now.

My trainers creak on a particularly worn-down stair, which groans and squeaks. Everyone immediately looks up at me in shock.

Talk about making a dramatic entrance.

Callum recovers first.

"You shouldn't be here!" he yells, stabbing one finger at me in a gesture that leaves me in no doubt about who he means. I'm standing a few steps up, so he has to tilt his head back to look at me, but I still feel very intimidated by his aggression.

I don't answer him. Partly because I can't think of the right thing to say, but partly because it's such an intense experience to be so close to the spitting image of Dan, who was the first boy I ever kissed. His lips, like Dan's, are full and pink, his lashes long and thick. But his aura is so different. Dan was easy and approachable; his brother is bristling like a hedgehog.

"You should pack up and leave right now," he continues, his tone raging.

"Callum, the lassie's our guest!" his father shouts angrily at him, but Callum's already spinning round, striding furiously away across the hall. Lucy shoots one nervous glance at me and then runs off in his wake.

I manage the last few steps down to floor level, though my legs are wobbling with nerves. Mr. and Mrs. McAndrew just look at me. Despite Callum's father's reminder to him about his manners to a guest in the house, I can tell from their faces that neither of them is exactly happy that I'm here.

Then I hear footsteps above me, running lightly down the stairs. I actually tremble in anticipation of someone else who might order me out of the house. It can't get worse, can it?

"Catriona," says Mrs. McAndrew, looking up, "your brother's just made a terrible scene."

A girl a few years older than me reaches the bottom of the stairs and holds out her hand to me. "Hi," she says. "I'm Catriona McAndrew. You must be Scarlett. Sorry about Callum, he's always been a bit of a drama addict."

If Callum and Dan take after their father (or took, in Dan's case), Catriona McAndrew is spookily like her mother: slender, almost frail-looking, though her grip on my hand is strong enough. She has the same flaming red hair, pulled back into a tight ponytail, and a sprinkling of freckles over the bridge of her nose, surprisingly pretty against her pale white skin. But she seems much more confident than her mother, and she's actually smiling at me.

"It's okay," I manage to say. "I mean, I understand."

"I'll show you round a bit, shall I?" she says. "This place is a real maze."

"Thank you, Catriona," her mother says gratefully.

"Good girl," her father adds.

"Come on," Catriona says, pulling gently at my hand. "This way. You could probably do with a bit of fresh air. Let's start by going outside and looking at the moat."

I nod and follow her.

I just hope she isn't planning on pushing me in.

Thirteen

SEEING DAN EVERYWHERE

"And here's the sea," Catriona says, gesturing grandly.

Though I heard the roar of the waves as soon as we crossed the drawbridge, I had no idea that Castle Airlie was built practically on the side of a cliff, with a sheer drop to the Irish Sea below. The drawbridge is on the far side of the castle, which is built in a triangle—two long sides, one short—with a central courtyard. I walked round the entire three sides while looking for a staircase. No wonder it seemed to go on forever. My bedroom is on the side that doesn't face the sea. I wish it did. I can't imagine a more stunning view than this.

I gasp at the dramatic sight. The Irish Sea is pounding the rocks far below angrily, gray waves breaking into white foam, a constant, relentless pressure that makes me realize how powerful the sea can be. Eventually, it will eat away at the rugged cliff we're standing on, sending it tumbling down to the edge of the water.

I take a step back. Catriona has been really nice to me, but that might have been just lulling me into a false sense of security before she pushes me off the edge. My fears about the moat were quieted when I saw how shallow the water was—Catriona says it's just a "decorative feature" now. But push me over the cliff and there's no way I would survive a fall onto those jagged rocks.

She laughs.

"Don't worry, you're safe enough with me," she says. "But maybe you shouldn't walk out here with Callum quite yet."

"He really hates me," I say sadly. "I can't blame him, I suppose."

"Oh, come on! We all know it wasn't your fault Dan died." I look at her.

"Do you mean that?" I ask, my eyes widening. I wasn't expecting anyone to say that, or at least, not so directly.

She looks straight back at me, red hair whipped across her face by the wind. Raising one hand to push it back, she says:

"Of course. It was just an awful accident."

I bite my tongue, because I know the truth. Peanut oil on the crisps at the party, enough to send Dan into life-threatening anaphylactic shock. And his EpiPen somehow removed, so that he couldn't save his own life.

But I can't tell her any of that. Yet.

Catriona sighs, turning to look over the sea again. She's wearing a sweater and a pair of faded old corduroy trousers that should be dowdy, but hang off her narrow bones in a way that actually manages to make corduroy look quite elegant.

"It's beautiful, isn't it?" she says. "I think it's the most beautiful view in the world."

"It's stunning," I agree, though secretly I find it more cruel than beautiful. The silvery sea pounding the rugged gray cliffs, the bare marshland around us: it's a stark and dramatic landscape, softened only by the sodden green grass underfoot. The castle behind us is equally stark, made of gray stone, with towers at each corner of the triangle studded with slit windows through which archers would have shot arrows at anyone trying to besiege the fortress.

"The moat was much wider then," Catriona says, reading my thoughts with unnerving accuracy. "It would have been really hard to prop up ladders against the walls. And there are hidden openings up above for pouring boiling oil over the heads of anyone who did manage to get a ladder up. This castle was never taken by anyone. It was impregnable."

"Wow," I say, staring up at the sheer stone walls. "It's— intimidating."

I'm not sure if that was the right word to use, but when I glance at Catriona I see that she's flushed with pride.

"It is, isn't it?" she says excitedly. "Lots of people think Castle Airlie is a bit—well, bare, I suppose. But it's one of the few castles no one ever managed to besiege successfully, and I'm weirdly proud of that."

"Did your family build it?" I ask, imagining McAndrew ancestors looking like Dan and Callum wearing kilts and fighting off would-be intruders with broadswords, like something out of *Highlander*.

Catriona doesn't read my mind this time. Instead, she wraps her arms around herself as if she's feeling the cold wind off the sea, and starts walking back toward the castle.

"A distant branch of the family did," she says. "In the thirteenth century. But eventually they only had daughters, and the castle's entailed."

I have to skip to keep up with her: she's walking fast now.

"That means it can only pass down to a male heir," she explains. "So it came down through one branch, and then another, and eventually to my grandfather."

"That's crap," I say. "The entail, I mean. My dad was a baronet but because he only had a girl, the title's died out. Not that I'd want a title, but it doesn't seem fair, does it?"

"No, it doesn't," Catriona says, giving me a sympathetic smile. "Are you interested in history, Scarlett?"

"Um, yes," I say, though it's a very general question. Still, she's being nice to me, much nicer than Callum, and I basically would agree to anything she said just to have an ally at Castle Airlie.

"Would you like to see the family portrait gallery?" she says, so enthusiastically that there's clearly only one acceptable answer.

"I'd love to," I say.

I can't help feeling that Catriona is incredibly poised for someone whose brother died six months ago. She's acting more like a tour guide than a bereaved sister. But, considering the drama going on with the rest of her family, maybe it's just a coping mechanism: and maybe, too, she's trying to overcompensate by balancing out the overheated emotions of some of the other McAndrews.

And, I reflect, I'd much rather have Catriona behaving as if I'm just another guest at Castle Airlie who needs the grand tour, than Callum stabbing his finger at me and yelling that I shouldn't be here. . . .

●   ●   ●

"Are you okay?" Catriona asks. "You've gone really quiet."

She's right: I haven't said a word in ages. Catriona has been doing all the talking as we've walked along the gallery, giving narration on portraits of McAndrew ancestors from Tudor ones in ruffs and doublets, to satin jackets, to ruffles and lace, to dark Victorian suits. But what's been keeping me so silent is the eerie resemblance that many of the men share. It's like seeing Dan everywhere—Dan, whose face I knew so well from afar, but only saw up close for such a short period of time. Now I can look at him as closely as I want, for as long as I want. I just have to visit this gallery, with its echoing mahogany floor and bottle-green walls hung with images of Dan in every conceivable historical costume that I can imagine.

"It's just . . ." I back up and sit down on a padded window seat in one of the bays built into the thick stone walls, probably to provide views over the Irish Sea. I can imagine it being really relaxing to curl up by the heavy old glass panes and watch the sea pounding at the rocks below the cliff.

"It's just that so many of these paintings look like Dan," I say.

"Oh, Scarlett. I'm so sorry." Catriona sits down next to me. Everything in Castle Airlie is on a large scale—there's plenty of room for both of us in the window bay. Catriona takes my hand. "I wasn't thinking. . . ." She looks up and down the gallery. "I'm so used to the McAndrew face, you see. To me, it isn't just Dan. It's Dad and Callum as well, and it was Granddad, when he was alive." She smiles at me. "Did you know Dan well? How long had you been going out?"

Oh, this is embarrassing.

"Um, we weren't going out or anything," I admit, curling up into a ball and hugging my knees. "We'd only just met, really."

"Was it sort of a whirlwind thing?" Catriona asks.

"I don't know what it was," I confess. "We just—we were talking and then we started kissing, and then he collapsed."

"It must have been terrible," Catriona says sympathetically.

"You shouldn't be comforting me," I say. "I hardly knew Dan, and he was your brother—it's so much harder for you."

"But you actually had to *see* him—you know—"

"Well, don't you two look really cozy," a girl's voice breaks in.

I jerk my head up, stunned that neither Catriona nor I have heard her approach. We must have been really absorbed in our conversation.

"Lucy!" says Catriona, looking as surprised as I am.

"Let me guess," Lucy says. "You're having a lovefest about how fantastic Dan was, right?"

I've seen her photos, and I saw her briefly earlier, crossing the hall. But close up, Lucy Raleigh is even prettier than

I thought. Her skin is smooth as satin, and with her up-turned nose and little pink mouth, she looks like a girl in one of those natural-ingredient shampoo ads, her long blond hair poker-straight and shiny as the diamond studs in her ears. She exudes the kind of confidence that Princess Plum and her cohorts have, the confidence of knowing that she's rich, beautiful, and privileged. And she's the girlfriend of Callum McAndrew, who, though incredibly hostile to me, is undeniably a very good-looking boy from a well-off family.

So why, when she has all these advantages, is she glaring at me like I'm dog poo on her expensive shoes?

"I didn't know Dan that well," I answer, choosing my words carefully, because I don't want to get caught out in a lie, "but I really liked him. Everyone seemed to like him, actually—"

Beside me, Catriona is nodding. But Lucy interrupts me, her hands on her hips.

"*Everyone liked him?*" she snorts. "God, if they only knew! They only liked him because he was so two-faced he'd tell people exactly what they wanted to hear. Dan would do anything, say anything, to get what he wanted."

"Lucy, *please*," Catriona starts.

But Lucy overrides her.

"You didn't even *know* Dan," she snaps at me. "You talked to him for five minutes and then you followed him outside to that terrace so he could feed you a load of compliments and snog you. Just like he did with every single girl he ever met. You didn't exactly make it difficult for him, did you?"

165

"Lucy, stop it," Catriona warns again.

But now I can speak for myself. Anger has loosened my tongue.

"Why are you being so nasty to me?" I demand. "Why are you doing this?"

"Because you ought to know that Dan was really a slag," Lucy insists, her blue eyes flashing. "You've probably built up this whole romantic fantasy about him, told yourself that if he were still alive, you'd be together. Ha!"

Catriona jumps up. "Lucy, you're going much too far."

But, awful though it is to hear that I was just one of many, many girls for Dan, I don't want Lucy to stop. If you're investigating a murder, you have to be prepared to hear a lot of things you may not want to find out. I knew that from the beginning. And if what Lucy's saying is true, it's a really interesting perspective on Dan—one that might help me discover who killed him.

"So what's this got to do with you? Why is it your job to go around setting the record straight?" I challenge her, hoping to provoke her into saying even more.

She takes the bait and bites down on it hard.

"Someone has to do it," she insists. "Even now that Dan's dead, nothing's changed. Everyone just keeps going on about Dan this and Dan that, but Callum's worth a hundred of him—"

"*Lucy!*" booms a voice from the far end of the corridor. Loud footsteps stride down the gallery, heavy thuds on the polished wooden floors. Callum McAndrew comes into view.

I catch my breath. If I thought he was glowering before,

I hadn't seen anything yet. His gray-green eyes are so bright with anger they're positively flashing sparks at us. Lucy's right: Callum is the complete opposite of Dan. I never saw Dan as anything but the happy, smiling charmer Lucy's describing, whereas his brother seems to have a perpetual scowl. He's like a thundercloud storming down the hall.

I wish fervently that Taylor were here for backup. She would square her shoulders and scowl right back at him, and seeing her do that would make me feel a thousand times better.

Or Jase. Having Jase standing next to me would make me feel totally safe.

I tell myself firmly not to be so weak and woolly. I chose to come into the enemy's lair all alone—I'll have to take the consequences. I can stand up for myself—I've done it before, in worse circumstances than these.

Brave words. But watching Callum's approach, I swallow hard and brace myself for what's about to happen. One thing's crystal clear: there's going to be a *lot* of shouting.

NOTHING'S FAIR

"What's going on here?" Callum McAndrew yells. He draws level with his girlfriend and slams to a halt. The heavy, wood-framed pictures on the dark green walls can't possibly be shaking just because one seventeen-year-old boy strode down the corridor. But it feels as if they are. Callum's fury is so powerful that it's displacing a lot of air in the gallery. It takes a lot of courage for me to stay exactly where I am, rather than shrink back into the protective embrasure of the window seat.

Lucy looks up at him imploringly.

"Cal, I was just defending you," she says.

"God, Lucy, why can't you leave this alone?" Callum snaps.

"Because it's not fair!" she protests, sounding suddenly very young.

Callum grunts.

"*Fair*," he says bitterly. "Nothing's *fair*."

He's standing next to a portrait of a long-dead McAndrew in a kilt and velvet jacket, both hands planted in front of him on the hilt of a sword, lowering storm clouds brewing thunder in the gray sky behind him, a strike of lightning splitting an oak tree in the background of the painting. The long-dead McAndrew, who was clearly painted in a very bad mood, is the spitting image of Callum, from the dark brows pulled down over the gray-green eyes to the stubbornly set jaw, even the stance of the broad shoulders and legs planted wide enough to withstand a gathering storm.

And I think of Dan, Callum's twin brother, dead and buried, and Callum standing here, so alive that lightning practically crackles in the air around him.

Callum's right. Nothing's fair.

He turns to Catriona. "And *you* shouldn't be encouraging her."

Catriona, quite unintimidated by Callum's looming presence, leans back in the window seat, wrapping her arms around her knees, and sighs:

"Cal, you can't go round policing what everyone talks about. Scarlett just got here. Of course she wants to talk about Dan, that's what she's *here* for."

"She'd better not be saying anything bad about him!" Callum narrows his eyes at me threateningly.

"If you bothered to say a word to me, you could *ask* me what I've been saying," I snap at him, really annoyed that he's talking about me as if I weren't here. "*I* haven't got anything negative to say about your brother at all."

Quite unexpectedly, Callum covers his face with his hands. "I can't do this," he groans. "Mum and Dad—everyone talking about Dan, and we're expected to be able to—God, sometimes I wish *I* were the one who'd died. I really do."

He turns his back, and it sounds like he's crying. Horrified, I can't move a muscle. I know that the biggest humiliation for someone as tough as Callum McAndrew must be to burst into tears in front of his girlfriend, his sister, and the girl he thinks killed his brother.

"Cal, come with me." Lucy puts her arm round his shoulders and guides him back down the corridor.

"Just tell her to stay away from me, okay?" Callum says in a voice now thick with tears. "Please? Just get her to stay away from me. . . ."

They vanish round the corner of the gallery. I'm torn between pity for Callum's obvious pain, and anger at his attitude toward me. The latter emotion is winning out: I can feel myself bristling up. I haven't exactly been seeking Callum out, and he's making it sound as if I'm following him all round the castle, pushing my unwanted company on him.

I look at Catriona, who's still curled up, hands wrapped around her knees. It could be a defensive posture, but she seems more comfortable than frightened. I have the feeling Catriona has seen this scene (without my participation, of course) quite often in the months since Dan's death. She pulls a face at me, a cross between a grimace and a grin.

"Lucy and Callum have been going out for two years," she explains. "She's really protective of him."

"I can see that."

Catriona grins, a proper one now.

"Yes, she doesn't exactly make a secret of it, does she? I think it gets on his nerves quite a lot. But Dan's death made Lucy go into overdrive—she fusses around Cal like a mother hen." She looks thoughtful. "It's weird—I didn't think they were getting on well at all before Dan died. In fact, I was sure they were going to break up. They don't have that much in common, really. But they've got closer and closer ever since. It's like his death brought them together." She shivers. "Everything in this family falls into before and after Dan died. That's the only way we classify anything anymore."

I nod. "That's exactly the way it is for me, too. Exactly."

We sit in silence for a few moments, each of us lost in our own thoughts.

"I'm sorry about Lucy going after you, Scarlett," she says eventually.

I shrug. "I never thought coming here would be easy."

That's true enough. But I don't think I'd quite taken in how hard it was going to be, either.

I glance at Catriona. She's actually looking quite sorry for me. So I take a gamble and ask her the question that's been dying to get out since she first offered to show me round Castle Airlie.

"Do you think I could see Dan's room?"

• • •

I stand in the middle of Dan's room, on one of the few patches of floor that isn't completely covered with random stuff, and swivel around slowly, amazed by what I'm seeing. I don't know quite what I was expecting, but it wasn't this. Catriona said that Dan's room had been left just as it was when he went down to London that last time, because their

171

mother couldn't bear to have anyone touch it, so I wasn't assuming it would be one hundred percent tidy.

Believe it or not, I've never been in a boy's room before. I actually had a shiver of excitement as Catriona walked me down the corridor and pointed at a door to indicate which one was Dan's. Finally, I'm entering boys' territory, a world I know barely anything about (no brothers, no friends with brothers of the right age). This was Dan's room, the boy I'd had a crush on for years, the only boy I'd ever kissed. And now I'm going into his world, seeing how he lived, where he slept, what his favorite things were.

Though the only reason I'm here is because he's dead.

It's exciting, but morbid. I can rummage here as much as I want: Dan will never come in to catch me. I can spy on him and learn his secrets, but it's meaningless, because he isn't alive for those secrets to matter anymore.

Though, surveying the room as best I can, I honestly doubt that Dan *had* any secrets. It looks as if everything he had is on public display. Actually, it looks as if he accidentally let off some nitroglycerine in here and the entire contents of his bedroom exploded and stuck to the walls.

I don't know where to even start describing Dan's room. Even though the room is big and has lots of light from the two windows, there's a dank, musty smell in here, probably from the piles of dirty clothes and smelly shoes festooning every surface, as if Dan got undressed by spinning very fast so his clothes got fired off his body in all directions. Maps are pinned all over the walls in the spaces between shelving units: London, New York, Amsterdam, Paris, Tokyo. Dan clearly had dreams of traveling the world, getting out of rural Scotland. There are stacks of CDs, tottering in precarious hand-built towers, and video games ditto, with a game box in the corner next to the old TV. Various guitars, mostly dusty, lean against the walls, with old hats propped on their heads. It should look cool, but actually I think it's a bit pretentious, as if Dan has copied something he saw in a magazine. It feels self-conscious. I'm embarrassed for him.

There's a corkboard on the far wall, above the desk. I pick my way toward it, nearly turning my foot on something that slides away from me, lurking beneath a pile of old jeans. The board is pinned with articles, film tickets, stubs of tickets to band gigs: Powderfinger, African Soul Rebels, Placebo, Papa Roach, and one called the Translucent Frogs of Quuup. Blimey. On the wall beside the corkboard are posters, ripped and faded: Spider-Man, a scary one for the next Batman film. There's a European Rail timetable on the pile of stuff on the desk. It's very thumbed about and greasy with use. I look at some of the books—lots and lots of Calvin and Hobbes comic books, arty books on graffiti. They're all pretty bashed about too. I don't think Dan took care of anything he owned.

On top of a pile of comic books, I see a mobile-phone charm and pick it up. It's a miniature TARDIS from *Doctor Who*, the TV program, a little blue police box in a transparent plastic shell. It's just the kind of thing I'm looking for: something small that Dan loaned me that I want to give back, my extra cover story for coming to Castle Airlie. Even if someone's been in Dan's room since he died, there's so much clutter here that there's no way they'll remember having seen this charm on his desk. I slide it into my pocket.

Then I notice something else on top of the pile of books: a library ID card, laminated, with a photo of Dan on it. I pick it up and look at the photo. Dan's hair flops over his forehead in that way that always made me flush, and just seeing this image provokes the same physical reaction in me now. I run my finger over the card, reading what's stamped on it: Dan's name, his London address, his date of birth.

It's in October. This month. I pull my phone out of my jeans pocket and check the date on the calendar: no, I haven't made a mistake. Dan's birthday is next Tuesday, the nineteenth.

Which means it's Callum's birthday too. Their eighteenth birthday, probably the most important, most exciting birthday anyone ever has. And Callum will be celebrating it alone, for the first time in his life.

I'm suddenly feeling a lot more sympathetic to Callum's angry outbursts than I was half an hour ago.

I put the ID down and look around me once again, trying not to panic. Because I'm scared that Dan's room is going to defeat me. There's just so much mess here that I don't know how to start searching it. I've got the charm, which is what I came for, but it seems really stupid to have the opportunity to look around for potential clues and not to take it. I start to walk toward the bed and hear something snap below my foot. When I look down, I see it's an old alarm clock that I've just broken. I didn't even notice it.

The bed is so nasty—I sit down on it and then jump up straightaway. The sheets smell as if they haven't been washed in ages, which, considering that Dan died six months ago, must be true. I bet, from the state of the room, they were pretty smelly even before he left for London.

This is the kind of thing that would really put you off dating boys.

I find myself fervently hoping that Jase's room is nothing like this.

Can't think about Jase right now, can't think about Jase . . .

I bend down and look under the bed. Piles of magazines about guitars, a big shoe box containing a pair of new Timberlands, never to be worn. Nothing that could possibly be called a clue. I straighten up again and notice, on a table beside the bed, a couple of boxes that stand out from the rest of the clutter. They're white with black writing and a yellow insignia that I've seen on Aunt Gwen's prescription bottles. I pick one up and open it.

It's full of EpiPens.

Just one of these would have saved Dan's life.

And I realize, strange though it is, that despite the investigation of Dan's death revolving entirely around the mystery of his disappearing EpiPen, and whose bag it was in, that I've never actually seen one.

Each EpiPen is packaged individually in a smaller box. I take one out and slide out its contents. It's a clear plastic tube with bright yellow labels on it, and inside is a long stubby pen, wider than my thumb, with a gray cap on one side and a black tip on the other. Tilting it, I can see that the needle comes out of the black tip. You just put it against your body, take the cap off, and press, and the needle injects you with a lifesaving dose of adrenaline. Nothing could be easier.

If you have your pen safe in your jeans pocket, where it was supposed to be . . .

Doing my best to repress the memory of Dan's tortured face, his hands frantically scrabbling at his jeans pockets for his medicine, I slip the pen back into the box and close it up. Dropping it back into the larger box, I close the lid and replace it on the bedside table. I take a deep breath, pushing every bad memory out of my head. I close my eyes for a moment, trying to center myself, and when I open them, I'm looking at the built-in bookshelves next to the bed. They're piled haphazardly with books, CDs, and various bits of electronic stuff: an MP3 player, a digital camera, a Polaroid camera . . .

Hmm. I didn't think they even made Polaroids anymore. Leaning in, I notice that there are a couple of packets of film for the camera propped beside it, still unwrapped and looking fairly new.

It seems a little odd that Dan would own a digital camera and still be buying film for a Polaroid. What would he need it for? I kneel on the bed and reach up to the shelf where the Polaroid is sitting. I take it down and look at it. Not much dust—there's way more dust on a lot of the books. This camera has been used a lot more recently than other things in this room. I reach behind to the far part of the shelf, to see if there are any photos there. Nothing.

I scan the shelves, but I don't see anything looking like a photo album. Not that I'd really expect Dan to have anything that organized. There are a couple of notebooks, but I flick through them and find no loose photos inside, just notes from what looks like research for essay projects.

I flop back down on the bed again—by now I'm getting used to the smell and the greasiness of the sheets—and look around the room feeling hopeless. I could be in here all day, going through everything, and still fail to find a few Polaroid photos: they don't take up much room. Clothes and stacks of magazines are piled up as high as the mattress in some places: all of them could have Polaroids inside. And there's an old steamer trunk at the foot of the bed, plus a huge wardrobe, both of which, I imagine, will be stuffed with more things of Dan's that would explode out if I opened them. . . .

I close my eyes and try to think what I would do. Where would I put photos I'd taken? Probably close to the camera, because why move them somewhere else? And if they were just casual photos of friends hanging out, they'd be in view. Or some of them would be pinned up on the corkboard. But they're not, which suggests that Dan didn't want them on public display.

So, by this logic, they would be hidden somewhere near the camera. I open my eyes again, looking straight at the shelf where the camera was resting. There are a couple of hardback books leaning next to where it was, held in place by the MP3 player. One's called *Schott's Original Miscellany*, and the other one's called *White Wings Over Vienna*.

Schott's Original Miscellany I've heard of: it's a collection of weird facts, the kind of thing boys like. *White Wings Over Vienna*, though, doesn't sound anything like a book a seventeen-year-old boy would read. Also, it doesn't sound anything like the titles of the other books in Dan's room: it's not a graphic novel, or a nonfiction tome on graffiti or street logos. I kneel up and pull it off the shelf, curious about its contents.

And as I do, the book tips toward me and flutters open, and something falls out onto the bed.

It's a Polaroid photograph.

I sit back down on the bed, opening the book, and immediately realize why the title was so incongruous. Dan must have picked it out simply because it was the right size, and fairly solid, not because he was remotely interested in the subject. Though you can't tell until you open it, the central part of the pages have been cut out with a razor, leaving a large section inside, large enough to conceal whatever you don't want people to find. Drugs, maybe. Or money. But in this case, it's a stack of Polaroids.

Of half-naked girls.

* * *

I don't know what I was expecting to find, but this has really shocked me. I dump the photos out onto the bed and turn them over gingerly, embarrassed and feeling a bit dirty to be even looking at them. It's not just that the girls aren't wearing much in the way of clothing. That would still be embarrassing, but not as bad as this. They're actually posing like the girls on the covers of men's magazines, their fingers in their mouths, their bottoms sticking out, their hands squeezing their breasts. Eww. This is so wrong. I shouldn't be looking at these. I reach one particularly salacious photo— of a girl lying on her back, hooking one finger in her

G-string and pulling it down, pouting at the camera—and actually feel myself blushing before I realize that it's Plum.

God. I look at it more closely. Plum has practically no breasts at all—they look like two flattened fried eggs. No wonder she was jealous of mine when they popped out earlier this year. She must wear a Wonderbra every day.

Then I feel creepy for poring this closely over a photo of a practically naked Plum. I flick back through the Polaroids to see if I recognize anyone else. There's Sophia, the countess who goes to St. Tabby's and hangs out with Plum's set, lying on her tummy, pushing back her hair with a fleshy white arm, looking awkward, as if she wants to be anywhere but on a bed with a camera in her face. I think another face is familiar, a girl I saw out with them that night at Coco Rouge, a skinny blonde with a big gummy smile who's as happy to be posing as Sophia is uncomfortable. And—oh my God—I think that's Nadia, though her back is toward the camera and you can't see her face. But those slender pale brown arms hung with gold bangles, lifting that mass of blue-black hair off the nape of her neck . . . it does look like Nadia.

She's standing in a bathroom, completely naked. No wonder she wouldn't show her face. A few other girls have done that too—hidden their faces in pillows, or turned so Dan couldn't get their face on camera.

But, as I reach the end of the stack, I see one particular girl who I'm sure wishes she'd turned her face away from the lens.

It's Lucy.

I goggle at the Polaroids—there are three of them, in a sort of rough sequence. Lucy's incredibly pretty face, with its round blue eyes and upturned nose, is unmistakable. She's in her underwear, like most of Dan's other photographic subjects, and it looks to me from the background as if she's lying on Dan's bed. Her legs are up in the air, propped against the wall in a pinup girl pose, and she has a cigarette in one hand and a glass of wine in the other. She's tilting her head back to let her long blond hair trail over the pillows in a messy, sexy tangle. She looks very attractive, but also very self-conscious, as if she's practiced lying like this in front of a mirror to get it exactly right.

There's absolutely no innocent explanation for these photos. Lucy, by all accounts, has been going out with Callum for a long time, and these look comparatively recent: Lucy's hair, her makeup, even the sophistication of her pose, all indicate that these couldn't have been taken a few years ago, say, before she and Callum got together.

I understand now why Lucy was so passionate on the issue of Dan's character versus Callum's. Whatever the circumstances under which these photos were taken, she must have asked for them back, and Dan must have refused.

And I think I understand the answer to my earlier question—why Dan had a Polaroid camera as well as a digital one. I bet he managed to convince a lot of them to pose for a Polaroid, rather than a digital camera or a mobile phone, because it makes only one picture. You can't post a Polaroid on a Web site, or send it to everyone with a click of a button.

You just make the girl feel she's really special, and you

kiss her and give her something to drink, and you gradually coax her into taking some clothes off, and you bring out the camera, and you say it's just for the two of you to giggle over, because she looks so pretty and you want to have her with you looking just like this even when she's not around. . . .

I shiver.

Could this have been me? Could I have been talked into taking my clothes off and posing for Dan, just like all these other girls?

And how many boys did he show these trophies to?

*　*　*

Five minutes later, I'm crossing the drawbridge once again, but this time on my own. I have to get out of Castle Airlie. It feels like a rat trap at the moment, with me as the rat, scurrying down corridors, jumping at my own shadow, not feeling safe anywhere.

I don't mean unsafe in the sense that anyone's going to step round a corner and swing a broadsword at my head—though there are plenty of swords hanging decoratively on the walls, and Callum certainly looks strong enough and angry enough to wield one in my direction. No, I mean that I've had quite enough shocks for one day. This morning, I fainted. It's barely lunchtime, and already I've learned, thanks to Lucy and then my very unpleasant discoveries in Dan's room, that Dan was probably just looking at me as another notch on his belt, another trophy to collect.

Ugh, those Polaroids. I shiver at the thought of them. I shiver at the thought of *myself*, giggly on a couple of glasses of champagne, agreeing to do some sexy poses for Dan's collection. It's all too easy to say you'd never do something; although I'd like to think that I'd be strong enough to resist, my brief experience with Dan and then Jase has showed me that a sexy boy can make your head spin in a way that makes you feel drunk even though you're stone-cold sober. What if I were drunk, and Dan asked me to do something I knew I didn't want to, but wanting to please him won over my resistance, because I was afraid to lose him? Maybe that was what happened to those girls.

Though I have to say that some of them looked more than happy to be posing for the camera. Plum in particular was definitely giving it her all.

Without consciously deciding where my feet should take me, I'm finding myself following the drive that winds past the castle. Turn right, and it leads to a walled area which must be where they park the cars; turn left, and it's a long expanse of macadam with no end in sight, lost in a thick stand of trees beyond the marshy grass that grows profusely around the castle. Unsurprisingly, I turn left, every instinct telling me to take the direction that leads out of here, away from Castle Airlie and any more nasty secrets it may contain.

I wish I could just keep walking. If I had my wallet on me, I almost think I would. What a temptation that would be—just keep walking till I hit the road, stop a car, ask the way to the station, wait for the next train back to Glasgow and then to London. Never look back. Leave the mystery of who killed Dan for someone else to solve. I know it wasn't my fault, and isn't that all that matters? And now I've seen what Dan was capable of, my zeal to solve the puzzle of his death has abated a little, I must admit. . . .

I've been walking very briskly, needing some physical exercise to clear out the skin-creeping sensations that have been itching at me ever since I found those Polaroids, and I've already reached the woodland I saw from the castle. The drive cuts straight through it, but it's much colder here, the thick growth of trees blocking out the weak autumn sun. I tilt my head back and see that the trees on either side of the drive have started to grow together, meeting high above, forming a sort of canopy that shuts out the pale silvery sky. Damp wraps round my shoulders, and any light that filters through the leaves is dark green and heavily shadowed.

Perfect. I step off the drive and onto the mulch that lines the floor of the grove of trees. It's covered with damp leaves, and I squat down and brush them away until I've cleared a decent-sized patch of ground—moist, fertile dark mud. Then I extract the Polaroids from my pocket, together with Dan's lighter, which was the other thing I took from his room, and, one by one, careful to hold them as long as I can over the patch I've cleared, I set fire to them and watch them curl, blacken, and burn away to shreds.

It smells horrible. This was another reason I had to come outside: I didn't want to be doing this in the bathroom and have people wondering why there was a nasty acrid smell, not to mention black smoke, oozing out from under the door.

I work my way through the stack of photos. But I leave the ones of Plum and Lucy for last. I hesitate when I reach them, debating whether I should burn them at all: wouldn't Taylor say that I should keep them? The ones of Lucy could be evidence, after all, if it was Lucy who killed Dan, part of her motive for hating him enough to want him dead. And I suppose the same could be said of Plum. Besides, what about keeping the ones of Plum in case she ever tries anything on with me again, just as she kept that video clip of Nadia? Maybe it's weak and stupid of me to want to burn them. But there's a vulnerability about her in these photos, no matter how much she's doing her porno poses, that embarrasses me and makes me want to get rid of them. No one should have photos like this of themselves in their enemy's hands. Not even Plum.

I decide to compromise. I'll burn all but one Polaroid of each of the girls. And if it turns out that neither Plum nor Lucy had anything to do with Dan's death, I'll burn those, too. But the risk that I might need one of these photos for evidence is too steep for me to run. It isn't only about me, after all: it's about catching a murderer. Even if the victim's turned out to be some sort of serial semi-porno photographer, that still wouldn't be justification for killing him.

I shove two of the photos into my back jeans pocket, buttoning down the flap for safety. Then I take one from the remaining small pile, hold it up, and set fire to the corner. It crumples slowly, plastic melting onto itself, the images of Plum pulling down her knickers and Lucy with her legs in the air forever faded and dissolved. And I feel so much better when it's a tiny crumpled piece of black gunk dropping to the forest floor that I know I made the right decision. I pick up the next one and hold the lighter to it eagerly—and then the next, and the next. When they're all gone, I feel almost as weightless as a bird in flight. And I know that when I've burned the last two, the release will be even bigger.

I wish I could do it right now.

I push the leaves back over the spot and mess them around a bit, so you couldn't tell they'd ever been disturbed. Then I stand up and look around me. I take a long, deep breath, thinking about chemistry class and the process of photosynthesis: trees making oxygen, cleaning out pollution, creating fresh forest air. I feel that I'm freshening my lungs, purifying myself of everything I just saw, making myself clean again.

And then, from nowhere, Jase's smile pops into my head, and I sigh.

He hasn't been in touch with me since our day at the lake. Not even a text asking if I'm okay, or thanking me for not telling my grandmother about what his loony father did.

So is that it? Is whatever was starting with Jase over before it really began?

I feel tears pricking my eyes, and I blink them back. At least this "relationship," for lack of a better phrase, had a better ending. At least nobody died.

I think about going back to Wakefield Hall after this, and what I'll say if I see him again. And then I jump right back to the present, because how can I think about going back when I still have so much to do here? And a tight time schedule, too? Well, one thing's for sure: I won't be asking to stay on longer. Thank God I'll be leaving before Callum's birthday, at least.

I realize how awful it must be for Callum: the normal excitement he would feel at being eighteen all destroyed, the excitement at every birthday ruined, because every single birthday from now on will also be a terrible reminder of his dead twin. No wonder he can't bear to look at me, the girl he thinks killed his brother, or at least had something to do with the mystery of his death. I'd probably feel exactly the same.

I clear my throat, and the sound is such a shock in the quiet of the woods that it startles me, even though it's a noise I've made myself. I shiver, and it's a purely primitive reflex, the fear of being alone in the woods, even though I'm not exactly lost—I'm just a few paces away from the drive. A car could come along at any minute.

But it won't. Because there's nothing around here at all but forest and marshland and Castle Airlie, far behind me, and I would hear a car from miles away. There's no car coming. I'm alone in this grove of trees. The sound of my breathing is the only noise besides the wind hushing the leaves overhead, and the occasional rustle of a bird landing on a branch.

And then I hear it: a twig, cracking as loudly as a pistol shot.

Followed almost immediately by the crack of what sounds like a shotgun firing.

I haven't jumped this high since I was doing gymnastics. I take a huge leap and hide behind the biggest tree trunk I can see. Flattening my back against it, I try desperately to

control my breathing and avoid making any sound whatsoever.

I'm hoping madly that I am just being completely paranoid. Because the alternative is much, much worse.

That would mean someone's shooting at me.

fifteen

LIKE A RAT IN A TRAP

My back is pressed so tightly to the tree that I can feel every scratchy sticking-out piece of bark digging into my spine. I don't care. I flatten myself even tighter against the trunk and make myself breathe through my nose to keep as quiet as possible. Even in this damp climate, the leaves overhead are drying out for autumn, and they rustle in the wind, dead dry things tumbling slowly to the ground. My ears are straining so hard to hear any sound around me that it feels like they're pointing out at the corners.

Birds land on branches, twittering softly to one another.

More leaves rustle above my head.

Nothing else.

And then, another shot. Closer now, and sounding, in this quiet forest, incredibly noisy. Its echoes reverberate through the trees, followed immediately by the equally loud noise of the birds that have settled on the branches above me taking off in a cloud of flapping feathers, squawking noisily.

This time, I'm so scared I don't jump. I don't think I

manage to breathe for the longest time. I'm in a cold sweat—my palms are clammy, but I'm too frightened to move even to wipe them on the legs of my jeans. My heart is thumping like a kettledrum, so loud it's hard for me to hear over it. So when I hear the rustle of leaves, I can't tell where it's coming from.

But I'm pretty sure it's not overhead.

I can't stay here. If someone's coming closer, stalking me, I'll be a sitting duck. I look down at what I'm wearing: trainers, skinny dark blue jeans, gray sweater. I pull up the neckline of the sweater and tuck it in over the top of my T-shirt to hide the latter's bright blue color. Good: I'm all dark shades now, nothing that would make me easy to spot. And it's lucky I'm dark-haired. A blonde would be much more visible.

Then I survey the ground. It's thickly covered in leaves—leaves that are sheltered enough by the tree branches above not to be moist with rain and humidity, which means they'll crackle when I walk on them. Anyone who might be stalking me with a shotgun (oh God, don't panic, Scarlett, don't panic) will hear exactly where I am.

I reach up instead and grab on to a branch, and pull myself up into a swing. I tuck my legs up into my chest and come up on the upswing in a tight ball, judging the moment till I'm at the right height to kick my legs out forward in a big jump, letting go of the branch as the jump takes me forward, my legs shooting out, my whole body flying through the air in a long line, back arching, arms back. And I land where I was aiming, by the roots of a nearby tree, close enough to the trunk so that there aren't fallen leaves lying there, and I come down fairly silently. My feet land first. Then my knees bend, my back rounds, and I squat down, hands touching the ground, and breathe through my nose as quietly as I can.

I listen again. Nothing.

I huddle a bit forward till my nose and one eye are sticking out round the side of the tree. I see tree trunks, the black tar of the road, and the gold and red and brown of fallen leaves. Nothing else. No flash of color that doesn't belong in a wood.

No shine of light on a shotgun barrel.

There's a tree very close to this one. I take a deep breath and do a big frog jump, landing in a squat again and managing to clear the fallen leaves. I have to move, but at least I'm limiting my visibility. Only dark colors—I reach up to check that the blue of my T-shirt isn't showing. And I'm making as little sound as possible. Someone hunting me would expect, after the first couple of shots, that I would run away in panic, scattering leaves noisily in my wake, or freeze with fear in my hiding place.

I'm doing neither, which may confuse them.

I really, really hope it confuses them.

This tree is too far from the next one for me to jump, though. I look up instead and form a plan. Climbing up the trunk, with the aid of all its knots and crevices, isn't too hard, though, as always, I wish I were barefoot. I'd take the pain of bare skin against scratchy bark and nasty little branches any day for the security of knowing that my rubber trainer toe isn't going to pop out of a place I've wedged it into because I don't have enough traction or control. At least my hands are bare. I reach the branch I want and scamper along it like a squirrel, on all fours, moving swiftly, and then I lift up, grab the branch of the next tree, and launch up, using my upper-body strength and my abs to tuck up my lower body and swing my legs over to the trunk, where they hang, scrabble, and miraculously find a foothold. I slide down the trunk, wincing as my sweater catches on a big knot, and land fairly silently at its base.

I look back. I'm quite a distance now from where I started.

Then I hear something that chills my blood. It's a heavy metallic click, faint but distinct. I've never seen anyone re-load a shotgun in real life, only in films. So maybe it's just my lurid imagination that is causing me to think that what I just heard was someone snapping the shotgun barrel back into place, having loaded in two more cartridges.

Maybe I'm imagining that I'm the target. Maybe some-one's just out shooting birds or rabbits or whatever people shoot in Scotland in October, and I'm just working myself into a frenzy because after all, someone's already killed one son of this family and got away with it, and now they might be trying to do the same with me—

Bang! Another shot. Birds squawk and scatter leaves. The shot was closer this time, I'm sure of it: the echoes last longer.

I look around me desperately. The woodland's still thick, but even if I reached the end of it that would be worse: back to the castle is wide-open grassland, making it much easier for someone to aim right at me and then claim it was a terrible shooting accident. At least in the forest, I have a lot of shelter. As long as no one comes around the tree where I'm crouching and puts a barrelful of birdshot in my stomach.

Bang! The second barrel fires. Forget my hands being sweaty now—my entire body is clammy with terror. Panic sweat is horrible: it feels like the fear is melting you down, weakening you, till you're paralyzed with it, your muscles too soggy to move.

I have to do something. I can't be caught here like a rat in a trap. And I'm scared, too, that if I don't move now, soon it'll be too late.

So I start to climb. This time I go up and up, swarming up the tree as quietly as I can, higher and higher, till the branches are thinning out so much I don't feel safe putting my weight on them. I wedge myself into a fork in the branches and wiggle around cautiously till I get as comfortable as I can. Which isn't very comfortable at all.

It's two in the afternoon now. By five, it'll be dark. I can come down then and make my way back to the castle under cover of darkness. If I have to wait three hours in a tree, even shivering with cold and with twigs digging into my back, I'll definitely choose that over Option B—possibly meeting a killer armed with a shotgun.

Castle Airlie is behind me and to the left. I can make out the gray expanse of the Irish Sea in front of me, and to my right the drive winds away out of the woodland, through an expanse of more marshy grassland and the occasional oak tree, round a rising hill where I lose sight of it. The canopy of leaves below me is so dense that I can't really see anything below me in the wood, no matter how much I peer down. Occasionally I think I catch a glimpse of some movement, but nothing I can identify. Still, if I can't see them, they can't see me.

I break off a twig that's trying to burrow into my leg, and settle in for a long wait.

I'm not exactly sleepy or tired, but there's something about sitting still for a length of time that makes your head nod and your eyes want to close. So when the sun briefly breaks through the cloud cover, and I see a sparkle of rare sunlight hitting metal in the distance, I have to blink and rub my eyes and focus closely to make sure I'm seeing what I think I'm seeing.

Not someone running with a shotgun, the sun glinting off the barrel. No one could move that fast. It's a car, coming down the drive. Toward Castle Airlie. Which means it'll have to pass through this stand of trees.

I'm out of the fork I'm wedged in and swinging myself from one branch to another like Tarzan, only I bet his hands were a lot more callused than mine from doing this on a daily basis. I'm skinning my palms—I'll have grazes later, I can tell. But right now, there's so much adrenaline pouring through me that I don't feel any pain, just a desperate hope.

I bound down to the forest floor, catch my breath, and start gingerly moving from one tree to another, ducking over so I don't make an easy target, heading all the time in the direction of the drive. I pause behind a wide oak, waiting, listening, relying on my hearing because I can't risk putting my head round the trunk in case the person with the shotgun sees me. For a while, I don't hear anything, and I start to think that maybe the car's going another way, one I couldn't see from my perch in the tree, and I panic: if it does, then I could really be in trouble, because I've probably made enough noise for the shooter to work out where I am—

Oh, thank God! The roar of an engine reverberates through the wood. I dash out onto the drive and stand there waving my arms frantically, hoping there's been enough time for the driver to see me. . . .

It's a big, beaten-up Land Rover, pale blue, with bars over the front to help herd sheep or something. All I know is that those bars look unbelievably scary coming at me fast down the drive. But I don't have any choice. I stay where I am, terrified but determined, flailing in demented sema-phore with my arms. The Land Rover screeches to a halt about two inches from my face, and Mr. McAndrew's head pops out of the window as he yells:

"*Scarlett!* What the hell are you playing at, young lady?"

His brows are drawn down just like Callum's; he's frown-ing at me just as furiously. And I can honestly say I've never been so glad to see anyone in my life.

sixteen

HOW IS THAT EVEN POSSIBLE?

"Who was firing a gun by the drive today?" Mr. McAndrew bellows as he storms over the drawbridge and into Castle Airlie. I follow on his heels, half skipping to keep up with him as he speeds furiously along the corridor and into the Great Hall. "Everyone! In the Hall! Now!" He claps his hands.

"Lachlan?" Mrs. McAndrew comes running down the main staircase, her voice anxious. "What's wrong?"

"What's wrong?" Mr. McAndrew shouts. "What's *wrong* is that someone was firing a shotgun in the trees by the drive today, according to Scarlett. Which is strictly forbidden, because we all know how dangerous it is. Someone could be walking there. Or what if it hit a car?"

"Mr. Mac?" says Moira, coming through a door at the back of the Hall, wiping floury hands on an apron. "What's all the fuss and bother now?"

Her hair is sticking up, and I'd guess she's been pushing it back with floury hands, pre-wipe, because it's got a white streak at the front which makes her look unintentionally comic.

Mr. McAndrew holds up his hand rather peremptorily, waiting for more people to arrive. I can hear someone in the gallery already, and sure enough, a few seconds later Catriona appears, a big terry-cloth dressing gown wrapped round her.

"Dad? What is it? I could hear you shouting from the shower," she says, leaning over the balcony.

"Where's your brother?" Mr. McAndrew asks, his jaw set.

Catriona shrugs. "Gone for a walk with Lucy, I think."

"Did they take a gun out?"

"No idea, sorry."

"Dad!" A door behind us bangs and Callum McAndrew strides into the Hall. I'm finding him more and more annoying. Why can't he just walk like a normal person? He seems to be perpetually surrounded by a dark cloud. He's wearing a greenish tweed jacket over a big cream Arran sweater and ancient jeans, pretty much exactly what his father's got on, but somehow he manages to make it look dashing, which is annoying, too. "What the hell's the row about?"

"Were you shooting by the drive just now?" his father says, beetling his brows at Callum.

Callum looks shocked. "Of course not. I was just out for a walk."

"What about Lucy?"

Callum drops his gaze, suddenly looking a lot younger. "We had a fight," he mutters. "She went home."

"Lucy wouldn't be shooting by the drive either, Lachlan," Mrs. McAndrew says. "Everyone knows it's not safe."

196

"Well, someone gave Scarlett a nasty scare," Mr. McAndrew says.

"She was walking in the wood?" Callum asks, casting a stern glance at me. "Dressed like that? In October? What an idiot!"

"Callum McAndrew!" Moira says, before his parents can get in first. "The lassie's up from London, what does she know about game shooting? Did anyone bother to tell her? Did you?"

Callum's eyes flash, but he doesn't say anything. Moira turns to me.

"You should always wear something bright when you're walking through the woods in the autumn, Scarlett," she says, smiling at me. "Or you're likely to get peppered with birdshot by someone out after a nice plump pheasant or two."

When Moira says my name, I remember how Dan said it suited me. He was the first person ever to say that. I'd always been embarrassed by it, thinking it was a name for a heroine, a really beautiful one, and I could never live up to it. Even since then, I've been a lot keener on being called Scarlett. Even if Lucy's right, and Dan just went after any girl who'd say yes to him, I still get warm inside thinking of him complimenting me like that.

"Though if she's walking along the drive, she should be perfectly safe in any case," Mr. McAndrew bellows. "I'm going to check the gun room now. And if I find anything missing, there'll be hell to pay."

He stalks off across the Hall, his wife watching him, her white forehead corrugated with concern.

I'm a bit concerned too. Because I can't help noticing that Mr. McAndrew's going toward what looks like the same door that Callum just entered through . . . which means that Callum, despite his denial, came from the direction of the gun room. I look at Callum, whose mother is putting her arm around him. Is he capable of shooting at me? Why would he do something like that—to scare me away from here? And why would he want me to go? He wasn't at the party the night Dan died, by all accounts, but Lucy could have been acting for him.

And then something strikes me so hard that it's almost like a blow. I must be the idiot Callum called me, not to have thought of it before.

Who was the older twin—Dan or Callum?

Which one of them would have inherited Castle Airlie if Dan hadn't died?

* * *

"Och, that'd be Dan," Moira says, kneading away in a big, rather chipped, china bowl, scraps of dough stuck to her knuckles. "But you know, he never cared about the land like Master Callum. It's an awful thing to say, but it was always Callum should have been the older. Everyone knows it. They popped out in the wrong order, no doubt about it."

Moira is paralyzingly blunt. I gape at her from my seat on a high wooden stool, which she gestured me to when I followed her into the kitchen. She sees my reaction and bursts out laughing.

"Och, there's no beating around the bush with me!" she

says. "You'll get used to it soon enough. I tell you, Master Callum loves Castle Airlie. It's in his blood."

"I haven't really seen that side of him at all," I say, which I think is pretty tactful and diplomatic of me, considering that I've only seen a single aspect of Callum: the loud, shouty, angry one. I consider that maybe this is because Callum was up to his neck in the plan to murder Dan and is shouting at me out of guilt, and perhaps also to make the point that he's a grieving brother, not a cold-blooded murderer. This is chilling, but it's only speculation. I sigh. I need a lot more facts.

"Mmm, I can imagine," Moira comments. "Well, you'll have to take my word for it. If you took Master Callum from Castle Airlie, you'd break his heart right there and then. Master Callum and Miss Catriona, they both live for being McAndrews of Castle Airlie."

"Catriona showed me round this morning," I volunteer. "She was really nice about it."

"Och, she's got the manners in the family, no doubt about that!" Moira says, laughing. "And plenty of brains! She's an architecture student, did you know? Such a bright girl. Keeps her cards close to her vest, too, that's Miss Cat. Master Callum's a terrible one for saying what's on his mind without thinking about it first. Miss Cat, now, she thinks about everything before she says a word. She'll go far, that girl."

Moira drives her knuckles down into the dough, expertly working the air into it. Her hands are really strong. I can see the muscles in her forearms moving as she kneads the contents of the bowl.

"Just like Master Dan, now I think of it," she continues. "He was a born politician. Very charming, Master Dan." She smiles reminiscently. "And always ready to tell you what you wanted to hear. But he couldn't hide that he was the only McAndrew who never liked it here—he couldn't wait to get down to the bright lights of London. That's why he was at school down there. Living with Mrs. Mac's sister, going to all the parties there, getting his face in the magazines. Well, you'd know about that, wouldn't you?" She looks up from her work and assesses me with a quick bright stare. "Drink up your tea, now." She nods pointedly at my brimming mug, which she insisted on making for me. "You puir gurul, all the surprises you've had today. You must be fairly shattered!"

It takes me a little while to realize that "gurul" is Moira's way of pronouncing "girl." I pick up the tea and sip at it gingerly. Moira has spooned about half a cup of sugar into it.

"Ever since Dan died," I say frankly, "it's been one surprise after another. I suppose I'm getting used to them."

Moira tuts her tongue.

"You're too young. You're all too young for this," she says sadly. "Look at us here! We should be planning for the party of a lifetime right now, have the house full of people, not be moping around shouting at each other. . . ."

"You mean for Dan and Callum's eighteenth birthday?" I ask, drinking more tea. It's horribly sweet, but it is actually making me feel better.

Moira nods.

"We had a wonderful party for Catriona's eighteenth," she sighs. "A huge ceilidh in the Great Hall, a band playing,

I had four girls in from the village just to help me with the food—och, they danced till dawn! And of course, for the twins, it'd have been even bigger, what with there being two of them."

She stops kneading the dough and turns away, wiping away what looks like tears with the sleeve of her sweater.

"It's hard to believe Dan's gone, you know?" she says through the wool. "I tell myself I'll never see him walking through that door again with his cheeky smile, coming over to give me a hug and then help himself to some biscuits when he thinks I'm not looking. But it's not easy. It's not easy."

I look around the kitchen to give Moira some sort of privacy. It's a huge, drafty room, with a gigantic black iron range set into the wall on one side, an equally gigantic iron hood above it. Various saucepans and pots are set on top, bubbling away, and Moira's warned me in dire terms to be careful going near it, as it's all too easy to burn yourself on it. The walls are painted pale blue, which must have been a long time ago, as they're very faded and stained now, and overhead, in the rafters high above the big battered wooden table, is a system of pulleys and wooden rods draped with drying clothes and tea towels. It's toasty warm, smells of baking, and is by far the coziest room I've seen so far in Castle Airlie—even if it is the size of an airplane hangar.

Buzz! I jump. I'm so wound up with everything that's been happening today that for a moment I don't realize the weird fizzing vibrations I'm feeling in my side are actually coming from my phone. A text just came in. *Jase!* I think instinctively, and have to stop myself reaching for it straightaway. God, I so hope it's him. These people, fighting all the time, this huge echoing castle, not to mention playing hide-and-seek with a shotgun this afternoon—I could really do with hugging Jase, feeling his warmth, being briefly enfolded in his strong arms and pretending, like some feeble heroine from a fairy tale, that having a boy close will make everything all right.

I know it doesn't work like that. I know you have to fight your own battles. But just for a few minutes, there's nothing I'd love more than to pretend that hugging Jase would solve all my problems.

Moira hasn't noticed my start. Reaching for a tissue, she blows her nose with a loud trumpet, shoves the tissue up her sweater sleeve, and returns to her kneading. I finish my tea in one big slurp, and, high on the sugar rush, climb down off the stool and put my mug in the deep sink that runs half the length of the kitchen.

"I think I might go lie down in my room for a bit," I say.

Moira nods vigorously.

"Now that's a guid idea," she says. "Dinner's at eight, as always. You get a bit of a rest." She indicates a door at the end of the kitchen. "Go up the servants' staircase. Pop through that, go up the stairs in front of you to the second floor, through the baize-covered door, turn left and your room's third on the right. Easier than going through the Great Hall, and you probably won't bump into anyone. Which is probably the last thing you want to do right now, eh, hen?"

I blush. "Well, um . . . ," I mumble.

Moira shakes her head. "Master Callum's still breathing

fire," she says sadly. "I'm not saying it was the right thing for Mrs. Mac to ask you here, especially not now. But once you entered Castle Airlie as a guest, that's how you should be treated."

I tense up, wondering where she's going with this. Is she going to say I should leave? Because suddenly I realize that, despite all the drama and upset here in Castle Airlie, not to mention being stalked this afternoon, I definitely don't want to go: I sense that the key to the mystery of Dan's death is right here, among these people. And I have to stay until I find it.

"Off with you now," she says. "Get some rest. At least you've worked up an appetite with all that walking! It's cock-a-leekie soup and brown trout for dinner, with oatmeal potatoes, so you'll have plenty to eat."

I mumble a thank-you and head for the door she pointed out. Halfway up the stairs, though, I reach for my phone, and my heart leaps just at the sight of the little yellow envelope at the top of the screen that says I have a message. I unlock it and click on the icon in one fast move, and it must say something really awful about me that I have incredibly mixed emotions when I see the message.

I should be over the moon that I haven't lost another friend. But I'm torn—although I'm incredibly curious about its significance, I'm gutted that Jase still hasn't got in touch with me.

On my screen are the words:

MEET ME WHERE CARS PARKED ASAP. LOTS 2 TELL U. HOPE UR OK! T

Taylor's *here*? At Castle Airlie? How is that even *possible*? I dash down the steps again and look around me. There's a door at the end of the corridor that looks as if it might lead outside. I know where the cars are parked, because that's where Mr. McAndrew left the Land Rover this afternoon. And I know, too, that there's another bridge over the moat at the back of the castle, for kitchen deliveries, because I saw it when Catriona and I were on our walk this morning. I nip down the corridor, grateful yet again for my trainers which allow me to move near-silently, and lift the latch of the door.

I push it. It opens into a wide, stone-paved room which must be the pantry, as it's lined with shelves stacked with tins and packets of food. I can see another door further along the wall which must lead to the kitchen, and then, across the room, is a big wooden door with a smaller one cut into it. Bingo! In a flash I'm tugging at the latch. It creaks a bit, but I lever it up as gently as possible and prise it open.

Cold air blows through the opening. I've found the way out.

seventeen

"I'M ON FIRE!"

It's already dark. Night comes early in Scotland when winter's on its way. The pantry door opens straight onto a wide concrete bridge. I dash over it and, taking a quick inventory of Castle Airlie's geography, turn left on the grassy bank that borders the moat. There's a well-trodden path along it and I run round it, keeping a steady pace until the brick wall of the old stables, where the cars are kept, comes into view. Then I slow down until my breath is back to normal again, or close enough that no one could hear me panting and realize someone was coming.

There might be someone else in the stables, someone who isn't Taylor. After my scare of this afternoon, I'm taking precautions.

I walk through the wide stone arch, careful not to make any sound. It's completely dark in here. I stand in the center of the stables, looking around me. Faint light gleams off the metal of the cars, but it's an overcast night, with barely any moon glowing through the clouds, and the shadows are pits of black, completely impenetrable. The cold in here is damp, unheated stone, with a faint odor of mold. It's very creepy.

"Taylor?" I whisper.

There's a stir of movement from the far corner of the stables. I turn to look and see Taylor's face hovering in the shadows in what looks like an optical illusion. As she walks toward me, I see it's because she's wearing a black high-neck sweater and black jeans, which make her body invisible against the dark background. She looks like a cat burglar or a ninja. Very cool—and suitable for secret rendezvous after dark. I suppose that's the exception to the no-black-in-the-country rule.

"Over here!" she whispers back, her face gleaming, pale and eerie. "Come on, let's go outside."

"Outside?" I say, baffled, even as I follow her back through the arch.

Taylor tuts her tongue.

"In there someone could sneak up on us," she explains, leading the way round the back of the stables. "Out here we can see anyone coming from miles off. I figured that out while I was waiting for you."

"Nice one," I say respectfully, before I remember that she's not supposed to be anywhere near Castle Airlie. "But what are you doing here?" I continue. "How did you even *get*—"

"Flew up to Ayr, got a cab to Airlie village, found a B and B, hired a bike," Taylor cuts in succinctly. "Told the nice lady at the B and B my mom and dad were joining me and we were going to tour the area for my half-term. Then I said I'd got a call from them and they were stuck on their dig in Turkey because their paperwork wasn't in order."

Taylor's parents have given her a large contingency fund for emergencies—I suppose this counts as one. I admire the cunning way she's used the truth to make her lie as plausible as possible.

"I figure I have a couple more days before she starts freaking out that my folks aren't showing up," Taylor's saying, "but you'll be going in a couple of days anyway, right? So we should be covered."

"But what are you doing here?"

She shrugs. "It was really boring at school without you. Practically everyone's gone home for half-term. Besides, I thought things over, and I decided that while I . . . maybe . . . overreacted before, I wasn't going to listen to what you said about needing to come up here alone. What a girl in your situation needs is backup." She raises her eyebrows. "And, considering what happened this afternoon, I'd say I was right, wouldn't you?"

"You saw what happened this afternoon?" My voice rises, and Taylor instantly makes a lowering motion with her hand to remind me to keep it down.

"I was bicycling along the drive," she explains quietly. "I thought if anyone stopped me, I'd just say I was a tourist and got turned around on all these roads to nowhere. I got to this kind of miniforest, and just as I reached it I heard a shot, and I thought I'd better take cover. So I got off my bike and just sort of stuck my head round a few trees to see what was going on. I saw you doing one of your show-offy gymnastic moves over a tree branch. I did think at first you were just trying to impress some guy"—I stick my tongue out at her, which she ignores—"but then I heard another shot, and you know, I sort of began to think that someone might be after you. So I sneaked in a bit—"

"Did you see who it was?" My heart is pounding. What a break it would be if Taylor could identify the shooter.

"Sort of," she whispers.

"What do you *mean?*"

"I mean I didn't see their face! Whoever it was had on a deerstalker hat and a checked jacket. And the person was definitely not that tall."

"Ugh!" I sag in disappointment. "Well, it couldn't have been Mr. McAndrew, because he was driving up the road and found me. And it can't be Callum, because he's even taller than"—I clear my throat—"Dan."

"Damn, I really wish I had seen the person's profile at least."

I realize there's a piece of information about Callum that she is still unaware of. "Oh my God, Taylor. You're not going to believe this, but . . . Callum is actually Dan's twin brother. I fainted when I saw him. And it's their *birthday* the day after tomorrow."

"*What?*"

I give Taylor a brief summary of recent events. She's dumbfounded.

"Wow. Well, we've narrowed the field down a bit, right?" she asks. "We know now it was probably a woman shooting at you."

I shake my head. "There are loads more women than men at the castle." I count off on my fingers. "Catriona: she was in the shower when I got back, but I suppose she could have dashed back before Mr. McAndrew turned up, though it'd be tight. Moira came out of the kitchen, but again, she could have sneaked in through the back entrance and just dusted some flour on her hair to make it look like she was hard at work making bread. (I really don't want it to be Moira—she's been so nice to me.) Then there's Mrs. McAndrew—she came down from upstairs but she could easily have just gone up and come back down again. And Lucy." I pause. "Lucy wasn't anywhere around, but she couldn't have taken a rifle from the gun room, because then it would be missing and Mr. McAndrew would notice. Perhaps she could have brought one from her house."

Taylor's looking at me expectantly. I give her a quick rundown of who everyone is, how they've been acting since I've come here, and the Polaroids I found in Dan's room. She nods at the end.

"So Lucy's the most likely suspect on all fronts," she hypothesizes.

"I guess. She seems pretty angry at me and despises Dan, not surprisingly."

"Boys can be so *gross*," Taylor says disgustedly. "And girls can be so *stupid*."

Speaking of which, Taylor blows up at me when I tell her that I burned most of the photos.

"I leave you alone for two seconds and you pull something that *dumb*!" she exclaims. "You should've kept them *all*, just in case."

I grin. "I knew you'd say that, evil genius. But I couldn't. I felt really sorry for them." I touch my back jeans pocket, feeling the photos safely buttoned in there. "I kept one each of Plum and Lucy, though."

Taylor rolls her eyes. Even in the evening gloom, I see the whites of her eyes gleaming.

"You're such a *softie*," she says in frustration.

I can't help laughing. "I really missed you," I admit. "I'm so glad you're here."

Taylor shuffles her feet. "Cool," she says gruffly. " 'Cause I thought you might be really pissed at me showing up like this. You know, sticking my nose in where I wasn't wanted."

I start to say something, but she cuts me off.

"And I want to say, I get that this is really important to you, okay? I'm sorry that I took over a bit. I can be bossy sometimes."

"*Sometimes?*"

Taylor fakes a punch at my stomach.

"I mean it, though. I'm so glad you're here," I say sincerely.

"Me too," she says, smiling. "Scotland is pretty fierce, and so is this castle."

"Oh God!" Taylor has reminded me of another piece to the puzzle. I fill her in on Moira's comments about Callum being a much better inheritor of Castle Airlie than Dan. Now Lucy has a rival, or maybe a coconspirator, in the most-likely-suspect category.

"Did everyone in the family think that?" Taylor asks.

"It sounds like it, from what Moira said."

"Huh. So someone could have killed him to make sure it went to Callum, because he'd look after the place while Dan would run it into the ground?" Taylor suggests. "This Moira person, maybe? I mean, a castle must cost a ton of money to run, and keep up. . . . Most people don't live in

210

theirs anymore, do they? They make them into hotels or something. So you'd have to really love this place not to sell it and make a fortune and then just go party. What if someone was scared that was what Dan would do if he inherited?"

"Yeah, but he doesn't inherit till his dad dies, does he?" I say. "It always works like that."

"But didn't you say it's their eighteenth birthday in a couple of days? Maybe when the heir turns eighteen, he gets a whole bunch of cash to spend, or something, and that'd mean the estate would be bankrupted? Or maybe he gets to be a coowner, and he could sell part of it?"

I gape at Taylor, even though I can barely make out her features.

"That's a really, really good theory, Taylor," I say in awe.

She makes a smirking noise. "I'm on fire!" she says smugly.

"I need to look at a copy of the will, or the deed, or whatever it is that would explain how the inheritance thing works," I say slowly. "I'll have to find out where they keep it."

"How are you going to do that?" Taylor asks curiously.

I pull a face. "I don't know, and I don't have much time to figure it out either. There's no way they'll let me stay longer than Tuesday, not with Callum and Dan's birthday coming up."

"Whatever it takes, Scarlett," Taylor says grimly. "You've gotten this far."

I nod, and duck a look at my watch.

"Oops, I should be getting back—it's close to dinnertime,

and I don't want anyone coming to look for me." I swallow hard. "Taylor, thank you *so much* for coming. You know, I didn't realize how alone I felt here until you turned up—it means so much to me to have someone here who's on my—"

I break off as Taylor pretends to gag and throw up in the bushes.

"I'm trying to be nice," I say coldly.

"Well, don't. It's making me want to puke. I've got your back, okay? We're good."

We look at each other for a moment. I want to give her a big hug, but Taylor's not touchy-feely at all: she'd hate that. Instead, I slap her on the shoulder and she slaps me back. It's tragic—we're like a couple of boys.

"See you round," she says.

"Will you be okay getting back?"

"Sure. I should get going too—Mrs. Drummond will yell at me if I'm late for dinner."

"Sounds like school."

Taylor grins. "The food's a *lot* better," she says happily.

She heads off to retrieve her bike from where she's hidden it behind the stables, and I jog back to the main drawbridge. Moira might well be going in and out of the pantry while she's cooking dinner, and I don't want to rouse her suspicions by having her spot me coming back in when I'd said I was going for a nap. I cross the moat and push open the door cut into the huge wooden gates, heavily decorated with wrought iron to make them near-impossible to break down, even with a battering ram. The latch lifts easily—this is deep countryside, where people don't lock up till they go to bed at night. But as I push the door open, it unexpectedly bumps into something, and I hear an "Ow!" as it makes contact.

Then it's pulled open from inside, and Callum McAndrew appears in the doorway, glowering at me.

I guess the shock of him looking like Dan is wearing off, because the first thought in my head here is, *God, doesn't he have any other facial expressions?*

"You hit me," he says unfairly.

"I didn't mean to. I was just opening the door."

"Well, I was walking down the corridor. I wasn't expecting anyone this time of night."

"It's not *that* late."

"What were you doing outside, anyway?" he demands.

I think about telling him to mind his own bloody business, but somehow I feel we've antagonized each other enough.

"I wanted some fresh air," I say. "I've had a bit of a weird day, so I thought I'd go outside and look at the stars."

To my surprise, his face softens, and I briefly glimpse a familiar grin.

"I do that sometimes, too," he says. "I've got to say, you're no coward, are you? Going back out in the dark after saying you got shot at this afternoon."

"I didn't say I got shot at," I correct him. "I just said someone was shooting in the wood, and I was scared I'd be hit."

I look him right in the eyes, though I have to tilt my head back to do it. When I met Dan at that party, I was in high heels, practically at eye level with him. Now I'm in my trainers, and Callum's towering over me. But I hold his gaze even though he makes me nervous—and not in a good Jase Barnes way.

"Come on," he beckons. "I'll show you where you can look at the stars without traipsing around outside in the dark. The last thing we want is you falling in the moat. You seem fairly accident-prone."

Callum turns and walks down the corridor, clearly expecting me to follow. While part of me feels like he's trying to be nice, another part of me wonders if Callum McAndrew may be tricking me into falling into a dungeon under the floor. (I've heard some Scottish castles have those—the lairds would listen to the screams of their enemies starving to death while they ate their dinner.) But I doubt it. From what I've seen of Callum, he's not afraid of face-to-face confrontation. He'd be much more likely to throw me into the moat himself than do anything sneaky or underhanded.

He's opening a door in the far wall of the corridor and holding it for me. Dutifully, I walk through, noting that when he's not yelling at me, he has the manners of a gentleman. And then I gasp.

I'm standing in the middle of the central courtyard, hidden in the center of Castle Airlie. But the word *courtyard* doesn't do it justice. It has a wide stone verge, but the center is a grassy lawn, dark and lush in the night air. Lights from the castle windows pool down long gold diamonds onto the grass, and above us the sky is bright with stars. It's a magical hidden garden.

"It's so beautiful!" I can't help exclaiming. I turn to Callum. "And it feels warmer here, too, or am I mad?"

"No, it always feels like the air's softer in here," he says. "Or it does to me, anyway."

Callum rubs his hand over his scalp.

"I spent lots of time in here when I was younger," he says. "Just playing games, or telling myself made-up stories about what might have happened here. I read all about the history of Castle Airlie, everything I could get my hands on. It was besieged in 1300 by the English King Edward I, did you know that? That was during the war with our King John." He grins, seeing my blank expression. "The *Braveheart* war," he adds. "Though the film made a lot of stuff up. But Sir William Wallace—that's the *Braveheart* guy—wrote in 1300 that Castle Airlie was 'so strong a castle that it feared no siege.' Isn't that amazing? It's built like a shield, three-sided, and he said it was a 'perfect shield in design and function.' And that he'd 'never seen a more finely situated castle.' Of course, he meant 'finely situated' in the sense of being impregnable, not that it was massively beautiful or anything. But it's still amazing to be mentioned that far back in history—"

He breaks off suddenly.

"I'm being a huge bore, aren't I?" he says, ducking his head in an embarrassed gesture. "I'm sorry. Girls hate it when I bang on about battles and sieges, apparently. You'd think I'd have learned by now—Dan used to tell me often enough."

"I was really interested, actually," I say, and it's nothing more than the truth. "I love all that kind of stuff."

"History?" Callum asks.

"Well, yes, but battles and sieges too. I'd have hated to live in those times, though," I blurt out. "No one would have let me fight. It would be so miserable to be hiding inside the castle watching all the men go out to fight and not doing anything myself."

Callum laughs softly. "Oh, you could have organized the defense. Pouring boiling oil on the invaders, pushing their ladders off the walls . . ."

"That does sound like fun," I admit.

To my surprise, I am smiling at Callum, and to my horror, I feel something inside me loosen and melt. Callum doesn't have Dan's softness or his approachability. His hair's cropped closer than Dan's, so it doesn't flop enticingly over his forehead, making you long to reach up and push it back. His shoulders are set square, his posture's straight as a soldier's; Callum lacks any of Dan's easy stance, his flexibility. He makes you feel every inch of his height. But in the soft shadowy light spilling through the half-open door and the lit windows overhead, I can see how handsome he looks.

"Talking of boiling oil, sometimes we light torches here in the courtyard, if we're having big parties," Callum says. "It's fantastic—the whole castle's lit up, and it looks so beautiful. You should see it like that."

Then he realizes what he's said, and catches his breath. I do too.

But I don't want to let him know I'm aware that his and Dan's joint birthday is coming up, in case it turns out he got Lucy to kill Dan so that he could inherit. This is chilling. I'm actually picturing him as the cold-blooded killer of his twin brother. Right now, standing next to him, that seems

216

really far-fetched. But *someone* killed Dan, I know that for sure. And so far, Callum has the biggest motive of all that I know about. More than Lucy hating Dan because he'd taken sexy pictures of her. Inheriting a castle that's worth a fortune—I can't imagine a bigger motive than that. Though of course, if Lucy killed Dan so Callum could inherit, that would be two birds with one stone for her. But would Callum know what Lucy did? Might he be innocent, or could he have planned the whole thing and stayed away from London and the party to give himself a solid alibi?

I'm suddenly freaking out that he might guess I know about their eighteenth birthday. If he did kill Dan, and he thinks I suspect him, I could be in real danger. My brain races, thinking of something to say that will change the subject from the potentially dangerous one of parties, but Callum gets in first.

"I know Mum invited you here so we could talk about Dan," he blurts out. "That's what she kept saying. She wants to talk about him all the time, and the rest of us . . . Well, I just leave the room when she starts up because I don't want to see her crying. I think Dad feels the same, but he has to stay."

I'm not really sure how to respond, so I stay silent, just observing him carefully.

He continues, "Ever since Dan died, she's been buried neck-deep in books about grieving. I don't honestly think it's helping much."

"I don't know what *would* help, though," I say, wondering why I'm trying to console him right now. "It's got to be awful, no matter how you deal with it."

I feel Callum's gaze on me and look up to meet his eyes. A sort of electric current passes between us, and I shiver.

"How are *you* doing?" he asks. "About Dan, I mean. It must have been horrible for you."

"It was," I admit, and I can't help being suspicious as to why he's finally showing me some sympathy. Even so, I'm also relieved that he's being nicer to me. "Really horrible. I didn't realize what was happening, and it was so scary. And I felt awful not being able to help him."

"You didn't know about his allergy?"

I shake my head. "But I hadn't known him that long," I confess.

"He didn't tell a lot of people," Callum said somberly. "He was a bit embarrassed by it. Which was stupid, because it wasn't his fault, you know? But that was Dan all over."

I'm puzzled. "What do you mean?"

"Oh." He makes a sound that's like a sigh and a laugh at the same time. "Dan had this thing about not wanting to seem weak. He was always like that, even when he was wee. He had to be the big man."

"Everyone at school looked up to him."

"Yeah, everyone loved Dan," Callum says, and as far as I can tell, there's no bitterness in his voice at all: he sounds sincere, happy that his brother was so well loved. "You did too, right?" he continues.

Funny—he's looking away now, as if he's not that interested in the answer.

I'm glad that it's dark so he can't see me blushing. "I really liked him."

"He'd charm the birds off the trees," Callum observes.

"That's what Moira would always say about him. Not like me."

I glance up nervously, but see he's smiling.

"It's okay. Dan was the charmer and I'm the grumpy one," he says. "You don't need to say anything. I haven't exactly been that friendly to you. In fact, I've been horrible. It's just that—"

"I understand," I cut in, mostly because I feel as though he's about to say something mushy that will make me want to drop my guard. "You were his *twin*."

"I still can't believe you didn't know about that," Callum says.

I shake my head.

"I did try to catch you," he adds. "When you fainted, I mean. I'm not a complete bastard. Sorry that I was too late. Does your head still hurt?"

I shake it again. "It's not too bad. I've got some painkillers if I need them."

"You went down slow," he says, remembering it. "Your knees sort of gave way, and then you fell back a bit, like you were sitting down, and then you just collapsed. I think you sort of sat on your suitcase as you were going down—that probably broke your fall."

"I must have looked really stupid," I say, unable to help being a bit appalled at this vivid description of my theatrics.

"Not really . . . Well, maybe a little bit. . . ." He's really grinning now. "You were totally out of it on the drive back. I had to take off my jacket and prop up your head, so you didn't get too bounced around."

"Who carried me up to my room?" I ask, blushing.

"Me, of course," he says.

I writhe inwardly. He knows how much I weigh. How *humiliating*.

"I'm sorry if I was really heavy," I mumble.

"You're not at all," he says, almost flirtatiously. "You're just a tiny wee thing." He looks down at me. "You barely come up to my shoulder."

Callum puts out a hand and runs it in a line from his shoulder to the top of my head. He's right—I'm no taller than that. But when his hand grazes my head, there's a sudden leap of my nerve endings, like a small electric shock, and I see his eyes widen slightly as if he's felt it too. For a brief moment, his hand lingers on a curl of my hair.

I didn't realize before how close he was standing to me. Maybe I've actually taken a tiny step toward him without meaning to, because I could reach out and touch him now very easily with just a small movement of my hand. I wonder what the wool of his sweater feels like, whether it's rough. . . .

I know it's my turn to talk, but I can't think of anything to say. Anything, that is, that wouldn't completely embarrass me. I just stand there looking up at him, feeling really confused.

And he just stands there looking down at me, for what feels like a very, very long time.

I can hear him breathing, soft and slow.

I can feel my heart, pounding a drumbeat in my rib cage, battering at the bones.

"Callum?" a girl's voice calls, heavily muffled by the thick stone walls. It must be Catriona. "Cal, where are you?"

I expect Callum to answer, but to my surprise he doesn't.

"Cal? Cal!" The voice is getting closer and closer. I hear footsteps now. "Cal!" She appears in the open doorway, and though the light's behind her, I can tell by the gleam of it on her hair that she's a blonde.

Which means it's not Catriona.

It's Lucy.

She walks out into the courtyard. I can't help feeling that if I were Callum, I wouldn't much like my girlfriend yelling for me all over the place like this. It's not exactly dignified of her, and it makes him look a bit little-boyish, like she's his mum and she's chasing him to do his homework or something.

"There you are," Lucy says, finally spotting him.

And as she starts walking toward him, she sees me.

"What's going on out here?" she exclaims.

"Nothing, Luce," Callum says, his tone resigned. "Scarlett and I were just talking."

"I thought I'd come back for dinner and maybe we could play some billiards afterward with your dad," she says coldly. "But I see you're *busy* at the moment."

"Actually, Lucy," he says impatiently, "Scarlett and I were having a talk."

"It's dinnertime," she snaps. "In case you were interested. I'll go and tell Moira you're coming."

Lucy turns on her heel and goes back inside. Callum looks at me. It's an awkward moment.

"I'm sorry," he mumbles. "She can be a bit . . ."

His voice trails off. It's the first time I've seen Callum McAndrew embarrassed. It makes him seem really human.

I'd quite like him like this, if it weren't for the circumstances.

"She's—I—" he says, and then he just looks at me, sighing and rubbing his hand vigorously over his skull in a way that would ruffle his hair if he had much to ruffle. Eventually he says, "I'll see you in there," and walks off.

I watch him go inside the castle. I need a few moments to catch my breath and settle down—my pulse is racing.

That was really odd. I could have sworn that Callum and I were just in that state of suspended animation where you might be about to kiss each other.

This is too weird. I couldn't deal with kissing Callum, I just couldn't. There's Jase, for one thing, and then there's the small matter of his being the twin brother of the boy whose murder I'm investigating . . . and the chance that Callum might have something to do with it.

I take a deep breath, and make a definite resolution never to be alone with Callum McAndrew again.

eighteen
"ICE QUEEN STARE"

Dinner was a disaster. Not the food, which was fantastic—
Moira is a world-class cook. I absolutely stuffed myself,
partly because all the running around today has made me
completely starving, and partly because the nervous tension
of sitting opposite from Callum, with Lucy next to him glaring at me, made me lower my head, concentrate on my
plate, and fork the food into my mouth as if I were a self-
feeding automaton. Moira—who doesn't sit with the family,
but serves the food—keeps offering me more, and I keep
taking it. She says how nice it is that I have a healthy appetite. I mumble something between mouthfuls.

It must be clear to Mrs. McAndrew that her attempt to
find closure by inviting me here is not a roaring success so
far. She tries to draw me out by asking me about myself, but
since I have a massively boring life, that doesn't get very far.
Lucy talks pointedly to Callum about people I've never met,
all through dinner, and when we've had pudding—a
rhubarb trifle so good that I'm now convinced the
Wakefield Hall catering staff are using some completely

different ingredient in what they claim is rhubarb crumble—Mrs. McAndrew stands up and says we're all going through to the Great Hall for coffee, so Moira can clear our pudding plates. But Lucy promptly insists that she and Callum don't want coffee and are off to play billiards, making it very clear that I'm not invited.

Which is fine, as I didn't want to go anyway. I do ask, however, if I can take photos of everyone on my mobile phone, and though I think they find this a bit odd, it's after dinner, and everyone (except Lucy) has mellowed out a little with the large quantities of fantastic food. I duly snap the assembled company; Moira, coming in to clear the plates, gets included, and is surprisingly flattered by the request. Catriona's the best sport, giving me a nice smile. Mr. and Mrs. McAndrew look understandably awkward, and Callum just stares at the phone, expressionless. Lucy scowls, but she's so photogenic that despite herself, the photo comes out so good that a model agency would sign her up immediately on seeing it.

Once Lucy and Callum leave, the rest of us walk into the Great Hall. Moira has set out a tray with coffee and biscuits, and we sit around the fireplace. It's drawing well, with a central log in it the size of a small tree blazing and crackling, set on a bed of burning pinecones. Mrs. McAndrew pours out coffee, and as we all set our cups down on side tables to let it cool enough to drink, I reach into my pocket and pull out the mobile phone charm.

"Um," I start hesitantly, "I wrote in my letter that I had something of Dan's I wanted to give back to you. It's not much, but here it is. . . ."

To my surprise, Catriona recognizes it immediately. "That's Dan's TARDIS," she says, picking it from my extended palm. "He *loved* this. Sometimes he'd make his phone ring just so he could see it flash and spin—remember, Mum?"

She hands it to her mother, who takes it silently. Mr. McAndrew, sitting next to her on the big sofa, puts his arm round her shoulders.

"He did love that," his father says. "I thought it was broken, though. Wasn't he complaining about that, Flora?" He gives her shoulders an affectionate squeeze.

"Oh, that's right," Catriona agrees. "It wasn't spinning anymore, he was really upset about it."

She looks at me inquiringly. I realize the reason the charm was in Dan's room: he'd taken it off because it didn't work. But I can't have them wondering why he took a broken charm back to London and then proceeded to lend it to me. I think quickly.

"He must have fixed it," I say, "because it was working when he put it on my phone. But, you know, it's been six months—it might not be working anymore by now. I haven't used it since he . . . um . . . ." I trail off, not wanting to say "he died" outright.

Mrs. McAndrew is still silent, peering down at the charm in her hand.

"I'm really sorry," I say, feeling awful at the deception. "I expect I should have just kept it."

"No, you did the right thing, Scarlett," Mrs. McAndrew says finally. A tear starts to roll down her cheek. "It's good to remember. . . ."

Her voice trails off as she reaches in her cardigan sleeve

and pulls out a hankie, mopping at her eyes. Catriona stands up, goes over, and kisses the top of her mother's head.

"I'm going up to my room now," she says. "I've got some stuff to do on the computer. Love you."

She crosses the huge Hall and runs lightly up the main staircase. I hear her going along the corridor, and then, in the distance, a door closing. I remember what Callum said about leaving the room when his mother started crying. Apparently he's not the only one.

"Thank you, Scarlett," Mr. McAndrew says over his wife's head, nodding gravely at me. "We spend a lot of time thinking about Dan but avoiding talking about him. It's good to have the happy memories."

Mrs. McAndrew dries her eyes and reaches out to me with the hand not holding the handkerchief. Awkwardly, I lean forward out of my overstuffed armchair and take her hand. She gives mine a gentle press. I'm horrified at how fragile hers is: I can feel the knobs and joints of her bones all too clearly through the thin flesh covering them, and they seem much too delicate to carry the weight of her rings.

"Thank you," she says, managing a smile at me though her eyes are still damp. "I know it's only a small item of Dan's, but it has made us all remember how much fun he was."

Wow, I think. I chose well when I picked that charm. Though maybe, on reflection, anything of Dan's that they hadn't seen in a while would have triggered this response. There must be so many memories bubbling just under the surface, waiting to rise.

"I—"

Mrs. McAndrew starts to say something else, and then stops. I sit looking at her, waiting. But gradually, with horror, I can tell that nothing's going to come out. No words, anyway. She makes an awful gulping noise, like a fish trying to breathe water and only getting air, and then, literally as if someone's turned on a pair of taps, her eyes flood with tears that pour down her cheeks in a sheet of water. I've never seen anything like it. I'm frozen in my seat with embarrassment and helplessness, because I know there's nothing I can do to make the situation any better.

"Flora, darling," Mr. McAndrew begins.

In one shaky but determined movement, she stands up, waving her husband away. Covering her face with her handkerchief, she walks jerkily across the Hall, her heels tapping on the exposed parts of the stone floor. Halfway to the stairs, she breaks into terrible sobs. I never want to hear anyone crying like that ever again. It's literally heartbreaking.

I stare, miserable, at Mr. McAndrew, whose face has gone gray. He looks suddenly very old indeed.

"I'm so sorry . . . ," I mumble, as Mrs. McAndrew, weeping, starts to go upstairs.

He shakes his head at me.

"Not your fault," he says sadly. "Not your fault at all. Flora wanted you to come. I just hope to God she's right, and it's helping to heal her. I worry that we're just opening up the wounds instead."

I don't know what to say. I just hang my head.

"If he'd just had his EpiPen with him," Mr. McAndrew says wearily. "He never let it out of his sight. But we've been over and over this a thousand times, and never been able to work out why he didn't have it that evening. I have to give up asking that question." He sighs. "There'll never be an answer, and it'll just keep torturing me if I don't give it up."

I wish very much I could tell Mr. McAndrew everything. But I can't. At the slightest hint that I suspect Callum—or Lucy, acting for him—he'll throw me out of the castle on the spot.

"I have to go to her," he says, standing up.

I nod, and will myself to burden Dan's grieving family even further. I don't have any other choice.

"Mr. McAndrew, I was thinking," I begin, "maybe you could show me round the castle a bit tomorrow? If you're not busy. I'd love to learn a bit about the history of the McAndrews and, um, what Dan's life was like here."

I've been practicing in my head throughout dinner, but it sounds a bit feeble now I come out with it. But my request goes down very well with Mr. McAndrew, whose eyes actually brighten at the suggestion.

"How nice," he says. "I could show you where Dan played when he was a boy, his favorite places."

"I'd like that."

"Excellent. Tomorrow morning it is, then."

Mr. McAndrew walks toward the staircase, moving slowly, like an old man. Drinking my coffee, I wait for him to climb it and disappear along the corridor. I leave ten minutes after he's vanished from sight, and then I head up the staircase too, and at the top take the direction in which I think Catriona went.

I'm feeling a nasty lump in my stomach as a result of

having upset Mrs. McAndrew so much, almost like a physical pain. I'm trying to tell myself that she would want to find out who killed her son, particularly seeing how much she's grieving for him, but I know that's a bit disingenuous of me. What if I find out it was Callum and Lucy conspiring to do it, so he could inherit? That discovery would probably kill Mrs. McAndrew.

But I can't stop. Not when I'm so close to the finish line.

I hear music coming from further down the corridor, a cool-sounding, electronic chill-out music that I hope is Catriona's. It sounds like the kind of thing she'd listen to. I reach the door and listen at it for a moment: no voices, which hopefully means it's not Callum and Lucy. And when I knock, it's Catriona's voice that sings out:

"Come in!"

I open it and put my head around the door. Catriona's sitting at a desk, her back to me, doing something on her computer. Squinting to see what it is, I identify it as being an architectural model in 3-D, and I must admit, I'm surprised at how poised she is. After the scene downstairs, I would have thought she'd be messaging some friends, writing about how difficult life is here, with her mother in tears, her brother angry with me, and his girlfriend throwing wobblies every two seconds. But no, she came right up here and started to work on something clearly pretty complicated and brain-taxing. Impressed though I am, I can't help finding this a bit cold.

But maybe she's used to the scenes by now, and this is her way of detaching herself from them. I remind myself that it's been six months since Dan's death: Catriona must be horribly accustomed to her brother's sulks and her mother breaking down in sobs. I suppose I can't blame her for deciding that, if everyone else is going to give in to their emotions, she's going to shove hers away and focus on her studies.

I still can't help thinking I'd have rung a friend, though, rather than playing around with computer models.

"Do you mind if I hang out with you a bit?" I ask. "Your parents went off, and I don't really think I'd be that welcome playing billiards with Callum and Lucy."

And I want to ask you lots of things about Callum and Lucy, and this seems like the perfect opportunity.

"Of course." Catriona saves whatever she's working on and swivels round in her chair.

"Oh wow." I can't help but gawp in awe when I enter her room. "This is *amazing*."

It's a huge, beautiful room, with lots to look at, but the centerpiece is a huge four-poster bed, its posts massive and heavily carved, hung with heavy green velvet curtains. I goggle at it.

"Isn't it gorgeous?" Catriona sighs. "I love it so much. I think it's my favorite thing in the world. Go on, have a look up from inside."

I climb up—all the beds at Castle Airlie are so high a child would need steps to reach them—and crane my head back. I see at once what she means. The inside ceiling of the four-poster is draped with more green velvet, caught up into a central swirl like a canopy. I'm eaten up with envy for this bed. You'd feel like a princess going to bed in it every night—drawing the velvet curtains, closing out the world.

"It's like being inside a really posh chocolate box," I say.

"Sometimes, when it's pouring out, I just curl up in there and spread out all my books and do all my studying in bed," she says. "It's lovely."

She smiles, but then her expression sobers as she asks:

"So, were Mum and Dad okay?"

"Not really," I admit guiltily. I've manipulated this family so much, I'm beginning to feel really bad about it. "Your mum was all right at first, but then she really started to cry and went upstairs."

"Oh God." Catriona pulls a face. "She thinks she can deal with it, but she can't, really. Poor Dad just follows her round nervously, trying to take care of her. We're all pretty worried about her, actually. Moira thinks she's a few steps short of a nervous breakdown, and Moira's always right."

I don't know what to say to this, so I look around her room instead. It's got a thick, pale cream and pink carpet, and the walls are pale green with delicate black-and-white prints hanging on them, all very elegant. Catriona has a dressing table by the window, a proper one with a mirror with folding wings on each side, lots of space for makeup and creams and brushes, and a matching chair in front of it. Beyond, in the far corner, is a pale green sofa, which has a little coffee table in front of it. And her desk, besides the computer, has a printer and scanner as well. It's all kept incredibly neat and tidy, which I'm sure is Catriona: she seems a very precise and organized kind of person.

"I can't believe how big your room is," I say.

She giggles. "I've even got a study next door for my drawings, and my own bathroom through that door." She points to it. "Mum and Dad put me in here after I got too big for the nursery, because they said it wouldn't be fair to make me share a bathroom with two boys. Lucky, eh? But you must have a lot of space where you are, don't you? Over dinner you were saying Wakefield Hall's really big."

"It is, but my grandmother closed off large parts of it when my dad died," I explain.

"Oh, that's sad. But they'll be opened back up again one day, won't they?"

"I don't know," I say. "Maybe."

She tilts her head to the side and her red ponytail tilts along with her, curling onto one shoulder.

"I'm studying to be an architect at Edinburgh. Perhaps I'll come to Wakefield Hall and help you restore up all the old rooms and make them beautiful again."

"That sounds great," I say to be polite, but I couldn't be less interested in what Catriona is studying. I have information I need to pry out of her.

But Catriona has a one-track mind. She's like Lizzie that way.

"I'm going to do my dissertation on Castle Airlie, of course. This place needs so much work." She pulls a face, her gray-green eyes crinkling up to amused slits. Unlike her brothers, whose eyes, though exactly the same color, are strikingly large and rimmed with thick black lashes, Catriona's are slanted over her equally slanted cheekbones. With her dead-white skin and flaming hair, she looks faintly Russian, or Tatar, like her mother. "It's a bit of a crumbling old ruin, really," she continues. "The plumbing is *Victorian*, the heating's a mess, and it's horribly drafty."

"My back did get awfully cold at dinner," I admit.

She purses her lips. "I bet your front got pretty cold as well. Lucy was doing her best ice queen stare at you. God, she annoys me. I'm worried that she's got her hooks so far into Cal he'll never get them out again."

Wow, maybe I won't have to pry anything out of Catriona after all.

"They've been going out for years, right?" I say, leaning forward to show how interested I am.

Catriona leans forward too, conspiratorially.

"*Actually*, she made a play for Dan at one stage, but he wasn't having any. And I don't think Cal ever realized. Dan wasn't at all the type to have a steady girlfriend—not yet, anyway. So there wasn't anything doing there. But now that Cal inherits—well, Lucy will never let him go. I'm sure that's why she was after Dan in the first place."

My eyes widen. "You mean . . ."

But I don't need to make the suggestion: Catriona's right there already, nodding away.

"She's in *love* with the idea of being the mistress of Castle Airlie," she says. "I bet she danced for joy when Dan died. God, what airs she'd give herself! It doesn't bear thinking about."

"Why is she round here all the time?" I ask. "It's almost like she lives here."

"I *know*." Catriona rolls her eyes. "Frightful, isn't it? Her dad lives in the village. He's got a nice house there, but nothing half as grand as this. It's sort of their country home—they've got a big place in London, too. Tons of money but not much class."

Catriona sounds very like my grandmother sometimes, I think.

"Lucy says she doesn't get on with her stepmother," Catriona's continuing.

"Is she a bitch?" I ask.

"Well, that's just it. She seems perfectly harmless to *me*," Catriona says. "I think Lucy makes up stories about her stepmum to get Mummy and Cal's sympathy and give her an excuse to be round here all the time. Which, as you've pointed out, she is." She sighs. "I keep telling myself Cal will go away to university and sow some wild oats, meet someone else, there's nothing to worry about. But I'm sure Lucy will follow wherever he goes. And Cal's the loyal type, more's the pity. He's loyal to Lucy now, even though I'm *sure* he can see what a nightmare she can be. I mean, she wasn't even invited to dinner, and here she goes again, turning up and just expecting Moira to set a place for her! Mummy would say she's always welcome, but Lucy behaves like she already lives here! Moira *hates* her," she adds unexpectedly.

"Really?" I widen my eyes. "Why's that?"

"Doesn't think she's good enough for Cal at *all*. Doesn't want to see her running Castle Airlie—God, no. Moira always wanted Cal to inherit, you know."

"She sort of told me that," I say.

"Did she? She must like you," Catriona comments. "Moira thought Dan would never settle down here, and I'm sure she was right. Dan was a complete playboy. He'd always rather be in London than stuck up here in the middle of nowhere—that's how he saw it. When Mum and Dad got down to London after Dan died, and Moira met them, apparently the first thing she said was: 'It's a tragedy for the McAndrews but a boon for Castle Airlie.' Mum was so upset she made Moira get the first train home."

I focus on the most important part of this whole story, the part that's a clue.

"Moira was in *London* when Dan died?" I ask, my ears pricking up.

Catriona nods. "Visiting her cousins. They live there. But she never saw Dan. He was too busy partying. And all his friends were like Lucy, you know? I met them a few times. All just interested in having the latest cool things before they were in the magazines. They were in this total competition to get stuff first and show it off at clubs on the King's Road. And when someone else got one too, they'd throw it away to anyone who'd take it and go out and buy something new instead. They were completely superficial. There was this one girl, Plum—God, she was an awful snob. I hated her. She pretty much ran the whole group."

"I used to be at school with her," I say. "She's so nasty I can't even tell you."

"I'm sure. So you can see why I don't want Cal settling down with someone who's friends with people like that. Ugh. She'd fill the castle with them and invite photographers from *Tatler*. Horrid."

Catriona's grimacing to indicate how much the thought distresses her. I can see how upsetting it would be. But I can't exactly see her killing Dan to avoid his bringing Plum and her set up to Castle Airlie on a regular basis—as motives go, that's the weakest one I've ever heard.

And Moira? Moira, who was down in London when

Dan died? Could Moira somehow have sneaked into Nadia's party and poisoned the crisps, in an attempt to kill Dan so that Callum would inherit Castle Airlie? Wouldn't she have stuck out like a sore thumb?

Well, I think smugly, *I've already planned the perfect way to find that out. . . .*

nineteen

"ALL GIRLS LIKE JEWELRY"

"It's nice that some young people are still interested in history," Mr. McAndrew says over his shoulder.

He's leading me up a narrow stone spiral staircase, and his words bounce around the walls, making his voice sound hollow and booming. There's something honest and bluff about him that I like. You can tell how much he's missing Dan by the tightness in his jaw, the sadness in his eyes. He really loved his son.

I wouldn't mind having a dad like Mr. McAndrew.

"I'm doing history A level," I lie. Damn, I've told so many of these, I'm losing track.

"Well, if you're studying anything to do with battles and sieges, this should be very useful," he says as I reach the top of the steps.

"Wow." I glance around me. We're at the top of one of the towers at the corners of Castle Airlie, and the view over the marshlands and the Irish Sea beyond is spectacular.

"Look here," Mr. McAndrew says, pointing to the windows. "They're all narrow, so that the archers could fire on the attackers without being afraid they'd get shot themselves. Just room enough for a crossbow and a bit of space to sight your target."

I nod appreciatively, clutching my stomach. I just stuffed myself on the most enormous breakfast ever, and that climb straight afterward is making me feel slightly queasy. Castle Airlie actually has a room just for breakfast. It's next to the kitchen and it's got a lot of silver servers all lined up against one wall, like in a hotel—if you lift the lids there's scrambled eggs, bacon, kippers (eww), fried potatoes, and grilled tomatoes. Yum. Plus, there was toast, butter, and five kinds of jam on the table, and big thermal jugs of coffee and tea. Despite it being pretty early—Mr. McAndrew had said to be ready at nine, so I got downstairs at eight-thirty—I ate so much I can barely breathe now. Big mistake.

"Would they pour the boiling oil from here, too?" I ask.

He laughs. "Imagine carrying a vat of oil up those narrow stairs. No, that was on the next level down. I'll show you."

He heads down the staircase again. I follow, cursing the impulse that led me to ask that. I wanted just to stand still and digest for a while. Oh well, if Mr. McAndrew's going to walk me round the entire castle, at least it'll help me work off some of my breakfast. . . .

He's at the foot of the stairs, looking enthusiastic.

"Dan loved everything about the sieges," he says. "All the children did. They'd play games reenacting them for days and days and rope in all their friends. Look, here's one of the oil slots."

He's indicating the stone floor of the corridor, just below

the window embrasure. I look down and my eyes widen. It's a deep trough slanting down toward the wall, so you could wrestle a big barrel of hot oil into position and then tip it over so its contents went flooding down into the trough.

"It used to be open to the outside, of course," Mr. McAndrew's saying. "So if invaders were on ladders against the walls, the oil would pour down on their heads. But they were all bricked up a long time ago, because of drafts." He chuckles. "Dan was very disappointed. He was a very blood-thirsty child. Thank God they were all closed, or he'd have been pouring things down there all the time."

"He sounds like he was a lot of fun," I say.

"Oh, he was a real scamp. Never serious for a moment, that was Dan."

I think about the Dan I briefly knew—always laughing and joking, seeming not to have a care in the world, and I can't help smiling at the memory.

Then I think about those photos I found in his room, trophies of the girls he'd been with, and my smile fades.

"Would you like to see the dungeons?" he asks. "The children used to play there a lot too. And they're quite dramatic, in a scary kind of way. Lots of gory tales about them."

He's looking so enthusiastic that I can't possibly say no.

"I'd love to," I say. "I'd really like to see as much as possible, actually."

Mr. McAndrew grins at me.

"You know," he says, "I've just thought of something I'm *sure* you'll like to see."

Mr. McAndrew swings open a green baize-covered door and holds it for me. We go down a couple of flights of back stairs and into a stone-paved corridor. I'm trying to keep a map of the castle in my head, just so I have the faintest idea of where I am, but then he pushes open another door and we emerge in a corner of the Great Hall. This takes me completely aback, as I don't even remember noticing a door in this corner before. Usually I have a good sense of direction, but Castle Airlie is completely confusing me.

"Let's just pop into the estate office on our way," Mr. McAndrew's saying. "I think you'll find it worth the detour."

We cross the Hall and go through a big mahogany door on the far side of the fireplace. Beyond it is a further door, and Mr. McAndrew fishes in his pocket and pulls out a key ring.

"I'm never in here on the weekends," he says. "I have meetings here with my factor—he's the one who really runs the estate—but it's kept locked up out of office hours." He smiles at me as he thumbs through the key ring, finds a Chubb key, and unlocks the door. "You'll see why."

He pushes the door open and holds it for me.

"So, do you like jewelry, Scarlett?" Mr. McAndrew chuckles to himself. "Silly question, isn't it? All girls like jewelry."

"Um, yes, I suppose," I say, unsure why he's asking me this.

Mr. McAndrew crosses the room and takes down a big oil painting of a stag at bay, revealing a big black safe set into the wall. He starts fiddling with the combination, his broad back concealing the lock, which gives me time to look around the room.

It's colder in here, as if it's not heated on weekends.

More oil paintings hang on the walls—mostly, I can tell, ones that aren't considered good enough to be hung in more public areas of the house. There's a huge old faded leather–topped desk, embossed in equally faded gold around the edges of the leather. It's so big that it's more like a table, with a pair of carved chairs, one on each side, so that two people could sit and work at it facing each other. A gilt-framed mirror hangs over the desk, its silvery glass discolored and tarnished with age.

Next to me are a couple of big wooden chests of drawers, but the chests are really wide and the drawers are very narrow. I slide one out fractionally and see that it's full of documents and old prints. My eyes widen: if I have to search through all these drawers and read the contents, I could be here for days. There's a pile of brown card folders on the desk, and I scan them quickly. Nothing looks relevant to me; they're all bills and invoices. But, beyond the desk, I notice another door, and, as quietly as I can, I cross the room and nudge it open. It's a windowless storeroom lined with filing cabinets: above them are built-in shelves running right up to the ceiling, stacked with labeled boxes. This is *exactly* what I'm looking for.

Behind me, I hear Mr. McAndrew is removing something from the safe, and by the time he's turned round I'm back by the desk again, my most innocent expression on my face. He's holding a dark red leather box, which I guess from what he just said has jewelry inside it. I expect glitter when he opens it, light striking diamond facets, but instead there's a pale, subtle gleam. I gasp. It's a pearl necklace: three strands of huge white pearls with what looks like a moonstone in the center rimmed with diamonds, and it sits there in its black velvet bed, glowing like the moon in the night sky.

Mr. McAndrew, seeing my expression, chuckles again.

"Spectacular, aren't they?" he says. "They've been in the family for generations. They're passed down to the wife of the current laird. Flora hardly ever wears them, though. Maybe for a Northern Meeting now and then."

I must have looked blank, because he adds:

"That's a ball with Highland dancing—reels, mostly. Tons of fun and very good exercise, you're jumping around all night. We have them here sometimes, in the ballroom."

An expression of such sadness momentarily settles on his face that I know, without being told, he's thinking that if Dan were still alive, they'd be having a ball for his and Callum's birthday. He sighs, as if he's pushing the thought away from him, and says:

"Callum's wife will inherit them one day. I hope she'll wear them more than Flora does. Flora thinks they're too big for her—she's quite fine-boned. And Catriona has the same build, so she's never cared for them either. We should get them restrung, I suppose. Pearls should be worn, you know."

"My grandmother says that," I chime in, glad that I have something to contribute to the subject. "She hardly ever takes hers off. She says they need the oil in your skin to stay shiny."

"Good girl," Mr. McAndrew says, smiling down at me. "Glad to see that some members of the younger generation know about caring for beautiful things. Lucy's always after me to borrow the pearls for a Northern Meeting, but I regretfully have to say no. They cost so much to insure, we're only covered if a member of the family is wearing them. Want to try them on?"

Speechless, I can only nod. He picks up the triple strand of pearls, comes behind me, and places it around my neck, clicking the clasp shut at my nape.

"They weigh *so much*!" I exclaim unguardedly. It feels like a pound of weight around my neck, cold and heavy and smooth as silk. I catch sight of myself in the mirror that hangs over the desk, and my eyes widen. Despite the fact that I'm wearing a sweater and jeans, with no makeup on, the pearls transform me. My eyes are huge and dark and luminous; my skin, pale from lack of sun, glows in the reflected light from the pearls; and my hair, piled up on top of my head with a big silver clip, almost looks, in the tarnished glass of the mirror, as if it's a proper style—as if I've had my hair put up so I could go to a ball.

My hand lifts to touch the necklace. I can't believe how magical it is. In one stroke, it's made me beautiful.

"You look very pretty, Scarlett," Mr. McAndrew says gruffly.

"My grandmother says you should wear pearls close to the face," I say, "because they're really flattering."

He chuckles. "My mother used to say the same thing," he says, "but what she meant was they make you look younger. Not something you're in need of right now." He smiles at me. "Right, I'd better take those off you before you get too used to them."

No! I scream inside. *I never want to take these off!* But I

243

stand there reluctantly as Mr. McAndrew undoes the clasp. The pearls slide off my neck slowly, heavy and slippery, as if they don't want to leave either.

"There's a matching tiara, too," he adds, coiling the pearls carefully back into their velvet nest. Seeing my expression, he bursts out laughing. "Shut your mouth, young lady, or you'll catch flies in it!"

I see in the mirror what he means—I *am* gawping at the idea of myself wearing the necklace and crowned with a pearl tiara. I'd look like a princess. Or Audrey Hepburn in *My Fair Lady*. But though the pearls are incredibly distracting, the cogs in my brain are still spinning, working out what I need to do to get access to those filing cabinets. . . .

"Women and jewelry—it's like a drug, isn't it?" jokes Mr. McAndrew, taking the jewelry box back to the safe. As soon as he turns his back, my hand darts out, and I tear a strip of card from one of the card-folder covers, choosing one at the bottom so no one will notice straightaway that it's torn.

Mr. McAndrew closes the door and turns the lock shut. "Even the young girls," he continues. "Take them to a museum and they'll walk straight past every other exhibit to coo and cluck over the shiny things."

Okay, he's teasing me, but it's in a nice way. It feels sort of like something your dad would say to you jokingly. I quite like it. No one ever talks to me like this.

And as he does, I'm quickly folding the strip of card back and forth on itself, so it's a bent strip of accordion pleats.

He hangs the picture back over the safe and turns to me. I palm the folded piece of card in my right hand.

"Well, there's nothing more to see here," he says. "Just boring old documents. Want to see the dungeons now?"

"Ooh, yes," I say enthusiastically, following him to the door. As usual, he holds it for me. I start to go through it, and then I stop and exclaim:

"Oh, do you have a cat? I love cats."

"A cat? No," Mr. McAndrew says, baffled.

I point down the corridor.

"I'm sure I saw something move down there. . . . It couldn't have been a *rat*, could it?"

As I hoped, this instantly galvanizes Mr. McAndrew. He shoots off down the corridor, letting the door fall against me, and as it does I take the folded-up piece of card and press it into the tongue of the door lock so the pleats open up a bit, creating a sort of basic spring. Then I ease the door shut, praying desperately that this trick, which I read about in a book years ago, will actually work. It's very lucky for me that this is a spring lock, rather than the Yale kind where the metal tongue slides back and forth when the key's turned.

"Nothing here that I can see," says Mr. McAndrew, coming back down the corridor. "Are you *sure* you saw something, Scarlett?"

"I *think* I did," I say, furrowing my forehead, "but maybe it was just a shadow."

"God, I hope so!" he says cheerfully. "There's always a worry about rats here, with the moat, you know. Really, we *should* have cats, or a couple of terriers—they're great for ratting, you know—but Flora can't abide small animals. Funny, she's happiest on a horse, but she can't stand anything smaller. Very odd. Shut the door, did you? Good girl. Right, off to the dungeons it is. And let's hope we don't see any rats down there. We *do* have the pest control people in on a regular basis, but it's never a hundred percent guarantee. . . ."

He sets off down the corridor, still talking, and I follow him, darting a glance back over my shoulder at the office door. I just hope that the piece of card worked, that the tongue of the lock is actually held back by the card so it can't slide forward and fasten the door shut. Because if the card hasn't worked, and the door *is* locked, not only will I not be able to get back in, but Mr. McAndrew or his factor will realize what I tried to do the moment they open the door again and the piece of card falls to the ground at their feet.

*   *   *

We don't see or hear any rats in the dungeons, thank goodness, because they're gruesome enough without them. Dank and echoey and very dark—since the moat runs all the way around the castle, there's no place that the occasional grate could be set into the ground to give some natural light. There is electricity rigged up down here, but it's pretty feeble, and there are scary shadows *everywhere*. I can only be grateful that Mr. McAndrew isn't the type of person who thinks it's funny to hide and then jump out at me, because I think I would actually wet myself in fear if someone were nasty enough to do that down here.

"I can't imagine playing down here when I was little," I confess to him, looking around me at the bare stone walls and the much-eroded stone flags beneath our feet, damp and worn down from centuries of use, probably by poor prisoners left here to starve to death. "Weren't they scared all the time?"

He laughs.

"I think Catriona used to give the boys a hard time when they were smaller," he says. "She'd bring them down here to play hide-and-seek. You know, when you're little, being a few years older is a big advantage. She bossed them around mercilessly."

This leads on perfectly to what I really want to ask about: their characters.

"What were they like when they were little?" I ask as we walk past a series of stone cells.

"Well, Catriona was a real explorer," Mr. McAndrew says. "She must know every inch of the place so well she could draw it from memory. I'm not surprised she grew up to want to be an architect."

"She seems keen on modernizing Castle Airlie," I volunteer, remembering Catriona's comments about the heating and the drafts.

"Och well," Mr. McAndrew says with a laugh, "she's young and enthusiastic, bless her. But it's not she who'll decide. Girls marry and leave, Scarlett. That's the way of it. It's men who inherit. Always has been here, always will be."

I can't help bristling.

"I'm going to inherit Wakefield Hall," I say firmly. "I don't really know what I'll do with it, but I know I won't marry and leave."

He smiles down at me.

"Wakefield Hall can't be entailed, then," he says. "Castle Airlie passes down the male line. So there's always a McAndrew at Castle Airlie. And now it'll be Callum. He loves Castle Airlie just as much as Cat does—but for him it's more about the history, the land. Preserving the McAndrew legacy. Dan . . ." He sighs. "Well, Dan was actually the least interested in the castle. Maybe it was because he knew he'd inherit it one day—he took it for granted a bit, perhaps. I liked to think that he'd go off to London, sow his wild oats, and come back to settle here. Meet a nice local girl, raise a family."

He clears his throat and looks at his watch.

"Good God, it's almost eleven. Time to leave for morning service. Are you a churchgoer, Scarlett?"

"Not really," I admit.

"That's all right. Flora is expecting me, though. She's become much more observant about church since . . ." He clears his throat again. "Well, anyway. I must get going."

We make our way through the bowels of the castle, and emerge near the main door. As we approach, I see Mrs. McAndrew standing just outside it, on the drawbridge, looking at her watch.

"Sorry, darling," her husband says, striding up to her and kissing her on the cheek.

"We'll be late," she frets. Her eyes look strangely unfocused, I notice, and her voice is a little wobbly.

"Not to worry," her husband says bluffly, not seeming to notice that she's in an odd state. "The vicar will wait for us. Didn't we just give a big donation to rebuild the bell tower?"

He extends his arm to her, and she leans on it as they

walk across the drawbridge. I take a couple of steps onto the drawbridge too, just outside the huge wooden doors, and stand watching them as they cross the moat and walk down the drive to the carriage house. The wind is stirring the moat water, and it laps a little at the foundations of the castle. I stay there until the Land Rover pulls out through the stone arch and away down the drive. I wait until it's disappeared into the grove of trees where someone shot at me yesterday afternoon, and I wait five more minutes after that, just to be sure that neither of them has forgotten anything and needs to rush back for it, listening to the rattle of the old jeep's engine fading away, till there's nothing left but the sounds of the water moving softly below me, and the breeze lifting the leaves of the trees.

And then I turn and enter the castle once more.

I'm so nervous that I get lost at least twice trying to find the Great Hall again, even though it should have been very easy by now. But once I reach it, the door that leads to the office passageway is unmistakable. I slip through it and find the main office door. Heart pounding, I push on it, gently at first, and then, when it doesn't yield, much harder.

The door's sliding open. I'm in.

Twenty

BEYOND DANGEROUS

I ease the door shut behind me, making sure it's locked, and then dash across the room and into the filing storeroom. The shelves run all the way around the room, right up to the ceiling, and above the filing cabinets are old cardboard boxes stacked here and there, and dusty piles of old ledgers. God help me if the entail is in one of those, because I'll never find it.

Most of the labels on the cabinets are incomprehensible to me, but I scan them in sequence, looking for something to pop out, and when, halfway through the alphabet, I come across LEGAL, my heart leaps. I pull out the drawer and start rifling through the categories. Disappointingly, it seems full of endless letters from the McAndrews' solicitor about zero-rate band trusts, codicils, land registry filings, and lots of things I don't understand and really hope don't hold secrets that I'm incapable of working out. But eventually I find a section marked ENTAIL/DEED OF TRUST, and I pull out the folder eagerly, carrying it through to the main desk in the office and opening it up, careful not to disturb the order of the various papers it contains.

Again, there are tons of letters from the firm of solicitors, the paper getting yellower with age as their dates go more and more into the past, the neat computer printing yielding to jerky typewriting. Though I squint dutifully at each one, I can't see that they have any bearing on the fundamental question of how the inheritance for Castle Airlie works. I look at my watch. God, I've spent half an hour in here already! How did I use up that much time? And how long does a church service take?

Probably an hour, I think. Add on a minimum ten minutes each side for the drive to Airlie village, and I still have a bit of time. But take off ten minutes for waiting for the jeep to disappear, and then making my way here, and take off another ten minutes for putting everything away and getting far enough from the office not to raise any suspicions, and that means I only have another half hour in here. And I've had thirty minutes already, which has flown by, and in them I've found nothing of any use whatsoever. . . .

Fingers trembling with haste, I rip through the rest of the folder, desperately hoping to find what I need. And there it is, right at the back in a plastic envelope, typed on the wobbly old typewriter, dated April 20, 1924, and titled:

COPY ENTAIL/DEED OF TRUST FOR CASTLE AIRLIE, AYRSHIRE
PREPARED FOR LAIRD MCANDREW ON HIS REQUEST

Laird, I know, is Mr. McAndrew's title. It's like *lord*, in Scottish, and it means you own an estate. And like *lord*, it's passed down through the generations. When Mr. McAndrew dies, Callum will be the next Laird McAndrew.

I read through the entire entail—it's only three pages, but the legal phrasing is incredibly dense and complicated. Then I go back and scan through it again. It's only on the second reading that I come to the crucial bit, and I read the sentence at least three times before I fully take in what it means. It's very long, like all sentences in legal documents seem to be. My brain is concentrating so hard that it feels twisted up into a tiny little fist. I don't think I've worked this hard on anything in my entire life.

Castle Airlie and its land and domain shall be given TO THE USE of the said Trustees TO THE USE of the existing Laird McAndrew for his life, without impeachment for waste; with remainder TO THE USE of the first and every other son of the Laird McAndrew according to their seniorities and the heirs male of the body of each such son; with provision however that should the said heirs male of the body of each son fail to attain their majority, which for the purposes of this entail shall be defined as the age of eighteen, the aforesaid estate shall pass with remainder TO THE USE of the first and every other daughter of the Laird McAndrew according to their seniorities and the heirs of the body of each such daughter, with the provision that such heirs shall take the name McAndrew upon inheriting.

My heart is pounding with what I think I've found out. But it's such contorted wording that I can't completely trust my own judgment. I get a pen and a piece of paper from the desk and I copy the sentence out, slowly, meticulously, double- and triple-checking to make sure I've transcribed every word, every clause, in exactly the right order.

And just then, I hear someone outside the door.

*   *   *

I freeze in position, my pen in my hand, as if I'm playing a game of musical statues all by myself. My ears are pricked up, desperately trying to hear if the person outside is just passing by—which I fervently hope—or about to come in— which would be the worst possible scenario.

For about thirty seconds, there's complete silence. But I could have sworn that I heard quiet footsteps on the stone flags of the passageway coming to a halt outside the office door. I look around me, quickly assessing potential hiding places. Behind a door's always good, but I can see both doors from here and they both open flush to the wall, which means there won't be any space behind them to squeeze myself into. I shove the pen into my pocket and close up the folder as silently as possible, getting ready to move if I have to.

The silence is still total. I'm just beginning to breathe

again when there comes the most ominous sound, in these circumstances, that I could possibly hear.

It's a key being inserted into the lock.

I move so quickly that I probably leave a vapor trail in my wake.

By the time the door swings open, I'm curled up in a tight ball in the best hiding place I can find.

I can't see anything but a small piece of very dusty, cob-webby wall. There's no way I can turn my head enough to see who's just come into the office. And since that's the case, I squeeze my eyes shut and pray that they don't see me either.

I hear footsteps, a rubber-soled tread which could be anyone's. I'm hoping it's someone who just came in to get something they need, which would mean that they'd grab it and leave straightaway.

Though, on a weekend, with Mr. and Mrs. McAndrew at church, I can't imagine who that would be. . . .

The footsteps walk slowly around the office. I hear a chair being moved, which probably means that whoever's come in is looking underneath the desk. I'm incredibly grateful I didn't duck under there, because that was my first idea.

There's nowhere else to hide in the main office. The footsteps move closer now, coming through into the filing room. The door is pushed open, against the wall, as if to check that no one's hiding behind it.

The dust where I'm lying, stirred up by my arrival, is ris-ing up my nostrils. The lining of my nose is itching. I'm fighting a powerful urge to sneeze.

Then the footsteps stop and make a sort of muffled

squeaking noise, which indicates to me that their owner is standing in the middle of the room, turning round, surveying it.

I staple my lips together and hold my breath. If I don't breathe, I can't sneeze.

I really hope that's true.

My chest heaves with the effort of controlling the itching in my nose, which by now has become so powerful that it feels like it could explode at any minute. For a brief second, I let myself wonder who it is standing so close to me, so close they could maybe even take one more step and reach out and touch me, and then the thought panics me so much I shut it down as tightly as I'm clenching my entire body at this stage, fighting the urge to sneeze with everything I've got—

I hear footsteps again. My heart leaps in my chest with fear. And then I realize that they're receding.

They move back into the office again. I'm still not out of the woods: if I sneeze now, they'll still hear me. I manage a huge swallow, more of a gulp, which seems to help.

And then I hear the office door being pulled shut again, and the lock clicking into place.

My right hand's cramped under my chest, and I take the risk of wriggling it up till it reaches my face, so that my index finger and thumb can clamp over the bridge of my nose. I squeeze it so hard it brings tears to my eyes, but the pain seems to stop any further impulse to sneeze.

I'm not going to move for at least five minutes. Whoever just came in here might still be inside: they might have shut the door to make me think it was safe to emerge from my hiding place. Or they might be waiting on the other side of the door, to see if they hear any movement inside the office.

I close my eyes and try to go Zen, ignoring the screaming of my cramped muscles and the soreness of my nose. I breathe slowly, gently, taking little sips of air through my lips, fighting the urge to cough as the dust particles trickle into my mouth. I try, actually, to relax as much as possible, because I know from gymnastics that it's much easier to hold a position when you relax into it than when you're tensed up. I pretend to myself that I'm falling asleep.

I don't know how long I wait. Long enough to be sure there's no one in the room with me: I'm sure I'd have heard movement by now. Long enough to take the risk that anyone standing outside the door, listening, will have decided that it was a false alarm and gone away.

Slowly, painfully, I unwind myself. My feet have gone to sleep, which isn't good, because I need them for climbing down. I manage to extend my legs a bit along the shelf, and I swivel my ankles in circles, grimacing at the pins and needles till I think it'll be safe to put weight on them. Then I edge them out into the air, lower them, and, grasping the edge of the shelf with my hands, I lower myself down, walking down the edges of the shelves below me as if they were the rungs of a ladder.

Thank God whoever built these shelves was a good carpenter. When I was panicking in the office, the only hiding place I could think of in which I might stand a chance of not being caught was to grab the highest shelf in the darkest corner of the filing room, haul myself up as fast as I could, and curl myself into a ball under the ceiling, hoping that no one would think to look up that high.

People generally don't, in my experience. It's always better to hide higher than lower. They're much more likely to look under desks than at the top shelf of a cupboard.

I retrieve the folder from where I hid it, under an old cardboard box. I take out the piece of paper on which I copied what I think is the crucial sentence, fold it up, and put it in my pocket. Then, as silently as I can, I slide open the D–H drawer of the filing cabinet marked LEGAL and reinsert the folder in the correct place. I close the drawer and pad quietly out of the filing room, into the office, over to the door. And then I stand there waiting, listening, for another couple of minutes, before I dare to turn the knob of the lock and open the door.

I'm holding my breath. A pulse is pounding a military tattoo at the hollow of my throat.

There's no one there.

I literally sag with relief. My knees buckle for a moment; I feel as wobbly as a baby animal taking its first steps.

And then I pull myself together and set off down the corridor—not back into the Great Hall, just in case someone's sitting on a sofa there reading a magazine, waiting to see if anyone comes out of the door that leads to the estate office. I go in the other direction, with no idea where this passageway might lead and not caring that much either. It has to go *somewhere*, after all. I'll follow it round and find my way out of Castle Airlie.

After what I've just been through, finding my way out can't be that much of a challenge, can it?

· · ·

I have an agonizing twenty-minute wait behind the converted stables before Taylor finally shows up on her bicycle. She's panting, her cheeks flushed, her nose sweaty, which means that she's really gunned it: Taylor's so fit that she only shows signs of real physical effort when she's gone way beyond what most people would consider normal exercise.

"What is it?" she gasps, swinging one leg off the bike, snapping off it, and propping it up against the wall of the stables in a single practiced movement.

I hand her my transcription.

"I copied it from the entail," I explain.

"What does it say?"

"You read it and see what you think. I want to make sure I've got it right."

It doesn't take Taylor that long to absorb its significance. She has a brain like a steel trap.

"Oh my God," she says, raising her head from the paper. "This is *horrible*."

I nod bleakly.

"If there were male heirs, but they die before they're eighteen, a daughter can inherit," I say. "It's a loophole, really. And then it goes down through her kids, but they have to take the surname McAndrew. So there's always a McAndrew at Castle Airlie," I add, remembering my conversation with Mr. McAndrew in the dungeons.

"So a daughter can't inherit otherwise?"

I shake my head. "I checked the rest of the entail. It looked like the estate just gets passed down through the

258

male line, to the next male relative. That means her kids couldn't inherit either."

"Sexist," Taylor says angrily. "Isn't Catriona the oldest kid?"

"Yes."

"So it should be her who inherits!"

I shake my head. "It skips over her and goes to the boys."

"Unless they die before they attain their majority," Taylor says, reading from the paper. "I wonder why they put that in the entail?"

"Maybe, when they drew it up, there were sons but they were all sickly," I suggest, having had some time to think this over. "You know, likely to die young. There was lots of infant mortality in those days—I think more children died young than made it to adulthood. And they were frightened that there wouldn't be anyone in their family to inherit the castle. So they wanted to make sure that if the sons all died young, it would go to one of their sisters, rather than going out of the immediate family to a distant cousin."

"It's as good a theory as any," Taylor says, shrugging. "So where's Callum?"

"I don't know."

"Well, we have to find him." It's the first time I've ever heard a note of panic in Taylor's voice. "It's his birthday day after tomorrow, right?"

"Yeah, but how can I confront him and tell him what we think? I've got no proof! I can't just start throwing accusations around. And if no one believes me, it could be really dangerous."

Taylor's face falls. "You're right."

"I think I know a way. Plus this, of course." I tap the piece of paper. "Yesterday evening, I rang Nadia."

"You did *what?*"

"I wanted to find out who was at the party when Dan died."

Taylor shrugs. "So? She couldn't have seen everyone."

She waves the paper at me.

"They've got security cameras in the hallway at Nadia's place," I say. "Upstairs, just outside the lift."

Taylor immediately gets it.

"You think they save it all?"

"It's a computer feed. The security guy archives it and backs it up. Apparently they keep it for a year. They've got tons of insurance, and Nadia's parents are really paranoid. That's what she told me. Also, she said they think it means she can't bring boys back, because they'd see."

"Well, that's pretty dumb," Taylor comments.

"Exactly. She just goes to the boys' places instead. But anyway, she said she'd look at the backups and let me know if anyone shows up from the photos I sent her."

"What photos?"

I wiggle my phone at her. "I took photos of everyone. Smart or what?"

"Good thinking," Taylor says respectfully. "Did you tell her we'd delete that video of her puking?"

Now it's my turn to shrug. "What's the point? She wouldn't believe us. No one trusts anyone. Basically, until she gets something on me or you, we've got the advantage. We can make Nadia do us favors, as long as we don't push it."

"We'd better just make sure she doesn't get something on us," Taylor says grimly.

I grimace. It isn't a pleasant thought.

"You ring her now," I instruct Taylor. "Tell her to get on with it, if she hasn't done it already."

"Me?" She stares at me. "What about you? What are you going to be doing?"

"I'm going back into the castle," I say. "I've got an idea about something I might find in Catriona's room."

"Be careful, Scarlett," Taylor warns. "Dan's already been killed, and you've been shot at. This is getting *beyond* dangerous."

She's right.

But the deed of trust isn't enough. It's only motive—it isn't proof.

And proof is what we desperately need right now.

Twenty-one

"PUT THE GUN DOWN"

I sneak back into Castle Airlie through the door to the larder and up the back stairs. I can hear Moira in the kitchen clattering pans around, but I manage to avoid her, and the back stairs are carpeted with an old drugget that muffles my footsteps. I reach the second floor without bumping into anyone, and gingerly push open the baize-covered door that leads onto the main corridor.

It creaks open gently, and I slip through it, easing it back into place. Still there's no one about: the house feels eerily deserted. I nip down the corridor to the far end, where Catriona's room is situated. Several knocks on the door, and no answer. I turn the handle and walk in, not wanting to call Catriona's name in case she's nearby and I alert her attention.

She's not there. I close the door quietly and dash across the room, throwing open Catriona's huge antique wardrobe, which is almost as big as my whole room back at Aunt Gwen's. She showed me its contents briefly yesterday evening, but I didn't get a close look at anything, just enough to admire the shoe racks built on one side, the long clothes rails, and the shelves on the other side with handbags and other accessories neatly arranged. Catriona actually doesn't have that many things, not like Lucy, who I bet has brimming drawers and cupboards stuffed full with designer gear. So it's easy to find what I'm looking for on the handbag shelves.

There it is: a Marc Jacobs bag, chestnut, leather, with a big limited-edition buckle with *MJ* on it, barrel-shaped, with two big side straps. I pull it out and rummage inside. I wasn't really expecting to find Dan's EpiPen inside it, and of course, it's not there. But there's other stuff. A lipstick. Some mint breath fresheners. One broken earring. A small folded *London* A–Z map. A postcard from someone called Fitz, sent from holiday in Sardinia. A paperback book called *The Fountainhead*, with a folded piece of paper serving as a bookmark. I open the book and pull out the paper, just to be thorough. On it is written:

Cat—want this bag? That bitch Plum just bought it too. I've only had it two weeks! God, I hate her! Keep it if you want or just give it to the charity shop in Airlie, I don't care. So pissed off. Luce x x

I turn the paper over. It's a receipt for a facial, and the salon where Lucy had it done has written in the date of her treatment. I do a lightning-quick calculation: almost a month before Dan's death. I can't imagine Lucy keeps old receipts for any length of time—she'd just chuck them out rather than have them cluttering up her pockets. So she must have written this note shortly after the date on the receipt. Which means she gave the bag to Catriona weeks before the night of Nadia's party.

I reconstruct the chronology. Lucy bought the bag, and doubtless showed it round to everyone she knew, excited about having the very latest, limited-edition, featured-in-all-the-magazines It-bag. Lizzie would certainly have noticed instantly that Lucy was the owner of the newest Marc Jacobs, even without being told: Lizzie has an encyclopedic memory for fashion trivia.

But then Plum managed to secure one too, and that made Lucy so angry that she gave the bag to Catriona rather than have the same one as Plum. (Lucy, I note in passing, must be absolutely loaded—because that bag must have cost a fortune, and if it was barely used, she could have sold it on eBay and got back most of what she paid for it.)

So, on the night of Nadia's party, the bag was in Catriona's possession.

I turn the bag over and examine it. It's a dark chestnut, glossy and polished, its flap decorated with gold studs. There are studs underneath, as well, so it doesn't get dirty when you put it down: the studs touch whatever surface you put it on, not the leather. So the underside is smooth and unstained.

But I can't say the same for the back of the bag. You have to look closely to see it, because the stain is small and faint and not much darker than the brown color of the leather, but it's definitely there. It's seeped into the leather enough that I don't think it would be possible to get it out now. I put my fingers inside and probe the lining of the bag. It's a pale beige material, but when I work my hand down to the place where the outer leather is stained, and pull out the lining, I can see that there's a much bigger stain on it. It looks greasy. There's some white residue around it, as if someone's unsuccessfully tried to clean it. I put my nose to it and sniff, but there's no smell. I didn't really expect one from six months ago, but I thought I should try anyway.

Grease. Oil. Peanut oil. I think about the bottle of peanut oil I found hidden in a cupboard, tucked away behind the bar at Nadia's flat. Someone brought in that bottle of peanut oil, so they could poison the crisps they hoped Dan would eat. And they left the bottle in the cupboard, because they couldn't risk the oil being found in their possession in case their plan went wrong. I stretch out the mouth of the Marc Jacobs bag, confirming that, as I thought, there's plenty of room to put a bottle of peanut oil inside. And if it were to have tipped over in the bag, and the plastic seal wasn't perfect, it might have leaked a little from its neck, and some oil might have seeped out. Enough to stain the lining, and to leak through and stain the leather, too. Proof, if someone analyzes this stain, that peanut oil was carried in this handbag.

I wonder whether whoever brought in that bottle of peanut oil wiped it clean afterward. At the time I thought they must have. But it would still be worth checking, if the police will take this seriously. And maybe, now that I'm accumulating all this evidence, they will. . . .

Just then I hear a noise outside in the corridor, and I jump about a foot in the air with shock. Slipping the bag back onto the shelf, I close the door, shoving the note into my jeans pocket. I look round me frantically for somewhere to hide. Next to the wardrobe is the door to Catriona's study: I slip in there, leaving the door open a crack, and put my eye to it.

The bedroom door opens, and someone comes in. Oh God, it's Catriona! I back away from the door, wondering if I'll be able to hide behind it if she comes into her study, hoping she isn't going to stay in her room for long. . . . Then I notice that her walk seems oddly wobbly. She crosses the room to the window, and as she turns to look out of it, I realize to my great relief that it's not Catriona after all. It's Mrs. McAndrew, back from church. They're so alike—the red hair, the slim build—but it's creepy to see what you think is a twenty-year-old and then notice all the lines and wrinkles on her face, like a horror movie where someone ages before your eyes.

"Catriona?" she says, but not as if she's expecting to find her daughter here. It's like she's asking a question to which she already knows the answer.

There's that same oddness in her voice that I noticed before, out on the drawbridge. Now, without her husband offering her his arm, she wobbles and grabs on to the window curtain to catch herself.

Oh my God. I think Mrs. McAndrew is drunk.

"Catriona," she says again, and then she starts crying.

I duck my head. The sight of her grief is too much for me. Has inviting me here to Castle Airlie tipped Mrs. McAndrew over the edge? I feel incredibly guilty. I want to go up to her and give her a hug, let her cry on my shoulder, but the shock of me appearing in what she thinks is an empty room might make things even worse. I'm probably the last person she wants to see, anyway. I'm a walking reminder of how her son died—in mysterious circumstances that must make it even harder for her to bear.

Though if Taylor and I are right in our theory of who killed Dan, and why, probably the only thing worse for Mrs. McAndrew than his death remaining a mystery would be for her to learn the truth behind it. . . .

I hear movement, and look back through the partly opened door into the bedroom. Mrs. McAndrew's making her way back across the room, stumbling as she goes. She stops in front of the door to the corridor and pulls something out of her pocket.

It's a hip flask.

She takes a swig from it, wipes her lips, and sighs in satisfaction, slipping the flask back into her trouser pocket again. When she leaves the room, she's actually walking better, as if whatever she drank has picked her up.

This is really, really sad.

I wait several minutes before easing the door open. Mrs. McAndrew is nowhere in sight. I dash down the main staircase, too impatient to double back to the servants' stairs, running down it two, three steps at a time. Finding that bag in Catriona's wardrobe has convinced me more than ever that Callum may be in danger right now. Only, because of the weird layout of Castle Airlie, I end up having to run around two sides of the castle in order to get to the kitchen. I should have taken the back stairs after all.

I'm breathing fast as I burst into the kitchen.

"Moira, have you seen Callum anywhere?" I demand.

Moira looks up at me, startled.

"Scarlett! What are you in such a hurry for, hen?" she asks. "Hold on—I'm just getting the last of this cake batter in the tin."

She's holding a big china bowl, tilting it over a metal cake tin with one hand, scraping it with a spatula with the other.

"Chocolate and raspberry," she says. "Master Callum's favorite."

"I need to find him," I say urgently. "Do you know where he is?"

"He took a gun out after breakfast," Moira says, opening the iron door of the huge Aga oven. A great rush of heat pours out, but Moira is completely unfazed. She slides in the cake tin and clangs the heavy iron door shut again. "Said he wanted to do some clay-pigeon shooting."

"Where would he go if he wanted to do that?"

Moira raises her eyebrows, hearing the hurry in my voice. But she doesn't ask what's going on, just nods to the kitchen door, saying:

"Out there, turn left, and walk along the cliff. You'll see the ruins ahead, where the old castle was. The clay-pigeon range's in front of the old ruined tower. You cannae miss it."

"Thanks, Moira," I say, and run for the door.

I've never been so glad in my life that I'm fit. I sprint across the concrete bridge and by the time I hit the cliff path I'm running—not a jog, a full-out run. It's further than I thought, but I keep up my pace, fast and steady. I'd hear my even, panting breathing if it weren't for the sounds of the waves breaking against the cliff below and the cries of the seagulls circling above my head, or swooping and diving for fish. I can't hear anything but the sea and the birds, not even the sound of a shotgun firing.

Which doesn't, of course, mean anything at all.

Eventually I see the first sign of the ruined castle: gray stone, half hidden by a huge oak tree. It's a tower, as Moira said, and it's so striking that I stare at it, forgetting to watch my step. I trip over a stone in the path and nearly go flying. I save myself with a huge, awkward jump, landing with both feet.

I stand and survey the tower. I'm almost under it now. And it's more than a tower, actually: there's a lot of the old castle that surrounded it remaining, though in a sad condition. Weeds are growing up between the stones, and it looks as if the oak tree is growing much too close to the tower for safety, because one of its branches seems to have grown through one of the walls.

I walk, slower, round the tower, looking up at the existing walls of the old castle. I'm searching for the clay-pigeon range, but before I find it, I hear a shot. From above me.

Birds fly up from where they've been hidden in the oak tree, shrieking to one another, their wings flapping loudly.

And my phone buzzes in my pocket. I have an incoming message.

From Taylor.

`WHERE R U?`

I text back frantically, my fingers shaking from nerves:

`TRYING 2 FIND CALLUM`

Taylor texts back almost immediately:

N MATCHED PIC FROM SECURITY CAM
SENDING NOW

I put the phone on Silent. I'm circling the walls now, looking for the way up into the tower. Finally, a gap in the wall. I dash through it and find myself in a grassy open area which must once have been the main hall of the castle, because still here are the stumps of wide stone pillars, wide enough to hold up a big vaulted ceiling.

And straight ahead of me is the base of the tower.

My phone vibrates against my hip bone. I drag it out and stab a button to see my incoming message. The window opens.

I stare, horrified, at the photo in front of me.

It's Moira, smiling at me above the stack of dishes she's carrying.

Moira's face showed up on Nadia's security cameras.

Moira was at the party when Dan died.

So how does Catriona fit into this? Maybe Callum isn't in danger at all. Or is Moira trying to kill Callum too so that Catriona can inherit?

I turn to dash back to Castle Airlie.

And then another shot rings out, high up in the tower. It can't be Moira up there—no way could she have got here before me, not with me running full-out.

I hesitate. It could be Callum up above, taking aim at birds. There's a perfectly innocent explanation for those shots. And as long as Callum and Moira don't meet up, nothing bad can happen. I've got to get back to the castle.

I'm just clearing the walls of the old ruin when my phone buzzes again.

SORRY SORRY SENT U WRONG PHOTO HERE'S RIGHT 1

And there's a photo attached. I click on it, and what I see terrifies me so much I let out a little scream.

It's not the photo I took of Moira and sent to Nadia, so she could match it against the security camera.

It's the one of Catriona.

*   *   *

I spin round and run back to the tower so fast I don't even feel the ground beneath my feet. There's a dark gap at its base, which, as I near it, resolves itself into a narrow entrance leading to a spiral stone staircase. I start to run up until a loose chip of stone turns beneath the sole of my trainer and tumbles down a couple of stairs. In my state of nerves, it sounds like a wrecking ball crashing through a wall. I stop dead, pressing myself flat against the stone wall behind me, only allowing my breath to ease out slowly, silently, through my nose, though my lungs are gasping for relief.

Above me I hear a voice, but I can't make out if it's male or female, let alone identify it. I think I hear footsteps, too, but the tower's close to the cliff edge, and the noise of the waves beating below us and the plaintive cries of the sea-gulls are loud enough to make it hard for me to distinguish any other sounds.

Which might work in my favor. I can't hear what's going on up there, but hopefully whoever's up there can't hear me either.

Steadying my breathing, I proceed up the stairs, taking more care on the crumbling steps. This tower isn't exactly safe: there are big cracks in the walls. But the steps seem to hold my weight well enough, and I don't have any choice. I have to keep going up.

Suddenly, a shaft of light strikes down the well of the spiral stairs. I must be near the top. Gingerly, I crouch down and creep up the last few treads. And then I raise my head fractionally, fractionally, till my line of vision is just barely at the level of the floor.

I see feet, first of all. Boots, jeans . . . I tilt my head back, looking up the body. It's Callum. He's standing further away from me than I anticipated, and I realize that the tower is only a staircase, that there's a whole upper level here that I couldn't see from the ground, probably because it was concealed by the oak trees. Behind him there's a crumbling stone wall, as far as I can tell. And no wonder it's light up here—the roof is completely gone. Nothing overhead but sky.

There's a shotgun propped against the wall next to Callum. His arms are by his sides, but there's a big window at his back and because of the light pouring through it, I can't see the expression on his face.

"If this is some kind of joke, it's *sick!*" he's saying, sounding completely incredulous. "I can't believe you'd do this!"

"It's not a joke," comes a voice from behind me. "Just do it, Cal!"

"You're crazy! You've gone completely crazy!"

Callum takes a couple of strides forward, and behind me, a shot rings out. The echoes are deafening in the stone room, and I duck down, clapping my hands over my head, terrified of a ricochet. Callum jumps back again, yelling something that gets lost in the sound of the blast.

It seems to take forever for the noise to die down. I wait till I'm sure that there isn't a bullet bouncing off the stone before I raise my head again. Callum's stepped further back, terrified beyond words.

"Just jump, Cal. It'll all be over before you know it." Catriona has lunged forward, almost level with the stairs now. I just have to tilt my head to see her. She has a shotgun in her arms, which she is aiming straight at Callum.

"Cat, I don't understand," Callum pleads with her, rubbing his hand violently over his skull. "Please tell me what's going on! Is it some sort of game? If it is, it's not bloody funny, okay?"

"Jesus, Callum!" Catriona yells. "Don't make me shoot you!"

"*Why? Why would you shoot me?*" her brother yells back.

"Because I can only inherit Castle Airlie if you're *dead*," says Catriona furiously. "Even though I'm the oldest of all three of us, I couldn't inherit, because I'm a girl. Did that never strike you as the most unfair thing in the world? Didn't it? Or did you just take it for granted that you should get Castle Airlie, because you're a *boy*?"

"But Cat, I wasn't going to get Castle Airlie either," Callum points out desperately, "because Dan is—*was*—half an hour older than me. How's that fair either?"

"I'm older than both of you! *Two years* older! It should have gone to me!" Catriona screams.

Callum covers his face with his hands. "Jesus, Cat," he says. "I had no idea you felt this way. I promise, I had no idea. You never said a word."

"There wouldn't have been any point," she says. "It wouldn't have changed anything. I mentioned it to Dad once, and you know what he said? 'Girls marry and go to live with their husbands, Cat, that's how it works'! Well, I'm never leaving Castle Airlie. *Never*. I'm going to make it perfect, I'm going to do all the work that needs doing and Mum and Dad have neglected all these years—"

"Cat, just put the gun down, okay?" Callum pleads. "You're not in a good state. Please, put the gun down and let's talk about this."

He takes a step toward her, his hand held out.

"I'll shoot you if you take one more step, Callum," Catriona snaps. "I swear I will. I've gone too far to stop now."

"What do you mean?" Callum stares at his sister, her eyes filled with rage. "Oh my God—*Dan?* You couldn't have. That was an accident, wasn't it?"

Catriona gives a dry, nasty laugh.

"*Right*," she says. "It *was* an accident, actually, believe it or not. I went along to that party with a whole group of

Lucy's friends, and I put peanut oil on every bowl of crisps I could find. It was so easy." She makes that awful laugh again. "I just dribbled some oil into each bowl before I poured the crisps—then I stirred them around a bit with my hand so they'd get some trace of oil on them. Nobody even noticed me. I'm not one of their group—and all they wanted to do was drink and smoke and get off their faces as quickly as possible. They couldn't have cared less what I was doing."

I hear her shift position slightly, her feet moving on the stone flags.

"They were Dan's favorite crisps, those blue ones he loved," she's saying. "I brought them to the party. I was sure he'd eat some, and of course, as we've all been told since the dawn of time, it just took the faintest trace of oil to send Dan into anaphylactic shock, right?"

"But he didn't," Callum says faintly.

"That's right, he didn't. Scarlett ate some instead. I saw her at the bar, talking to him. Then, when she kissed him, she still had some peanut oil in her mouth, and that was enough to trigger the shock. Amazing, isn't it? It made things so much easier for me," she adds. "All eyes were on her. No one even looked at the crisps. I couldn't have planned it better."

"Cat—" Callum starts. His voice sounds awful now, rough with shock.

"And this'll be an accident, too," Catriona interrupts. "You were up here shooting and the floor gave way by the window. It's all crumbling anyway, everyone will believe that."

"And what if I don't jump?" Callum asks hoarsely, sounding so doubtful that I can tell he still doesn't believe she'll make him do it.

"Then I'll shoot you, like I said, and leave you to bleed out. Make it look like you tripped and shot yourself with your own gun. That'll be a much nastier death, Cal. I'd jump if I were you."

"No one will believe I'd be that clumsy," Callum says furiously.

"What else are they going to think? That *I* shot you?" She laughs, a bitter laugh quite devoid of any amusement. "Come on, I'll be their only child left. They'd believe *anything* before they'd think I killed you and Dan!"

"You won't get the castle anyway, Cat, even if I do jump," Callum says, sounding frantic now.

"Oh, yes I will," Catriona says coldly. "There's a clause in the deed of trust. If all the male heirs die before they attain their majority, Castle Airlie passes to any surviving sisters. I only realized it six months ago, but I started making plans straightaway. I had to get it done before your eighteenth birthdays."

She takes another step toward Callum. If she's going to make it seem that he shot himself by accident, she'll need to shoot him at close range. And that's going to bring her close enough to me that I could reach out and grab her ankle. I weigh the odds.

If I knock her over, the gun could go off and any of us could get shot. But if I don't, she'll kill Callum.

Callum may still have some doubts about the seriousness of Catriona's resolve to kill him. I don't. Callum's brother, Dan, died in my arms. I know, more than anyone, that Catriona's already murdered one brother.

She won't hesitate to kill Callum now.

I have to take the risk.

I raise my right arm and snake it out across the floor, reaching for Catriona's ankle. But just as my fingers touch her boot, she takes another step. I make a grab for her and miss by a fraction. I fall sprawling onto the cold stone as Catriona fires the gun. The blast is so close it's like something slamming into my head. My brain is spinning with the reverberations. When I snap my eyes open again, I see dust hanging in the air, fine stone chips from where Catriona fired and a ricochet hit the floor.

But I don't see Callum. Just the empty air where he was standing.

A terrible scream bounces off the crumbling walls and flies into the air.

It's me. I'm the one who's screaming.

Twenty-Two

A SHEER DROP DOWN

I scramble to my feet and sprint across the floor to the place where I last saw Callum, shoving past Catriona on my way. It's take her down or find out what happened to Callum, and that's no choice at all. I have to see Callum, or what's left of him—

I pull up short a bare foot before I tumble to my death. Oh my God. I didn't quite understand why Catriona was telling her brother to jump, because the tower isn't that high. But this ancient building backs onto the cliffs, and there's a sheer drop down where the wall has long since fallen away. I'm teetering on the edge, the stone floor crumbling away beneath me, looking at the rocks below and the gray sea pounding them, white frothy foam surging up the sharp teeth of the cliffs.

But what I don't see is Callum's body lying down there. My heart is pounding.

And then I hear something, a movement just below my feet. In a flash, I drop to my knees and crane my head over the edge.

Callum's hanging there, both hands wrapped around a stone block protruding from the wall. His eyes widen as he sees my face appear directly above his.

"Scarlett!" he manages.

"Hang on, Callum!"

I look down. There's nowhere for him to jump—it's nothing but bare rock below him. Behind me, I hear the sound of a shotgun being racked up. I swing round.

Catriona's pointing the gun at me. I've never stared down the business end of a shotgun before, let alone when it's aimed at my chest. The sight of those two shiny black barrels is the most frightening thing I have ever seen in my life.

"You too," she says, gazing straight into my eyes. "You're going over the edge as well. Jump."

I remember lying on Catriona's bed last night, laughing and joking with her. Thinking how nice she was, how normal. Last night I was almost sure it was Lucy who had killed Dan, for Callum's sake.

Now I look into Catriona's slanted gray eyes and I wonder how I could ever have liked her. Because all I see in there is sheer, terrifying madness.

I brace myself. I'm going to hurdle two steps, hit the floor in a roll, and kick her legs away from her. I know I can do it. She won't expect how fast I can come at her. Nobody who hasn't seen a gymnast sprinting toward them realizes what a head of speed we can power up from a standing start. I'll be on her before she knows it, and as soon as I'm in my forward roll, I'll be below the gun barrels. If they go off, she'll be firing above my head. And Callum, hanging far below floor level, will be safe from any stray shot.

I switch my weight to my toes, lifting up slightly, poised perfectly to burst into action—

"Scarlett! Help!" Callum yells desperately. And I hear a terrifying slipping sound, like nails sliding down a stone block.

I have no choice. I have to help him. What good will it do me to take down Catriona if Callum's falling to his death below us?

I drop flat on the ground in a single movement, dragging myself over the edge, dangling my arms over to reach him. One of his hands has slipped over the block and is reaching up, flailing the air, trying to get a grip on something. I grab it and dig my fingers tightly into the muscles of his forearm. His hand closes just as tightly over my arm. Wow, he's strong. I know I can pull him up, I know I can, if Catriona just leaves us alone.

"Oh, how sweet," Catriona mocks. "Saw one brother die and now you can't watch the second one go? Who d'you like more, Scarlett? Dan or Callum? Dan was the charmer, but Callum's worth twice of him, you know. Just ask anyone."

To my horror, I see Callum's face, upturned toward mine, crumple in pain as she taunts me. Tears are welling up in his eyes as Catriona insults Dan. I feel his grip slip a little, his fingers slide down a fraction toward my wrist, and I take a deep, deep breath, grab him even tighter, and haul him up with every atom of strength in my body.

"Hold on!" I yell savagely down at him, right into his face, that handsome face that's so like Dan's but so different at the same time, so full of a strength that Dan never cultivated. "I've got you! I'm not letting go!" I give another haul, one hand digging into a crack in the stone floor, the other one dragging at Callum's dead weight, the lats down the side of my arm and back screaming in protest, until suddenly I realize he's not a dead weight anymore.

Somehow, I've lifted him far enough that he's managed to find a foothold that's taking a lot of his body weight. The strain on my arm loosens enough that I can afford to reach my other arm down now, not needing to cling to the ground for dear life, and Callum, seeing instantly what I'm doing, lets go of his clutch on the stone block and grabs mine instead.

God, he's heavy. I grit my teeth and heave him up, clenching my stomach muscles tightly to help my back take the strain. I feel Callum come up higher; I feel him get a better foothold in whatever crevice in the rock below he's found to grind his boot into, and I have a surge of excitement, knowing I can pull him up. I can save his life when I couldn't save Dan's.

"Oh no," Catriona says above me. "No, no, no! Sorry, but I didn't come this far to back out now!"

And I feel the barrel of the gun, cold and hard, against my temple.

"Drop him," she says. "Drop him and I promise I won't kill you."

She must think I'm the biggest fool in the world if she even imagines I'd believe her.

But I can scarcely call her bluff.

The barrel presses closer against my temple. I flinch, despite myself, and my grip on Callum loosens for a second.

"Do it," he calls up to me.

His eyes are looking up directly into mine. Gray and clear and trying to tell me something, frantically, with everything he's got.

"Do it," he repeats. "It's okay."

He starts to let go his grip on my forearms, and I scream: "No! No! I won't let go!" and tighten my grasp on him so convulsively that I can feel my whole upper body trembling with the tension.

"Then I'll make you!"

Catriona's voice rises to a high-pitched, insane-sounding scream. She drags the shotgun barrel from my forehead. The relief of having it gone is intense, but it's instantly replaced by fear of what she'll do next. Though I can barely lift my head with the strain of holding Callum, I crane my neck back just enough to see her from underneath. Looming over me, her shadow falling over us, she reverses the shotgun, holding it by the barrels, and lifts it above the edge of the abyss, about to bring the stock down on my and Callum's clasped hands.

I close my eyes and hold on to him with every atom of strength I have left, though I know it will do no good. We're completely vulnerable.

I glance down at Callum again, and he stares up at me. He's stopped trying to let go of me now. And somehow, we're gazing at each other, and all I can see is Callum's gray eyes, thickly fringed with silky dark lashes, wide-set under his strong dark brows. I notice for the first time that he has speckles of gold-green in his gray irises, like mica chips that catch the light, and a moment of utter calm passes between us, and I stop panicking. For that moment, that long moment, I don't think about anything but looking down into Callum's eyes.

I wait for Catriona's blow to come, and hold on as tight as I can to him.

Suddenly Callum's face below me lightens—but not in expression. The shadow over us has lifted. Catriona's moved. And in that second, something falls heavily across my foot, and I hear signs of a struggle, a shotgun barrel hitting stone, gasps and grunts and fists landing on flesh.

I have no time to look round, no time to do anything but concentrate, fiercely, on dragging Callum up. I lock my back and curl up my abdominals, and, with everything I've got and more I don't, I haul away at Callum's arms in a series of long, miraculously powerful pulls that run right down my shoulders, into my back and my hamstrings, as my toes dig desperately into the stone floor scrabbling for a toehold, forcing me to stay there and not be pulled over the edge.

I can feel the cords in my neck standing out with the terrible effort, my teeth locking together in a grimace. Callum's face below mine is strained into a rictus of concentration as he swings his body up and walks up the wall, using my hands to steady him, higher and higher till he's got high enough to grab the edge of the floor and use his powerful arms and shoulders to heave himself over—

The shotgun goes off behind me.

I scream, though I'm so exhausted with the strain of pulling Callum to safety that all that comes out is a dry little croak.

Callum drags himself onto the floor beside me, panting as if he's run an obstacle course. He grabs hold of me, patting his hands up and down my body, his eyes wild.

"Scarlett! Are you all right? *Scarlett!*"

I nod mutely. My entire body is burning with the agony of straining my muscles way beyond their natural limits, but I think I'd know if I'd been shot.

Or would I? With the amount of adrenaline pumping through me, would I really know? And would Callum know if he'd been shot? The thought scares me so much I sit up and scan him with equal, wild-eyed panic. I can't see any blood on him, thank God. . . .

It sounds mad, but we're so intensely focused on each other, after what we've just been through, that it's not until we've ensured that we're both unharmed that we even think to look around us. Catriona's sprawled on the floor, facedown, several feet from us. The shotgun barrel is just visible below her. And across the room, body at a weird angle against the wall, head twisted round, is—

"Taylor!"

I jump to my feet, all pain forgotten, and race across the room. If Taylor's been hurt saving our lives, I'll never forgive myself.

"Taylor!" I kneel down beside her. "Taylor, are you okay? *Taylor!*"

I take her head between my hands and turn it gently, my heart pounding with fear. Please, please tell me she hasn't broken her neck.

Taylor's eyes snap open like someone in a horror film coming back to life. I scream again, something I'm doing much too much this afternoon, but again, all I produce is a hoarse croak.

"*Ow!*" she says crossly. "Stop twisting me!" She gets her hands under her and lifts herself up. "My back hurts really bad," she complains.

But suddenly there's a howl from Callum, so raw and wounded that I spin round, terrified that somehow he's realized that, after all, he's been shot.

He's kneeling beside his sister's body. He's turned her over, and she's lying in his arms, her head flopping back over his arm at an angle just as odd as Taylor's was. But Taylor didn't have a huge red stain on her chest, a stain that looks as if it's spreading out even as I stare, horrified, at Callum. He puts one hand against her neck, looking for a pulse. And I see from his expression, simultaneously horrified and also, awfully, relieved, that he can't find one.

Catriona is dead.

I get up and walk slowly toward Callum, as slow as if I were walking through water, because my entire body is screaming with pain. And when I reach him, I kneel down beside him and put my arm around him. I don't know what I'm expecting, but he turns to me, and awkwardly, over Catriona's body, he leans into me and puts both his arms around me. His head sinks till it's resting on my shoulder. With my other hand, I stroke his hair, his poignantly short stubbly hair, and I take the weight of him on me, holding him as he sobs against me, his tears wetting my sweater as I burst into tears myself. The relief of finally letting my guard down, sobbing my heart out, while Callum and I hold each other, is unbelievable.

Taylor is as white as a sheet as she looks at Catriona's body.

"I grabbed her, and she tried to hit me with the gun. I ducked and she tripped and sent me flying . . . ," she says. "I tried to get the gun away from her, but she wouldn't let go, and then she fell against it and it went off. I didn't mean . . ."

"It wasn't your fault, Taylor," I manage to say to her. "You saved our lives. It wasn't your fault."

I take my hand from Callum's head and hold it out to her. Wincing, she makes her way across to us and kneels down beside us, looking at Catriona, holding my hand.

I can't be sure, because I know how much Taylor would hate it if I ever caught her crying. So, deliberately, I look away.

But I'm pretty sure that tears are pouring down her face too.

Twenty-Three

IT NEVER LASTS

I see the turning to Prestwick airport up ahead, and look over at Callum as the Land Rover slows down and eases into the left-hand lane. It's too noisy in the jeep to have any sort of conversation that doesn't involve yelling. This is a really old model that Callum told me proudly has been "in the family" for thirty years or so. It looks like it's held together with duct tape and rubber bands. Callum handles it very confidently, but then, I suspect he's been driving it round the estate since he was fourteen or so, like most country boys.

It's a huge relief not to be able to talk for the moment. There's been so much talking in the last twenty-four hours: doctors, police, the McAndrews, telling the same story over and over again, how I went out for a walk and met Callum, how we decided to go up in the tower and do some target shooting, and how we found Catriona there, victim of a fatal accident, having obviously tripped and fallen over her own gun. Only Moira, having seen me in such a hurry to find Callum an hour before, knows there's more to the story than that, and Moira's not telling. I don't know how much Moira suspects, if anything, but certainly she didn't say a word to the police about me seeming distressed or desperate to find Callum. And the police, clearly brimming with sympathy for the poor McAndrew family, with two such terrible tragedies happening in the short space of six months, were all too happy to take Callum's and my word for what we found in the tower, and take Catriona's body away on a stretcher.

They said it's very unlikely there will be an inquest, and even if there is, I won't need to come back to Castle Airlie. I've got nothing to tell the coroner that Callum can't: anything I'd say would be a line-for-line corroboration of his story.

I won't be coming back here ever again. I've been involved in too many of this family's tragedies. The sight of Mrs. McAndrew hearing that a second child of hers had died in a horrible accident was almost too much to bear. I don't think she'll ever truly recover. Mr. McAndrew looks like a ghost of himself, gray and faded; his hair actually went several shades whiter overnight. Callum, I think, is still in shock. I don't know if it's really sunk in yet that his sister killed his brother and tried to kill him, all so that she could inherit Castle Airlie. He's been so busy telling lies and trying to take care of his mother that he hasn't had much time for himself.

And we've been no use to each other. What we went through was so horrible that our eyes are still wide and frightened. The memory of looking at each other, sure we were both about to die, is unbelievably vivid. I could hardly get to sleep last night; I barricaded my door from the inside with the chest of drawers, even though I knew that this night was the first in Castle Airlie that I couldn't be in any danger, because Dan's killer was dead. I sat up shaking and whispering to Taylor on the phone. We talked half through the night about nothing at all, just to hear someone else's voice, a friend's, not to feel alone after what we'd gone through that afternoon. Poor Taylor had to go back and spend the night at the B and B by herself. No matter how hard we tried, we couldn't think of a plausible story that would cover her presence at the scene. I wanted to go and spend the night there with her, but we all decided that would look weird too. And considering how desperately we were trying to pass off Catriona's death as a freak shooting accident, the last thing anyone wanted was any kind of suspicious circumstances that might lead them to think there was more to the story than we were telling.

Taylor asked me last night, or maybe in the early hours of the morning, whether I wished I'd never started out on the path to investigate Dan's death. And I had to say no—because if I hadn't, Callum would be dead too. In an awful way, that makes everything really simple. I can't have any regrets. As Taylor pointed out, who knows if Catriona would even have stopped at just killing her brothers? Who's to say that, having got away with two murders, she wouldn't have grown impatient at not inheriting the castle as soon as she'd like, and turned her focus on her father, too?

Trust Taylor to be able to look the worst possibility clearly in the face.

No, I was right to want to find out who killed Dan, even

though my quest started out being only an attempt to clear my own name. I look back at the naive girl who, six months ago, kissed a boy for the first time, only to see him drop dead at her feet, the girl who was a passive participant in her own life, and I'm amazed to realize that I hardly recognize her. I've come so far since then; I've learned so much about myself and what I can do.

I really like who I am now. I like this Scarlett. I'm strong and I can think on my feet; I can be sneaky when I need to. I'm brave enough to kiss a boy and funny enough to banter with him. But why did my growing-up have to be at such a high cost? Why did Dan have to die? Why did Taylor have to cause Catriona's death, even by accident, and why did Callum have to find out that his sister was trying to kill him?

I shiver. I have to stop asking myself this kind of thing. Because something else I've learned is that some questions don't have satisfactory answers, and asking them is like bashing your head against a brick wall till you're bleeding.

With much clashing and grinding of gears, Callum slows down the Land Rover on the ramp and pulls it to a halt outside the Departures entrance. I expect him to jump out and drag my suitcase out from the back, but he stays where he is, turning to look at me.

"Scarlett . . . ," he begins, clearing his throat. "I don't know what to say."

"It's okay," I mumble, embarrassed. "I don't know what to say either."

"But there's stuff I *have* to say to you," he insists. "I was a bastard to you from the moment you arrived. I didn't want you there and I made it really clear." He sets his jaw, obviously not enjoying this apology. "And it turned out you were the only person who was really on my side."

"Well, I was—"

"Trying to find out the truth about Dan," he says, finishing my sentence. "And you were right not to tell any of us what you were doing. We wouldn't have believed you until it was too late. You saved my life." He looks down at me, his eyes full of emotion. "I can't ever repay you for that."

"It's okay. Really," I say awkwardly.

"And that's not all." He rubs his hand over his head. "That afternoon when you were in the woods by the drive, and you thought someone was shooting at you?"

Oh my God, I think, *if Callum's about to tell me that was him, I don't think I'll be able to handle it.*

"It was Lucy," he confesses. "She just told me last night. You know, when she came round and we had that fight?"

I nod. We didn't sit down to dinner last night; Moira just made sandwiches and put them in the breakfast room in case anyone was hungry. Which mostly, of course, we weren't. But Lucy came to see how Callum was, and they had a screaming fight which culminated in Lucy storming out and yelling at Callum all down the main staircase. I stare at Callum now, unable to believe that it was Lucy shooting at me in the wood. From the moment I realized that Catriona had killed Dan, I assumed it was Catriona who had done that, too, though I couldn't work out why she would have wanted to shoot at me.

"She said she was jealous of you," Callum's admitting.

I don't understand.

"Jealous of *me?*" I blurt out.

Callum colors up.

"She said she didn't like the way I looked at you," he mumbles.

Oh. I feel myself blushing too.

"So I broke up with her as soon as she told me," he continues. "I mean, that's just insane—she could have killed you! And she got really angry when I broke up with her." He sighs. "I had no idea she was capable of anything like that. She said all this stuff like she was sure you'd been snooping in Dan's room, and in Dad's office—she was really paranoid about you."

I don't say anything. I'm not going to tell Callum that Lucy was right: that I *was* snooping, that she's not as paranoid as Callum thinks. Because if Lucy is lunatic enough to take a shotgun and start firing it in my general direction, she's not the kind of person Callum, or anyone, should be going out with, and I shouldn't do anything to encourage him to see her in a better light.

"Oh Callum, I'm really sorry this happened now," I say hopelessly. "It's awful that you've had a breakup on top of everything else."

I can feel how alone Callum is, having lost his brother and sister, and now with no girlfriend to comfort him.

He shrugs. "I didn't have a choice," he says sadly.

We sit quietly for a minute or so, and then someone behind us honks their horn. Callum jumps down from the Land Rover and hauls my suitcase out of the back. I climb down—going a bit slower than normal, because I'm sore all over—and join him on the pavement.

"Thank you again, Scarlett," he says, looking down at me, his gray eyes very serious.

"It's okay," I mumble, thoroughly embarrassed.

He holds up a hand to stop me.

"I owe you from now on. I mean that. I promise that if you ever need help, wherever you are, you can just ask me and I'll come. That's a promise. You can always count on me."

I look up at him, speechless. And then he bends down, puts his hands on my shoulders, and kisses me, very gently, on the lips. I'm so shocked and surprised that I just stand there as he holds me close for his kiss. I'm much too confused to kiss him back: there's his similarity to Dan (though that's faded considerably, the more I've got to know Callum, and the more I've found out about Dan). And there's Jase, too, the unresolved business with him. If this were Jase, I'd be kissing him back with everything I had, and it's partly because of Jase that I can't really respond to Callum, because I'm so confused right now about what I feel.

I never knew before that you could be attracted to two boys at the same time. Now I know you can. I feel like I'm strapped to the steepest learning curve in the world, and I don't know when it will ever stop.

I should probably be pushing Callum away, but I'm not. I can't. This kiss is incredibly comforting somehow: very sweet, very soft. It's so good to be close to someone, held against his body, that I drink it in, aware that I have no idea when I'll get this kind of comfort again. All I can hear is Callum's breathing; all I can feel is his hands on my shoulders, his warm lips against mine. I lift one of my hands to stroke his head, his soft short hair, and tell myself it's to soothe him, though I think I've been wanting to run my hand over that short hair ever since I saw him.

And as I do so, I think, like a cold stab to my heart, the voice of reason and sanity: *I will never do this again. I will never be kissed again by Callum McAndrew. I will never touch him anymore, ever, in my life.*

Finally, he lifts his head. We pull away from each other and stand staring into each other's faces. The noises of the outside world flood in: honking cars, people shouting to one another and pushing past us, the whine of airplanes above our heads. We had such a brief moment of pushing everything but us away. I think that's what the kiss was really about for both of us, a moment to forget all the horror we've just lived through. Catriona's dead, bloody body. Callum's parents, white-faced and old-looking. The truth of how Dan died. For the moment of the kiss, we weren't thinking about it: we were just two warm bodies, touching, giving each other a basic, primitive relief, like animals, and I'm more grateful for it than I can say.

But it never lasts. The world shoves its way back in whether you like it or not, and its presence changes everything.

"You know we can't—" Callum starts, but I'm already nodding.

I know we can't. How could we? Even if it weren't for Jase and my feelings for him. Callum's brother died after kissing me. I saw Callum's sister try to murder him, not to mention me. Too many terrible things have happened be-tween me and the McAndrew family.

I bend over to grab the handle of my suitcase. I can't look at Callum anymore. When I first saw him, all I could see was Dan. But now Dan's face has dissolved from my memory, replaced by Callum. Those life-and-death minutes I spent holding Callum over the edge of that drop, looking down into his face, will never leave me.

I turn away from him and walk through the automatic doors into the terminal. I'm determined not to look back, but a few steps in, I can't help it. I swing back and look over my shoulder, hoping he's not still there.

He is. He's watching me walk away. I raise a hand to him. And as he lifts his hand to wave goodbye in return, he smiles at me, such a sweet smile that the tears prick at my eyes and I have to swallow really hard.

It's the first time Callum McAndrew has ever really smiled at me. And it'll be the last.

* * *

Taylor's waiting for me in the coffee shop. She looks as exhausted as I feel, like she slept in her clothes. There are dark circles under her eyes and her skin, usually a thick milky white, is grayish, as if she's been in a basement for days, without natural light. She's wearing low-slung com-bat trousers and a chunky Arran sweater she bought in the village, and there's a small rucksack propped by her chair, probably containing nothing but changes of underwear and socks, plus her toothbrush. Typical of Taylor to travel really light.

Her expression, as she catches sight of me, is appalled.

"What happened?" she asks, jumping up. "You look like someone else died."

"Callum just kissed me goodbye," I manage.

"Oh *no*," Taylor says, getting it immediately. "You can't—"

"I know, I know," I say, wearily.

Taylor sits down again, pushing a coffee toward me.

"I got you a gingerbread latte," she says. "I thought you might need cheering up."

This is such a deliberate understatement that, despite my misery, I can't help cracking a little laugh. I sit down and take a swig of my latte.

Taylor grimaces. "What was it like at the castle this morning?"

"Moira was going round clearing the drink bottles from the bar in the Great Hall," I say sadly, "because Mrs. McAndrew was really drunk last night. Moira didn't say anything, but I'm sure it was so that Mrs. McAndrew couldn't get hold of any more alcohol."

Taylor frowns.

"I heard Mr. McAndrew this morning, making the funeral arrangements," I continue, "so I think that means there won't be an inquest. He sounded awful." I gulp. "Catriona is going to be buried next to Dan."

"That's cozy," Taylor comments, which I think is really flippant of her, but I let it pass.

"And you know I told you Callum and Lucy had a huge

fight yesterday?" I finish. "He told me just now he broke up with her."

Taylor's eyes widen.

"He didn't waste much time," she says. "Breaking up with Lucy last night and kissing you this morning."

"Taylor, *please*. It wasn't like that. Apparently it was Lucy firing at me in the wood, can you believe it? I was sure it was Catriona, but no, it was Lucy. She wanted to scare me away."

"Crazy sister, drunk mother, crazy ex-girlfriend," Taylor says mockingly. "Callum likes the crazies, eh?"

"*Taylor*—" I say, really cross with her now.

"I'm sorry!" Her face crumples. I've never seen her like this before; she actually looks like she might be about to cry. "I had nightmares for hours about Catriona lying there all covered in blood—I don't think I actually got much sleep at all. I kept waking up, but then I'd go back to sleep and start dreaming about her all over again. . . . I know I'm making stupid cracks, but I'm freaking out!"

I reach out and take her hand, holding it tightly. I can see that she's trying to hold back tears. We sit for a while in silence, Taylor's jaw working as she swallows hard, choking down the lump in her throat.

"It wasn't your fault," I say again.

Funny how that phrase keeps popping up. I hope Taylor finds comfort in it, as I once did.

Taylor is still unable to speak, but she's squeezing my hand so hard it's almost painful.

"And . . ." I hesitate to say the next thing, true though it is. "It was the best thing that could have happened. For everyone. What if Catriona hadn't died? She'd have denied everything. We'd have had to take it all to the police. Even if she got convicted, think of the trial—everything coming out—it would be so much worse for her family than her dying in what they think was a tragic accident."

Taylor nods slowly, her pressure on my hand releasing slightly.

"I just wish it hadn't been me," she says in the weakest voice I've ever heard her use.

"You saved our lives," I say. "Callum and I would have been killed without you."

"I still can't quite believe it," Taylor says, her voice still small. "You investigate stuff, and you know someone got killed, but it's still unbelievable when you come face to face with a murderer."

"I know. I still can't quite believe it either."

"*Passengers on the eleven-forty-five flight to London Gatwick, the flight is now ready for boarding at gate ten,*" comes a voice over the loudspeaker. "*Passengers on the eleven-forty-five flight to London Gatwick, the flight is now ready for boarding at gate ten.*"

"I guess that means it's time to go home," Taylor says.

We stand up and Taylor slings her rucksack over her shoulders. Then we look at each other, and, ignoring the boarding call that's still going out over the loudspeaker we take a step toward each other and collide in the biggest hug ever. We wrap our arms around each other's bodies and practically squeeze the other one to death, like two boa constrictors in a death match. Our marathon hug says everything we're not saying out loud, and it's exactly what we both needed. When we eventually separate, both of our eyes are a little damp.

I pick up my latte. It's probably cold by now, but I could still do with the sugar rush.

"I never thought I'd say this," Taylor says as we head toward the security line, "but I'm actually looking forward to getting back to school, you know?"

"Oh, I know, me too," I say, my tone heartfelt. "Nothing to do but work—"

"No life-threatening dramas," Taylor adds.

"Just eating cauliflower cheese—"

"Farting like drains—"

"Being really bored—"

"Oh, come on—you've got a gorgeous guy waiting back at school for you," Taylor contradicts me as we show our passports and boarding passes and file into the line waiting for the scanning machine.

I roll my eyes. "Yeah, right. How long's the flight?"

"An hour and a quarter."

"Well, I'd better get started with the Jase update now, then. There's a lot to tell you."

Taylor manages a half grin at me. It's by no means her best or biggest grin, but it's a start, and it's a lot better than the way she looked a few minutes ago.

"There's always something happening to you, Scarlett," she says.

"No more, I swear." My mouth curls up into a bit of a smile as I grab my little suitcase and put it on the belt for the scanner. "Honestly, I want to lead a really boring life from now on."

"*Right*," Taylor says, her grin enlarging by the moment. She twists her shoulders, sliding off the straps of her rucksack. "We'd go crazy in a month, and you know it."

We're smiling at each other properly now.

"No, really," I insist. "I mean it."

I empty my pockets into the little plastic tray and walk through the scanning arch—no beeps, no alarms, no drama. There you go. It's a start. And as I put my phone and keys and loose change back into my jeans, and lift my bag off the rollers on the other side of the belt, I watch Taylor walk through the arch in her turn. She's still grinning at the thought of us leading boring lives. A security official says something to her and she nods, following them over to one side.

"Random check," she calls over to me. "Or maybe they just don't like Americans."

The security official smiles as she starts tracing lines along Taylor's body with her wand. And I have a rush of gratitude that Taylor's my friend, so powerful that I feel a lump rising in my throat. I dig my nails into my palms in an effort not to cry; it's the last thing either of us needs. No more tears. Instead, I scoop up Taylor's phone and change, sling her rucksack over one shoulder, and walk over to a row of seats to wait for her. She looks over to check that I have her stuff, but it's just a reflex: she doesn't really need to.

Taylor knows I've got her back, and I know she's got mine. If I ever had any doubts about that, after Castle Airlie they were washed away. We're a team, always will be. Whatever happens from now on, we know that for sure.

And right now, that's more than enough for me.

epilogue

It's not that long or difficult a journey back from Scotland, but after staying up most of the night, it's enough to exhaust Taylor and me. After chattering all the way on the plane trip, we've run out of steam by the time we're standing on the train platform waiting to get the Gatwick Express to Victoria station. By the time we're on the Bakerloo tube line, last stop Wakefield, Taylor has dozed off with her head lolling on my shoulder. I wake her at the terminus and we trudge up the drive, barely exchanging a word. At the big entrance gates, we wave each other goodbye before Taylor heads off to her room—she's planning to sleep all afternoon.

I should do the same. But I can't. For Taylor, Wakefield Hall is just her school, a boring old pile of stone and mortar surrounded by acres of grounds. For me, apart from being my home, it's something even more important: it's where Jase Barnes lives. And the closer today's journey has brought me to him, the more my anticipation has built.

I need to see him. I need to find out what he's thinking about us and whether he wants to go on seeing me despite his dad's intense protests (that's putting it lightly). My kiss with Callum this morning has made me even keener to learn whether the future holds anything for me and Jase, strange though that may sound. Because I have to put everything to do with the McAndrew family as far behind me as I possibly can, so I have any kind of chance of moving on with my life. Dan and Callum McAndrew are the past, and they have to stay that way.

I turn off the drive into the gatehouse and walk through the door. Thankfully, no one is here to greet me.

I go upstairs, put my suitcase in my room, and apply some careful, you-can't-really-see-it's-there-but-it-makes-a-difference mascara and lip gloss. Then I spray on a little light perfume, change my sweater for a dark green one that doesn't look like I slept in it, and nip back outside again. Aunt Gwen is in the sitting room listening to the radio, and doesn't even turn her head to acknowledge me, though I say "Hi!" in passing. Honestly, I could slit my wrists on the kitchen floor and she'd step right over me to get to the kettle.

I make a circuit of the grounds, but I don't see anyone. There are very few girls here at half-term, and none of them, clearly, is keen enough on fresh air to go for a walk on a blustery, late-autumn day. The sky's gray and heavy enough with clouds that I can't see the sun at all, just a faint lightening on the horizon where it must be. Leaves are rustling across the lawns, and though I'm hoping to see Jase pushing a wheelbarrow, I don't see him at all, even in the distance, down the long avenue of lime trees, or beyond the Great Lawn, over by the hockey pitches. I walk past the gate to the lake enclosure, but it's securely padlocked from the outside, and though I climb up the gate a little and peer over it, there's no one in there. The Wakefield Hall grounds feel dead, abandoned. It's impossible to realize that, next week, they'll be full again, of girls engaged in battle on the sports pitches or bouncing balls off the stone terrace walls. Right now, it's as if no one were ever here.

The emptiness and the gray skies are having a miserable effect on my mood. They also make me feel braver, though, because, having spent a good forty minutes doing—let's be honest—a thorough search of the grounds for Jase, I can't just give up and walk away. I think about texting him, but what if he doesn't get back to me for ages? I'll be on tenterhooks till he does: every time my phone beeps, my heart will jump right up to my throat.

Castle Airlie, and any thoughts of the McAndrews, are closed off to me now. There's nothing back there for me. There's only here, now, and that means Jase. Still, I have a feeling this weird stuff with his father has ruined everything. . . .

Despite my doubts and the threat of Mr. Barnes's terrifying temper, I eventually find myself, having done a circle of the entire school, walking down the path that leads to the Barnes family cottage.

I tell myself I'm just going slowly, one step at a time.

I tell myself I can turn around straightaway if I see Mr. Barnes, and hopefully he won't see me first.

I tell myself I'm an idiot to be doing this at all.

But my feet keep going.

And as I come round the slight bend in the path, the

first thing I see is a flash of color, but lower to the ground than I was expecting.

It's Jase, in a bright red sweater, crouching down beside his motorbike, adjusting something on one of the wheels with a wrench. I didn't think I made any noise, but he looks up, and when he sees me, a smile breaks across his face.

I let out a whoosh of breath I didn't realize I was holding. I realize I was scared that his reaction might be a lot more negative than that.

But almost instantly, the smile fades. He stands up, wiping his hands on a greasy rag, and walks quickly toward me, gesturing for me to go back the way I came. It isn't till we're well out of view of anyone who might come out of the Barnes cottage that he says, "Sorry—it's just that my dad's at home," looking incredibly uncomfortable.

At least he's brought his dad up straightaway, which means we're not going to be skirting round an elephant in the room, trying to pretend it's not there.

"I came to look for you the day after—um, you know," Jase is saying. "But you weren't around. I haven't seen you for a while. Did you go away?"

I realize that means he's been looking for me regularly, not just the day after the lake incident with his dad. He's noticed my absence. And that makes me feel better about his not texting me. Maybe he didn't know what to say; maybe he was waiting to see me in person. There's so much I don't know about boys and how they think. But I can tell that he's happy to see me, and that he's nervous, which are both good signs, because that means I matter to him at least a little bit.

"I went to Scotland to see, um, some friends," I say. "It was all really last-minute."

He nods. Perhaps he thinks I went away to avoid him and his dad for a few days, but there's no way I can explain the truth of the situation. No one will ever know about Catriona but me, Callum, and Taylor. We made a vow to each other over Catriona's dead body, and we'll never break it.

"Did you have a good time?" he asks.

I gape for a second or so, my mouth hanging open. You'd think I'd have expected this question, but Jase looks so gorgeous, slightly sweaty from working on his bike—a grease smear on his forehead, his red sweater rolled up to the elbows, showing off his muscular, golden-brown forearms—that the sight of him has temporarily frozen my brain. I gulp, and get myself back on track.

"Um, not really," I say weakly. "There was a bit too much family drama."

Understatement of the year, I think. And then I realize what I've said, unthinkingly: after all, the last time I saw Jase, family drama was exactly what we were going through.

He looks really uncomfortable.

"I'm so sorry!" I exclaim, blushing, and I reach out to touch his arm. "I didn't mean—"

"No, it's okay," he says. "My dad's—" He heaves up a deep sigh. "He's never exactly been easy to get along with. But since Mum left, he's been a nightmare. I don't know why he was like that with you. I've tried to talk to him but he just starts shouting and throwing things."

I grimace. The image of Mr. Barnes shouting and throwing things is, frankly, frightening.

"I'm really sorry about it all," Jase adds. "I didn't have any idea he was going to mind me hanging out with you."

"Me neither," I say.

He looks at me seriously, his golden eyes hypnotic as they stare into mine.

"Your gran probably wouldn't be that keen on it either, to tell the truth," he adds.

I know he's right.

"Well, they're both stupid, then," I hear myself saying defiantly. "It's none of their business anyway."

His eyes widen. "You mean that?"

I nod fervently, and then blush again, embarrassed by my vehemence.

"Scarlett—" he starts, taking a step towards me.

I look up at him, completely forgetting to breathe.

And just then, we hear a car, coming up the gravel drive, the churn of its wheels grating against the loose stones shockingly loud in the silence. Jase pauses and we both look in the direction of the drive, even though we can't see it. We're standing by the new school block, close to the dining room entrance; the old part of the school building, the original Wakefield Hall, is on the other side of the new building, hidden behind a high ivy-covered wall. That's where the drive stops, in a large gracious turning circle with a fountain in the center.

With a final scraping of wheels on gravel, the car slows down and comes to a stop. A door opens and someone gets out. Jase and I exchange a quick, wary glance. A few days before, he and I would barely even notice something as standard as the arrival of a car at Wakefield Hall: it wouldn't have registered on our radar. But now, having acknowledged that, if we want to keep seeing each other, we'll have to do it despite our families' disapproval, we've instantly become sensitive about being seen together.

It sounds romantic. It isn't. It's really annoying.

Another car door opens. More footsteps on gravel, and then the boot opens. Just a girl coming back to school early, bringing luggage with her. But maybe Jase and I should move away from the school block to somewhere a little less in the main line of passage. I'm just about to say something when we hear:

"Hello? Hello!"

It's a girl's voice: loud, privileged, impatient ... and oddly familiar.

"*Hello?* God, this place is a bloody desert. *Hello!*"

"I should go and see who that is," I say reluctantly to Jase. Odd though it may be, I feel a sort of hostesslike obligation, since Wakefield Hall is, after all, my home as well as my school.

He nods. I make a wait-here gesture and start toward the arch in the wall. I'm only a few paces through it when I stop in amazement, unable to believe what I'm seeing.

Parked in front of the Hall's imposing front entrance is a black Mercedes from which the driver is unloading a stack of Louis Vuitton suitcases. Beside it, fishing in a huge leather handbag, is a girl in a white fur jacket, skinny jeans, and a big beret into which her hair is bundled and which partially hides her face. As I get closer, she pulls a cigarette case out of her bag, extracts a cigarette, and bends over to light it.

It's Plum Saybourne.

And as she turns to survey the mass of suitcases, dragging on her cigarette, she catches sight of me.

"Scarlett!" she drawls, puffing out smoke from her nostrils like a cartoon dragon. "How *delightful* to see you. Of course, it's not exactly unexpected, is it, since you actually *live* in this bloody backwater. God, I can't *believe* I'm going to be stuck here for the next two years."

Behind me, I hear Jase come up, but I'm paralyzed by Plum's words. Literally. I'm frozen to the spot.

"Oh, didn't you know?" Plum asks. "I got chucked out of St. Tabby's. Bloody hypocritical bitch of a headmistress, after all the money my family's given that school. I wanted to hire a tutor, but Mummy threw the most enormous tantrum at the idea of me on the loose in London. She's got the idea that your grandmother will straighten me out." She raises her eyebrows and expels more smoke from her nose. "I'd *love* to see her try. So here I am, at this godforsaken place that time forgot." She gestures, one sweep of a black-gloved hand, at the imposing mass of Wakefield Hall.

And then she looks back at me, and sees Jase standing by my side. Her eyes widen, and then she smiles at him—a long, slow, predatory smile.

"Well, *hello*," she murmurs. "I'm Plum Saybourne. And who are you?"

"J-Jase Barnes," he answers, and there's a bit of a stammer as he says his name.

Plum's magic works on everyone.

"I'm glad to see there's at least *one* consolation in this hellhole," she says, fluttering her eyelashes at him.

"You should go in and see my grandmother," I say firmly, determined to get rid of her. "Inside and up the stairs. There's a door marked HEADMISTRESS'S OFFICE. Her secretary, Penelope, works there. She'll tell my grandmother you're here."

"Oh, the excitement! My heart is *pounding* in anticipation," Plum drawls with sarcasm. "Well, better get it over with, I suppose."

Dropping her cigarette to the gravel and not bothering to stub it out with her high-heeled boot, she walks toward the wide stairs that lead up to the front door, smoke curling upward in her wake. Over her shoulder, she calls to the driver:

"Can you start bringing those in? It's bloody cold out here."

To my great annoyance, Jase swivels his head, watching her go. Only after she's disappeared inside does he turn back to me.

And we stand there, looking at each other, as Plum's driver carries her bags inside.

ABOUT THE AUTHOR

Lauren Henderson was born in London and lived in Tuscany and Manhattan before returning to London to settle down with one husband and two very fat cats. She has written seven books in the Sam Jones mystery series, which has been optioned for American TV; many short stories; and three romantic comedies. Her nonfiction dating guide, *Jane Austen's Guide to Dating*, has been optioned as a feature film by the writer behind *Ten Things I Hate About You* and *Ella Enchanted*. Lauren's books have been translated into more than twenty languages. With Stella Duffy, she has edited an anthology of women-behaving-badly crime stories, *Tart Noir*; their joint Web site is www.tartcity.com. Lauren has been described as both the Dorothy Parker and the Betty Boop of the crime novel. Her interests include trapeze classes, gymnastics, and eating complex carbohydrates.